I0604160

The Secrets We Carry

Journal
of a Girl in Trouble

A Novel Based on True Stories
By CLAY CORMANY

The Secrets We Carry
Journal of a Girl in Trouble
Copyright © 2025
by Clay Cormany

All rights reserved. No part of this publication may be reproduced, distributed, or transmitted in any form, or by any means, now known or hereafter invented, or stored in a database without the written permission of the publisher, except in the case of brief quotations embodied in critical articles and reviews. Names and places have been changed and/or merged to respect the people and places. This novel is a collection of True Situations merged together into one story.

Ordering Information:
Special discounts available for book clubs.
For details, contact the publisher at director@vanvelzerpress.com.

Paperback ISBN: 978-0-9898486-3-3
Hardback ISBN: 978-0-9898486-8-8
eBook ISBN: 978-0-9898486-4-0
Library of Congress Control Number Available from Publisher
Printed in the United States of America
FSC-certified paper when possible

VanVelzerPress.com in collaboration with Phoenix Farm

For Claire & Other Victims

The Hallway

*H*e came around the corner suddenly, unexpectedly, sending shock waves of fear through her body. *Oh no! Of all the bad luck! What if he sees me with this thing? I've got to ditch it! But how?*

If she kept on, she would be walking right into him. Just ahead, on the right side of the corridor, was an open door. She felt pretty sure it led to the language lab. *Too far.* Across from the open door a blonde leaned against a locker and chatted with a boy wearing a letter jacket. He seemed eager to get as close to this blonde as possible. Even if she were brave enough to butt into their conversation, it wouldn't stop Red Lion from seeing her or what she held in her hand.

There didn't seem to be any chance of escape except to turn around and walk away, but with almost no one else in the corridor, he would still likely catch sight of her in just a few steps when he looked up from his phone.

Then another classroom door – behind her – flew open. She swung around and saw an overweight kid carrying a backpack, clumping toward a drinking fountain. He dropped the backpack to the floor and bent down to it. She couldn't see the kid's face but that didn't matter. In a few seconds, Red Lion would be looming over her. *There's no choice.*

Swiftly and as stealthily as possible, she glided up behind the kid while he still gulped in water, slipping the compromising item under the flap of his backpack. She took only five more steps before Red Lion saw her. A smirk of recognition creased his lips.

"Why hello," he said in a low voice. "What a nice surprise."

Chapter 1

Collin Morris was tired. Tired of listening to his father rail on about the unfairness of a job market that took away his job two months ago and now kept him from getting another. Tired of listening to his sister Eleanor complain about Roger who she "loved to the moon and back" but who should have given her an engagement ring long ago. Tired of being a fat teenager no girl would ever date. Tired of the diet that was supposed to stop him from being fat but after a month took only three pounds off his waistline. So, after eating miniscule portions of baked chicken, steamed broccoli and brown rice, Collin asked to be excused.

"What're you doing the rest of tonight?" his mother asked.

"Homework."

"On a Friday? I thought you'd be getting together with Herbie."

"Herbie was sick today. He texted from his allergist's. Sore throat, puking, even hives. All that good stuff."

"Poor kid," his father interjected. "With so many allergies, seems like he's always got something wrong with him."

"No one's still picking on him because he's biracial, are they?" Collin's mother flashed a worried look at him.

"No, not really."

"Yeah, but Herbie still has problems choosing friends," Eleanor added, unhelpfully. She'd been on Collin's case nonstop the past few weeks, from taking forever in the bathroom to using her playlists without asking. He knew she had a right to be upset with him, but that didn't mean he could ignore this insult.

"Don't be so hard on Herbie. He's always had a crush on you."

Eleanor's nose crinkled in disgust. "Seriously?"

"Yeah, and I bet you get a ring from *him* before you get one from

Roger."

If they'd been younger, Eleanor might have retaliated by flicking a spoonful of rice at her brother. Now, almost 21, she responded with a glare that would make a pit bull tremble.

"Colly, don't be so mean," his mother chided.

"Okay, sorry, but please chill with calling me 'Colly.' You make it sound like I'm a dog."

Before the dinner table drama escalated, Collin got up and headed upstairs. Once in his room, he decided to delay starting on homework until he finished the *Scarlet Angel* comic. He still read comics, but now mostly when he was alone in his room; he kept them a secret from everyone but Herb. It allowed his mind to escape the real world. He'd tried to move on, act his age, but loneliness always drove him back to this escape.

The angel had just rescued a teenage girl from the clutches of Vorman, a warlock slave-dealer, after slicing off the lock of her cage with his celestial sword. But the superhero wasn't out of trouble yet. As he and the girl approached a graveyard surrounding the warlock's cave, the ground began to shake. From behind them, Vorman shouted an incantation:

> Evil ones, hark, though dead you may be
> Rise from your tombs and listen to me.
> In life you were wicked, in death you'll be worse
> As you come together to carry out my curse.
> Find Scarlet Angel and the slave I have lost.
> And return them to me no matter the cost.

With the girl in his arms, Scarlet Angel dashed through the graveyard. Grey hands, grimy with mold and dirt, shot out of the graves and clawed at his feet and legs. Scores of zombies, rotting flesh hanging from their faces, stomped after the angel and the rescued girl.

How will he get out, this time? Collin wondered. He knew that under the terms of his exile from heaven, Scarlet Angel could fly only if no danger was nearby. If he broke that rule, he'd never be accepted back into heaven.

Collin turned the page and read on. In the end, the zombies trapped the angel and the girl against the gate at the far end of the graveyard. As the zombies closed in, Scarlet Angel grabbed his celestial sword. Vorman's undead minions had torn holes in his jeans and jacket, but the sword remained on his belt. Lowering the blade to his feet, the angel tapped the ground six times, then, hoisting it skyward, he swung it around his head six more times.

Suddenly, the celestial sword jumped out of the angel's hand and split into ten separate swords, which then rained down on the advancing ranks of zombies as if they were arrows from heaven. Zombie heads, arms, legs, feet and torsos tumbled and bounced around the angel until not a single zombie remained. After the carnage ended, the ten swords blended together a few feet above the angel's head before easing down into his hand.

Vorman, his bulging eyes flaring red, screamed in rage from the other side of the cemetery. "You won this time, Scarlet Angel, but I know you can only call on heaven to help you seven times, and you just used your sixth. After the seventh, you'll be mine." Then the warlock disappeared in a cloud of black smoke. But as a leader of the worldwide slave market, he would be back.

When he recovered enough strength, the angel flew the girl home and placed her into her own bed. He used his bandana to wipe dirt off her face and hands, then opened a window.

"Who are you?" the girl asked as he prepared to leave.

"No one who you'll remember," he answered before vanishing into the night.

It was true. When the girl woke up, she would recall Vorman, the zombie army and the Scarlet Angel as nothing more than faint images from a nightmare. No one he helped ever remembered him. That was part of the price he paid for being a disobedient angel not bad enough for hell, but not good enough for heaven. He could only return to paradise if he proved himself worthy by helping humans in trouble or despair.

Collin closed the comic and tucked it away on his bookshelf next to a dozen or so other recent issues of the *Scarlet Angel*. Other comics were there, too. *Alien Dusk*, *Western Warrior*, *Meteoria*. Collin empathized with the Scarlet Angel more than the others. Like the angel, he was a faceless nobody. Someone easily ignored and, if noticed, easily forgotten.

Collin picked up his backpack and turned it upside down over his bed.

Six books tumbled out along with paper clips, ballpoint pens, a dented water bottle, a packet of tissues, an unwrapped charging cable, a copy of his school's newspaper, *The Ram Courier*, a three-ring notebook and an unopened Omega-3 deluxe snack pack. He started to put the books away.

First came his copy of *MacBeth* with a picture of a blood-stained crown on its cover. "Out, damned spot!" Collin cried, staring at his right hand. He chuckled as he let the book plop onto his writing desk.

Next came his French III textbook, which he lifted a foot or so above his desk before letting it fall on top of *MacBeth*. "*Je laisse tomber mon livre sur le bureau!*" More chuckles.

The American History text followed. "And so, my fellow Americans," Collin intoned in his best imitation of a Boston accent. "Ask not what your country can do for you – ask what you can do for your country." Then switching decades as well as parties, he pointed to his left. "Mr. Gorbachev, tear down this wall!"

He had no homework in Earth Science, but when he picked up the textbook for that course, Collin couldn't resist additional theatrics, being a nerd – or at least a wannabe nerd - to his core.

Collin added his Algebra II text to the stack without any comments or antics. He couldn't be amused by any subject he was on the verge of flunking.

What the heck is this? Collin plucked the last book off his bed and studied it. This was no textbook. It was too small with no title on the brown cover or along the spine. A thin strip of matching brown elastic stretching across its front kept the book closed and gave it a touch of mystery.

A journal. Whose and how did it get in my backpack? The only way to find out was to look inside. Still, Collin hesitated. Eleanor kept something similar—a diary—during her high school days. The one time he peeked into it, he learned about people she liked and didn't like, the crush she had on her Spanish teacher, her fears about not getting into college and lots of other things she probably wanted to hide. Whoever owned this journal probably also had things to hide. On the other hand, if he didn't at least look at the first page, he'd never know who to give it back to.

Carefully, as if unlocking a tiger's cage, Collin opened the book and flipped to the first page. There was no name on it. In fact, the page was blank except for a sort of title:

Journal of My Secrets by A Girl In Trouble

Who would call herself a girl in trouble? With no clue as to the journal's owner, he turned his thoughts to the second question: *How did this thing get in my backpack?*

Collin rewound the whole day from the moment he left his house to the time when he walked through his front door after school. In class, during restroom stops and walks through the hall, he either carried his backpack or put it within easy reach. And during lunch in the cafeteria… *I did leave my backpack at the table when I went to get some apple cobbler.* The guys he ate with (Fred Givens, Eric Mowery & Ronnie Kleinschmidt) could be pranksters. Whoopee cushions and fake vomit were more their style, but this time maybe they got creative and slipped this phony journal into his backpack while he hunted for an off-diet dessert.

That made sense. This diary had to be a joke. Inside would be mushy confessions of love for him from an unidentified babe. She'd tell how she worshipped him from afar for many months, but could no longer hold her feelings in. She would describe in heart-thumping detail how much she longed to put her arms around him, kiss him, run her hands through his hair and across his chest. Maybe even sleep with him. But it would all be fake.

Collin tossed the mystery book to the floor and dug into his American History homework. As he read about JFK's assassination and the 25th Amendment, Collin let his eyes drift down to where the journal lay next to his trashcan. It seemed odd his lunchtime companions didn't use some cheap notebook for their joke. This journal's brown cover was made of felt and besides the elastic band across the front, a silky bookmark hung from the binding. *Would those clowns spend money just to mess with me?*

Once finished with the 1964 election and needing a break before the agony of Algebra, Collin picked up *The Ram Courier*. He read articles about additional security cameras being placed in the hallways and the principal's leave of absence due to cancer, but skimmed over sports scores and club news.

Then curiosity got the better of him. Putting the newspaper down, he snatched the journal off the floor and fanned through the pages from start to finish. He was astonished to see writing on all but the last few.

Returning to the beginning, he went beyond the title to the second page, the third page, the fourth and the fifth, reading every word laid down in precise, delicate handwriting. By the time he read forty pages, he was shaky and his heart beat so fast he wondered if he could get a heart attack at his age.

He slapped the volume shut and let it fall back onto the floor. He still didn't know whose diary it was or how it ended up in his backpack, but one thing he did know for sure…

This is no joke.

Chapter 2

"**Y**ou found what in your backpack?" Herbie's surprise came through despite his raspy voice.

"You heard me. A girl's journal."

"What girl?"

"I don't know her name, but she's a junior like us. Calls herself 'a girl in trouble.'"

"How did it get in your backpack?"

"Don't know that either." Collin sensed his friend's growing interest.

"Okay," Herbie said after a short pause. "Why not turn it into Lost and Found? If she really wants it back, she'll probably check there anyway."

"I guess I could, except..."

"Except what?"

"Except if the journal goes to Lost and Found, the office secretaries will read it, and there's stuff in there she won't want them or anyone else to see."

"Is she pregnant?"

"If she isn't, she could be soon."

Herbie's gasp seemed to burst out of Collin's cell and echo through his bedroom. "How much of it have you read?"

"Almost half. Enough to know she's not joking about being a girl in trouble."

There was another pause. Collin figured Herbie wanted at least a few details about the girl's trouble. He hadn't planned to share details, but suddenly needed for his one and only real friend to be in on this too. "She's got this boyfriend she calls Red Lion. She cheated on him with another guy, and now he's real demanding on her, if, um, you know what I mean."

"He wants her to put out?"

"Yeah, right. Anyway, she wants to dump him, but he's got something on her that makes it hard for her to do that."

"Maybe she feels guilty for cheating."

"I think it's something else. Something really big. But there's no way of knowing until I find out who she is."

"And I take it you want me to help you find out?"

"Well, yeah. You're my best friend and the smartest guy I know."

"Get real, big man. I'm your only friend and the smartest student in the school... except for Winifred Scoles."

Collin sighed. "Right."

"Let's start with how it got into your backpack. Did you have the backpack with you the whole day?"

"Yes, except at lunch. When I went for some apple cobbler, I left it under the table."

"Is apple cobbler on your diet?"

"I can have a half cup of fresh fruit at lunch."

"Cobbler counts as fresh fruit?"

"Close enough!" Collin waved his hand around in frustration. "What's that got to do with where my backpack was?"

"Nothing. Just curious. But maybe that's when the mystery girl put it into your backpack."

"I can think of three reasons why that's impossible."

"Three?"

"Yeah. Fred, Eric and Ronnie. The Three Stooges of Bridgeview High. If any girl even came close to our table, they'd have yakked their heads off about it or they'd have scared her away to begin with."

"Okay, let's look at this a different way. You said you always had the backpack with you except at lunch. Could you always see it?"

"Yes, when I'm in class, it's beside my desk or under it. When I go from one class to another, I carry it."

"You don't put it on your back, do you?"

"You've seen me. I wear it on my back only when I'm going to school or leaving. Inside of school, I haul it around on one shoulder. It's too much trouble to keep putting it on and taking it off."

"What did you do between classes before and after lunch? We'll rule out the boys' room since I don't think any girl would've followed you in there. You must have stopped at your locker at least once."

"Twice. Before homeroom and then before seventh period."

"And you saw your backpack?"

"Yes! I kept it between my legs or right next to them."

"I'm sure you would've seen a girl crawling around your legs."

"I'd have done more than see her." Herbie's questions were kind of annoying, but Collin knew he didn't ask them to be nosy. A girl crawling around his legs would have frozen him in hot disbelief.

"Did you make any other stops between classes?"

"You mean like look at a bulletin board or display case?"

"Yeah, or maybe talk to someone or get a drink from a water fountain or something."

"Hmm… I talked to Jimmy outside of homeroom and to Mrs. Rowland in the hallway after English. Bill asked me about a homework assignment right before Earth Science and I didn't exactly talk to Blake, he talked to me, sort of. Called me a lard butt who should make the world a better place by drinking cyanide-flavored Kool-Aid."

"Ah yes, Blake Emerick—living proof evolution can work backwards. Anyone else?"

"I don't think so. And anyway, with all those guys, I kept my backpack right next to me. Oh, yeah, one more thing. I stayed late after seventh period to get help from Ms. Riley."

"Algebra II?"

"Yeah, afraid I'm going to flunk it. Anyway, after I finished talking to her, I got a drink of water."

"Don't you carry a water bottle?"

"It was empty by then."

"When you got your drink of water, where did you put your backpack?"

"Right next to me or maybe a little behind."

"But if you bent over a fountain, you couldn't watch it."

"I guess not, but I only stayed at the fountain about ten seconds."

"Was anybody behind you, waiting to take a drink after you?"

Collin thought for a moment. "You know, for a second, I thought somebody was waiting for me to finish, but when I got done, no one was there."

"I'd say that's probably when the diary got slipped into your backpack."

"What? I mean, come on! Like I said, it only took a few seconds to get that drink. She'd have to move faster than an Olympic sprinter to get her journal into my backpack."

"I'm no expert on girls, but I bet they can move pretty fast if they want to."

"Maybe you're right. For all I know, this girl's a track star for reals."

"Did you see anyone else in the hallway after you finished your drink?"

"No… well Gail and Luke were about to suck face by her locker. There might have been one or two others; I can't remember who."

Herbie stayed silent, thinking. Collin almost felt the flow of energy through his friend's brain as his analysis of the mystery turned in a new direction. After over a minute of silence, Herbie asked, "She didn't put her name in this thing?"

"Right."

"Any other names in it besides this Red Lion guy?"

"Well, yes and no."

"Huh?"

"She does talk about teachers but just uses the first letter of their last name like Mrs. O or Mr. B. With other people, she uses their first and last name initials."

"How about dates? Most people start each entry with the month and day each time they write."

"Not her, except for sometimes mentioning a day of the week."

"What about room numbers, classes, places she goes with Red Lion?"

"There's nothing about room numbers, but she does talk about the classes she's taking."

"Like what?"

"English, Spanish —"

"Spanish makes sense. Mrs. Oswald teaches Spanish. I'm betting that's who Mrs. O is."

"She doesn't say much about where she and Red Lion go on their dates. Except sometimes it sounds like they go to a motel."

"A motel? Doesn't sound like a date; it's… I don't know… like something from a trash TV talk show."

Collin glanced at the brown book. "If you read this thing, you'd see it's worse than anything on trash TV. What should I do with this thing, Herbie?"

"It depends on what you want to do for her. If you just want to return it to her, take it to Lost and Found or, better still, put a notice in *The Ram*

Courier saying you've found a brown journal and offering to give it to its rightful owner. On the other hand…" Herbie's words hung in the air for a few seconds before he finished his sentence. "… if you want to help this girl escape from her scumbag boyfriend, you'll need to find out who they are."

Collin fell silent. No girl had ever expressed the slightest interest in him, much less ever needed him for anything. His few efforts to get a date either ended in polite rejection or outright humiliation. He didn't even risk admiring a girl from afar lest she catch him gawking. Yet now, through some twist of fate, he'd been given the chance to rescue a girl in desperate trouble, to be – he hardly dared think the words—her hero.

His mind drifted back to an old comic book he once found in his grandmother's attic—*The FBI Story*. It was filled with true cases of G-men tracking down bank robbers, bootleggers and cold-blooded killers. The G-men were real heroes, not make-believe ones. The stories were all based on true events. That's what he needed to be. A real hero like an FBI agent. Yet, how could he be anything to this girl in trouble if he didn't even know who she was?

"Hey, big man, are you still there?" Herbie's voice brought Collin back to the here and now.

"Yah, I'm still here and I told you. She doesn't put her name anywhere and—"

"I get that, but by finding out the classes she's taking, what teachers she has, we can probably still figure out who she is. And once we know that, we can probably identify Red Lion, too."

"And then?"

"And then… I don't know. Let's find out who these people are first."

Collin felt relief Herbie used the word "we." He considered the two of them a team whose combined talents could solve this mystery and rescue this girl from her evil boyfriend.

"Come over tomorrow and you can read the journal for yourself."

"I will if I'm feeling better."

"Oh yeah, I forgot you missed school today. What is it this time?"

"Crushed croutons in a salad my aunt brought over last night. There were so many other things in this salad, nobody noticed those little crusty fragments of bread until it was too late."

"Uh oh. Were the croutons made from wheat bread?"

"They sure were. I nearly croaked. Spent four hours at the ER and two more at my allergist's."

"Well, I'll bring the book over to your place if you want so my sister doesn't go crazy about germ exposure since she thinks everything is contagious."

"Yah, that might be better. Come around one. That'll give you time to read the rest of the diary."

"Sounds good, see you tomorrow afternoon."

Collin put his cell away and cast another glance at the little brown book. It seemed fitting for it to be on top of his Algebra text. Both books, in their own way, bewildered and frightened him. As for reading the rest of it, he decided not to for now. If he did delve deeper into this girl's life, he wanted Herbie to go with him – and share his horror.

Chapter 3

Collin pushed the door open and peered inside the bedroom he knew almost as well as his own. There were beautiful framed photographs hanging on the walls. Herbie took most of them himself. The subjects varied from mountain & cloud formations to human creations like bridges & buildings. Straight ahead was Herbie's desk, clear except for a lamp and a laptop. The westward-facing window in front of the desk had its shade pulled down, probably to reduce the glare from outside. Like so many other things, too much sunlight caused Herbie to get a headache.

At the desk was a weathered solid-maple captain's chair once owned by Herbie's great-grandfather, a Jamaican fisherman. An aluminum folding chair had been pulled up next to it. To the left, an overloaded bookcase nestled against a dresser covered with pill bottles, ointments, inhalers, epinephrine autoinjectors and an insulin pen. The wall above the dresser held a poster of Herbie's hero: Albert Einstein… sticking out his tongue. To the right of the desk, Herbie stretched out on his bed, nose buried in a copy of Stephen Hawking's *A Brief History of Time*. His glasses and bushy eyebrows made him look like a tall owl.

"I thought you already read that book," said Collin, closing the door behind him.

"Twice, but there's always the chance I missed something."

"You could always go back to *Blue Marvel and Cyborg*."

"I stopped comic book heroes years ago." Herbie pushed his thin five-foot-five-inch frame out of the bed and tossed the book back onto his pillow. "But I guess you've got something new for us to read today, don't you?"

"Wish I didn't."

"Let's get started."

Collin placed the journal on the desk and prepared to sit in the folding chair but Herbie motioned him toward the more-comfortable captain's chair. "You have center stage, big man, so you get the seat of honor."

"Thanks."

Herbie gripped the desk with both hands and eased himself into the aluminum chair; he obviously hadn't fully recovered from his latest allergy attack. Collin opened the journal to the first page. Herbie read the title. "Nice handwriting," he said. "I'd say this girl cares about what she does and how it looks." Herbie steadied his glasses and turned to the second page.

Dad's stroke was worse than we thought. Yesterday we found that out the hard way when he fell, trying to go down the steps to the patio. At first, we thought he just got cuts and bruises but an x-ray showed he broke his wrist. "Could have been a lot worse," the doctor said. Sure, but could have been a lot better, too. Now he has a cast on his right wrist and can hardly hold a spoon or fork. At breakfast he was dropping so much cereal on the table, mom ended up spoon feeding him like a baby. Dad also gets dizzy sometimes, which is what caused him to fall in the first place. At least his speech isn't so slurry as it was right after the stroke. Mom's hoping to get rehab for him. Question is will our health insurance cover it? Mom's already stressing out about money. She plans to go back to subbing, maybe be a tutor or library assistant. Should I help out more? Get a part-time job on weekends or after school? That might be a good idea if I wasn't so stressed out about school, especially Algebra. If I flunk it or even get a D, my chances of a scholarship will sink. GS offered to help me, start having study dates again, but that's how my troubles started! So goodbye college! No future career in journalism for me. Better start learning to flip burgers now.

Herbie paused. "She sure hates Algebra, doesn't she?"

"A girl after my own heart."

"Who do you suppose GS is?"

"I have a theory, but keep reading for now."

Over the next several pages, the girl seesawed between her father's physical struggles and her mother's working as a substitute teacher and an English tutor. Then, halfway down page 14, she shifted to a new topic.

Red Lion wants me to come over for sex tonight. He didn't say so, but I know that's what will happen because that's what always happens now when I see him.

Herbie paused again and looked at Collin. "So this is where Red Lion comes into the picture. The nasty boyfriend. I thought you said they went to a motel for their dates."

"The motel comes later. Keep going."

The whole thing is kind of funny. If I were a character in a book, people would laugh at me. "What an idiot she is!" they'd say. And the more they read, the more they'd laugh. It's Wednesday morning now, a few clouds but mostly sunny, pleasant. But I never wanted the day to start. Now that it's started, I don't want it to end. Is there a way to stop the earth from spinning? I can't stand this. My stomach feels like it's filled with acid eating away at my guts. I'm gunna puke! The waiting, the dreading. The hoping that something happens to keep the night from coming. Maybe a tornado could whisk me away to Oz. Ha! I'd tell Dorothy she was lucky she only had to deal with a wicked witch. But it's my fault. The whole thing is. Red Lion's right to treat me this way. Caught me cheating. No excuses! No escape! Have to admit I've always wanted a boyfriend. But not this. I want this to end. But how? I can't get away or he will destroy my whole life.

"Interesting," said Herbie. "Her handwriting is neat, but she's kind of disorganized. Like she has a lot to say but not much time to say it."

"I'd say it's a scared writing style," Collin replied.

"I wish she gave us a clue to her identity or to the identities of Red Lion or GS.

"I might not know who GS is, but I think we can guess what he did."

"We can?"

"He's the guy the girl cheated with; the guy Red Lion caught her with. That's my theory, anyway."

"Well, she does say having study dates with him is how her troubles began, so maybe you're right."

Herbie forged ahead onto the next page where the girl continued to fret over an upcoming "date" with Red Lion.

Stomach pain is easing but a headache has set in. Palms are sweaty and my mouth is dry with a salty taste covering my tongue. Legs twitch. Toes curl inside my shoes. Fingers drum on my desk. Typical when a date with Red Lion is closing in. How to end this thing? Maybe try to make myself uglier than I already am. Skip showering and brushing teeth for a couple of days. Let my hair go and not shave my legs, which I hate doing anyway. I read somewhere girls in Europe don't do this. Aren't they the lucky ones! Red Lion probably wouldn't care, as long as I do him. But mom would. She's got enough on her hands with dad and work. She doesn't need the added worry of a daughter looking crappy.

Then abruptly she shifted attention to some of her classes.

Hardly slept at all last night. Just as well. Would have had nightmares. Maybe I can snooze during Mr. A's class. His lectures are so long & boring! Already know most of the stuff he talks about anyway.

"I wish we knew what happened between these last two paragraphs," said Herbie.

"Yeah, it'd sure help if she put in the dates when things happened."

"At least we have our first clue to this kid's identity." Herbie reached down under his desk and pulled out a copy of Bridgeview High School's latest yearbook.

"What did that run you?" asked Collin.

"Nothing. It's a freebie for being the chief photographer." He thumbed to the pages featuring members of the faculty and then passed his finger over the photos of three men. "These're the only male teachers whose last names begin with A."

"Aren't a few of the new teachers men?" Collin asked.

"Just two, I think. Mr. Hamblin and Mr. Schrader. And since those names don't begin with A, we don't need to worry about them."

"Right, professor. Even my pathetic, barely average brain figured that out."

"Good for you. You're coming along nicely, big man." Herbie grinned at his friend before pointing at the first of the three photos. "Mr. Alejandro teaches industrial arts. Lots of girls taking his class now. Most of his work is hands-on. You know, demonstrating stuff. Not much lecturing."

"Yeah," agreed Collin. "You can't sleep in a class like his."

Herbie shifted his finger to the second photo. "Coach Alexander is even easier."

Collin nodded. "How much lecturing does a gym teacher do?"

"Not much, but he does yell a lot." Herbie moved to the third picture. "Here's our prime suspect: Mr. Armistead, American History."

"I've got Mr. Petrie for that class, and you have Ms. Danforth, right?" asked Collin.

"Yeah, but I know a couple of guys who have Armistead."

"And?"

"Well, the man does know a lot, but he blabs about things students don't need to know."

"Snooze-time."

"For sure."

Herbie continued reading. There were more complaints about Algebra and new complaints about filling out college applications, as well as expressions of sorrow over a friend who moved away.

Should I e-mail SM about what I'm going through? What

for? What can she do 1,000 miles away in Denver? Besides, she might not even believe me.

When Herbie reached the 19th page, Collin let his eyes drop toward the bottom. He knew another teacher's last initial appeared there. After a few seconds, he found it. "Read this." He tapped the paper.

Hope Mrs. R doesn't call on me to read anything out loud. Can't stand The Scarlet Letter. So much misery & hypocrisy, but compared to my life it's slapstick comedy.

Herbie's eyebrows went up and he stroked his chin like a wise old man. "So, she's in one of Mrs. Rowland's English classes. You have Mrs. Rowland, don't you?"

"Yeah, second period."

"We read *The Scarlet Letter* in AP English back in October."

"So did my class."

Herbie stroked his chin harder. "Which means she started this diary at least five months ago."

Collin nodded and flipped the page. "Things start to heat up pretty soon."

When they reached the top of page 22, Collin tensed up, knowing what came next. He squirmed in his seat and rubbed his hands across his eyes. *Do I really want to help this girl or am I a sick voyeur who should be locked up?*

The SC. Third time here. Red Lion uses same phony names for us. Room 104. What does it matter? Might as well be on the roof. Maybe I'll write a memoir someday about all this. More like a horror novel, except it won't be fiction. The worst of it is the way Red Lion leers at me before he actually touches me. His head juts forward and he stands there grinning and gloating, nose flaring, like a predator sizing up its prey. Finally he –

Herbie brought his hand down, blocking the lower half of the page. "Do we really need to read this to find out who this girl is?"

"No." Shame shot through Collin; he felt his face flush. "I shouldn't have read it last night, either, but at least I can tell you there's nothing about teachers here."

"And what do you suppose she means by the SC?"

"Seacrest Motel, I'd guess."

"If you're right then this Red Lion's got to have a car and money, too."

"He wouldn't need much money. The Seacrest is a real dump. Anyway, let's jump to where she talks about her classes and teachers again."

Collin flipped ahead to page 29 and pointed to some sentences in the middle. "Here you go."

Got to get new Spanish dictionary. Spilled ketchup on old one. That's what happens when you have to read Mexican poems during lunch because you were busy with other things last night. No time to eat but usually can't stand the slop they serve us anyway.

"Aha, this does help." Herbie said. "We figured out her teacher is Mrs. Oswald, right?"

"Right," answered Collin. He picked up the yearbook and returned to the faculty section. "The one other teacher whose last name starts with O is Mrs. O'Brien, who teaches English and we already know —"

"Mrs. Rowland is her English teacher," said Herbie.

"Right again!" Collin bubbled with excitement. *Wow, we're really thinking like a team.*

"Wait," said Herbie, pointing to the writing under Mrs. Oswald's name. "She teaches Spanish I, II and III. Which one is our mystery girl in?"

"A junior would be in third-year Spanish, wouldn't she?"

"Not necessarily. You don't need a foreign language to graduate anymore, so this might be her second year or even her first." Herbie frowned and went back to the brown book. "Let's not worry about that for now. Last night, you said the girl wrote about another teacher, a Mr. B."

"Yeah." Collin thumbed ahead to page 40.

Red Lion giving me a break next couple of days. Bless his sweet black heart! But compassion isn't what motivates him. He's just too geared up for the Rams football game with Westport, our big rivals. Keeps saying "we're gonna kick the hell out of them!" I don't give a ram's ass. Two tests coming up. I'm ready for Mrs. O's but not Mr. B's. Maybe study for it during lunch. The caf is serving beef stew today. Dog vomit would taste better than that crap. I'll settle for their brown lettuce salad.

"She sure hates cafeteria food," said Herbie.

"Some of it is pretty gross."

"Guess that's one good thing about having so many food allergies. I just bring my own lunch to school." Herbie refocused on the teacher photos in the yearbook. "There're four possible Mr. Bs the mystery girl could be talking about."

The boys ran down all the B teachers, their schedules and topics.

There wasn't an obvious one like there had been for English.

"Whichever class it is would be after her lunch, anywhere from fifth period to eighth period."

"Right!"

"What did you find out in the second half of the diary?"

"Umm... I haven't read it yet."

"Why not?"

Collin's head drooped. "I feel like I've violated this girl's privacy enough. I only wanna read more if we can't figure out who she is from what we already have."

"I get you, big man." Herbie closed the yearbook and slipped it back under his desk; Collin put the bookmark near the journal's middle and closed it.

A long moment of silence followed.

Then Herbie reached into his top desk drawer and pulled out a piece of notebook paper and a ballpoint pen. He wrote on the paper for about a minute and then pushed it toward Collin. "Here's what we know about the mystery girl so far. We'll call her Hester, you know, like Hester Prynne – another girl in trouble."

Hester, Junior at Bridgeview High School
Mr. Armistead for American History

**Mrs. Rowland for English
Mrs. Oswald for Spanish I, II or III
Mr. Blount for Computer Science or Mr. Browning for
Algebra I or II (after 4th period)**

"It'd sure help to have attendance lists for these classes," said Collin. "Then we'd see which students had all four of these teachers and pick out the ones that could be Hester."

"I think I can get that."

Collin stared at his friend. "How? Hack the school's computers?"

"Don't need to hack anything. I'll get them through MYSTUDENT."

"What?"

"It's an online system that lets teachers keep track of their students and record their grades."

"If it's for teachers, how can you use—"

"I got the password to it earlier this year when I did a research project comparing the courses students took with their extracurricular activities. Unless they changed the password since December, I should get in."

Herbie pulled his laptop over in front of him and began typing. "Damn!" he said, slumping in the aluminum chair. "They did change the password. This will take longer than I hoped, but we'll still get in."

Collin's eyes rolled. "How?"

"Oh, I'll find a way. I always do with problems like this." Herbie folded his hands behind his head. "Can you come over tomorrow about two?"

"I think so."

"Good. I should have the lists by then."

Chapter 4

*W*hen Collin got to Herbie's room the following afternoon, he noticed the dresser had nothing on it except a box of thumb tacks. He also saw a stack of papers on his friend's desk. He picked up the one on top. *A class list!* He read the heading. *Rowland, English II, Second Period, Room 145. Students Enrolled: 23.* Below were the names of the students, including his own, in alphabetical order, last name first. Several had e-mail addresses next to them.

"Guess you figured out the password," Collin said to his friend, who stood halfway into his closet, apparently searching for something.

"Easy peasy," Herbie's muffled voice carried back to Collin. "The password in December was 1940RHS#1. The new one is the same except the RHS is now lowercased and the #1 is changed to #2 probably because we're in the second semester."

A scraping sound followed by a thump came out of the closet.

Collin knew his friend kept all sorts of things in there—folding chairs, camera equipment, picture frames – so he couldn't tell what made the noise.

Herbie came out with an old bulletin board in his hands. He placed it on the dresser with its back leaning against the wall. The board covered the lower edge of the Einstein poster, giving the impression the great scientist, with his derisive expression, mocked their efforts.

Collin handed the top few lists over and Herbie tacked them in a row across the top of the bulletin board.

Herbie stepped back from the dresser and folded his arms. "Now, let's see which junior girls are taking English from Mrs. Rowland and American History from Mr. Armistead."

Working together, the two teens identified 49 girls in the four English classes taught by Mrs. Rowland. Of that number, 18 also had Mr.

Armistead for American History.

"Let's thin the ranks of our suspects a little more," said Herbie. "Let's cross check them with Mrs. Oswald's Spanish classes."

Collin scowled before complying. "Don't call them suspects. They're victims, or at least one of them is. We'll be the FBI guys, the good guys helping the innocent. Well, the kinda innocent."

Herbie gave an exaggerated bow. "Please accept my deepest apologies for this unforgiveable slip of the tongue. I now realize it is a horrible affront to the—"

"Just pin the Spanish lists up, dickwad."

Herbie took down the first set of lists and pinned up the Spanish, Algebra and Computer Science classes. That cut the list of possible Hesters from way too many, to seven, to four. Herbie wrote their names down on a sheet of paper and pinned it to the bulletin board.

Jane Tarquinio
Leah Jennings
Wanda Stenholm
Carmen Harper-Hawkins

"Do you know any of them?" asked Herbie.

Collin studied the names for a half minute before answering. "Not really. Don't have a clue who Jane is. Wanda is in my English class, but I've never said a word to her. Leah… don't know her either. And Carmen, well, I know who she is, don't you?"

Everyone from the custodian to the principal knew or knew about Carmen Harper-Hawkins. Student council president, homecoming queen, track star and a hundred other things. Carmen seemed the last person in the world to be a victim of sexual abuse.

"You never know," said Herbie. "Everyone's life is like an iceberg. Only a small part of us can be seen by other people."

Collin stretched out his legs, trying to channel a professional agent. "Come on, Herb. Carmen would never let herself be pushed around by a scumbag boyfriend. Anyway, I don't think she has a steady boyfriend, does she?"

"Well, I'm not going steady with her."

Collin let a thin smile creep onto his face. As far as he knew, Herbie had never even been on a date, let alone expressed interest in a girl before. He figured some girls would be drawn to Herbie since his friend, though short looked just fine and was super nice. His caramel-colored skin and his edgy dreadlocks gave him a sharp, put-together look; all except for his bushy eyebrows. Like Collin, Herbie had been bullied sometimes – in his case because of his race. That experience was probably why he was shy and mostly quiet.

"Let's see," Herbie said stroking his chin. "Danny Sullivan took her to homecoming, didn't he?"

"He escorted her onto the field for the crowning ceremony, but I don't know if they ever went out."

"Maybe they didn't. Anyway, I've seen her with at least two other guys since then. You know, Frank what's-his-name on the basketball team, and that foreign exchange student from Scotland. I doubt she's under any guy's thumb. If anything, she makes them do whatever she wants then leaves them."

"It looks that way, but then we don't really know what an abused girl looks like, do we?"

Collin shrugged. "No. Every girl is a mystery to guys like us."

"You mean nerds?"

"Yeah, except I'm not even a genuine nerd. You got to be super smart to be a nerd."

"You're smart enough, big man." Herbie unpinned the list and laid it on his desk. "Let's go back to the diary for a minute. Does it mention homecoming, student council or anything else that might point to Carmen as the writer?"

"Not a thing."

"Still, you've only read about half of it, right?"

"Right." Collin realized his partner in this was heading in the right direction, no matter how much he wanted to take the high road, it looked like to get more clues, he'd have to read more of her private, secret thoughts.

"Her writing is still the only place where we can find more about Hester's true identity." Herbie's bushy eyebrows went up. "Unless you want to ask these girls face-to-face if they have a cruel boyfriend who demands sex from them."

"No fracking way. But I still don't like getting deeper..."

"I know you don't, but unless we go further into her words, we're going to be stuck right here with too many choices."

"All right," said Collin. "Let's meet up after school tomorrow to read more of it."

Herbie sighed. "It's got to be Tuesday. I have a doctor's appointment tomorrow right after school."

"Which doctor this time?"

"Dr. Schultz, the allergist."

"I thought you saw him last Friday for your wheat allergy."

"I did. Same doctor, different allergy – strawberries, I think."

"Lucky you."

Chapter 5

Because he did a lot of online job hunting, Collin's father often let him drive the family car to school. Today, however, Mr. Morris had two job interviews, so Collin took the school bus – something he didn't like to do. The ride itself didn't bother him. It was who he met when he got off. Dull-witted, tough guy, born-loser bully Blake Emerick rode a different bus than Collin's, but the two of them always seemed to reach the unloading zone at the same time. Today proved no exception.

"Hey Morris, guess what?" Blake yelled, as they crowded through Bridgeview High's west entrance.

Collin ignored him.

"When I got off the bus, I thought there was an eclipse of the sun. But then I realized it was your big butt blotting out the sun." Blake flashed a gap-toothed grin that quickly morphed into a sneer.

Collin almost never responded to Blake's insults, but today, he felt differently. Being an FBI agent was the first real path to having a real life that seemed possible. He could do that and still not be in totally great shape. He could be an agent that helped people. But not if he let himself be pushed around. "That's amazing, Blake. Truly amazing."

"What? That you've got a big butt?"

"Nah! That you know what an eclipse is."

Collin didn't know where this sudden burst of courage came from, but he took advantage of the bully's startled silence to dash off toward his locker. Learning to push back was one thing, standing there to get pummeled was another.

During English class, Collin tried to listen to Mrs. Rowland discuss MacBeth's downfall from unrestrained ambition, but his gaze kept drifting one row ahead to where Wanda Stenholm sat. Everything from her flower-printed backpack to the neatly combed hair draped over one shoulder of her navy-blue sweater seemed normal, even dull. *That may not mean anything,* thought Collin. *Hester's not going to carry around a sign that says **"Abused Girl, Please Help."** More likely, she's going to hide the fact she's at the mercy of some creepy guy.*

Later in the cafeteria, Collin watched Carmen eat her lunch at a nearby table. Twice boys came over and sat next to her for a few minutes. Collin guessed they were asking her for a date. The first left with a sagging face. The second bounded away with a giddy smile and a fist pump. It seemed impossible Carmen could be Hester. *She could have any guy she wanted as a boyfriend. Wouldn't need to put up with one who treated her like shit even if she did feel guilty about cheating on him. And yet, Herb's right. Everyone's life is like an iceberg. Maybe there's a darker part of this girl's life we can't see at school.*

In fifth-period study hall, Collin took a break from wondering about Hester and read an old issue of the Scarlet Angel. He loved this issue: *Stovok's Pit* where the angel was trying to rescue Yuri, a young boy being used as a slave laborer in a Russian silver mine. His hero first had to discover where Yuri was kept. That wasn't easy because Stovok, the greedy mine owner, controlled a whole network of cages and cells where he imprisoned his slaves when they weren't working. Only by becoming a slave himself was the angel able to find the boy, free him and take him home after a torturous journey through the Ural Mountains with Stovok in hot pursuit. At the end, after returning Yuri to his family, the angel despaired about the other slaves he left behind at the silver mine.

"How many are still there? A hundred? No – more like two hundred. Two hundred boys and girls who will continue to work their lives away for that slimy leech Stovok who doesn't care what happens to them as long as he gets full wagons of silver."

Then Scarlet Angel heard a voice from heaven.

"You saved Yuri, didn't you?"

"Yes, but he's just one child."

"When you save one, you give hope to others."

Those final words gave Collin's spirits a lift. Hiding the comic at the bottom of his backpack, Collin smacked his fist into his palm. *Hope I get the chance to punch Red Lion someday. Maybe I should start some martial arts classes. I bet that will help me get into the FBI and pound a few bullies into next week if they keep messing with me.*

***

*T*he lift Collin got from the Scarlet Angel didn't last. As the day wore on, frustration crept over him. He knew Hester had to be close by, even if she just passed him in the hall once a day. He decided to repeat the route he took last Friday afternoon in the hopes she might be around him again. So he stayed a little late in his seventh period Algebra class and then got a drink from the same fountain he used Friday. Shifting his head as he sucked in water, Collin scanned the hallway in both directions. He saw Gail and Luke snuggling up again by her locker. This time two boys rushed past him and entered the language lab across from the lovebirds. There was no Hester to be seen anywhere.

He arrived to his last class – French III – two minutes late and more frustrated than ever.

"*Pourquoi êtes-vous en retard, Monsieur Morris?*" asked his annoyed teacher.

"*Je suis désolé, Madame Haas. J'ai dû aider un ami avec un problème.*"

"*D'accord. Veuillez vous asseoir.*"

Collin took his seat, feeling totally honest with saying he'd been late because he helped a friend. *She doesn't know it yet, but I'm the best friend Hester has.*

Chapter 6

Collin's family seemed in good spirits at the dinner table that evening. His dad talked about a second interview he landed with a local contractor, his mother bubbled with enthusiasm over a painting she finished and hoped to sell and Eleanor glowed with confidence about a birthday dinner Roger planned for her.

"He's made reservations at the Moravian Bistro," she gushed. "This has got to be it! This has got to be the moment he's been waiting for to propose."

"The Moravian Bistro?" His father whistled. "If Roger did buy you an engagement ring and then gets you a fancy dinner, he'll be broke before you can send out invitations."

"Oh Dad, don't be so depressing. Right now, Roger probably has more money than… than…" Eleanor's words caught in her throat.

"Than us? Than me? Is that what you wanted to say?" His father's mood turned sour.

As she so often did, his mother jumped in to head off trouble. "Who cares whether Roger makes more money than you, Ted? That's not what will make him a good husband for El."

"I suppose not," said his father, his tone still bitter.

Collin, who just finished another borderline-starvation dinner, tried to help by changing the subject. "What would you like me to get you for your birthday, El?"

"Huh?"

"What do you want for your birthday?"

His sister crinkled her nose. "I don't know. Whatever you can afford, I guess." A mischievous smile came over her lips. "Don't give me any comic books, though. I don't need to be rescued by the Scarface Angel or whatever that guy's name is that keeps you stuck in elementary school."

"No problem," said Collin; ignoring insults was his superpower. *But Roger might need to be rescued if he doesn't give you a ring pretty soon.* He pushed himself away from the table and picked up his plate and silverware.

"Colly, remember to scrape off your plate and put it in the dishwasher," his mom called after him.

"Sure. Or I can lick it off like any other dog."

* * *

Around 8:30, with most of his homework done, Collin gave Herbie a call.

"How'd your appointment go, Sir Isaac?"

"It wasn't strawberries this time. Turns out I've got vibratory urticaria," Herbie replied.

"What?"

"I'm allergic to vibrations."

"You're making that up!"

Herbie let out a prolonged sigh. "That's why my arms got covered in hives when I tested my dad's new power drill a while back. Dr. Schultz said it's genetic. I've probably had it my whole life, but with all my other allergies, it kind of got overlooked until now."

"Did you get some medicine for this… this vibratory whatever?"

"Yeah, some antihistamines. Mom says with all my pills and medicines, I'm going to need my own personal medicine cabinet. She laughed about it, but I know she's more worried than ever about me."

Collin almost said he didn't blame her, but stopped himself. It would be better to focus on their mission right now and keep Herbie from feeling bad about this new health issue. Herb's voice was giving away that he felt down about one more problem being stacked on his shoulders.

"I still don't know who Hester is," Collin lamented. "I watched Wanda in English and Carmen at lunch. As far as I can see, Wanda isn't shook. Doesn't act sad or scared, doesn't have any bruises I can see. And Carmen! Man, she can't even take a bite of salad without some guy hitting on her. She waves them around like her own personal slaves. I can't believe any guy would push her around. If he did, ten others would beat the shit out of him."

"I guess it goes back to us not really knowing what an abused girl looks like, which is why we probably won't find her unless…"

Collin gripped his phone harder. "Unless we read the rest of the journal and find more clues about her. Can you meet me at the Bridgeview Library right after school tomorrow?"

"The school library stays open for an hour after the last class. You don't want to meet there?"

"No. If Mrs. Hennessy sees us with a book that isn't a textbook or from the school library, she'll get nosy. If she realizes it is a real student's journal, she'll take it from us."

"Okay. I'll meet you at the front desk tomorrow around four. One thing, though."

"What?"

"Don't bring an electric drill."

* * *

Collin thought about Hester and Red Lion. It didn't make sense. *If you liked a girl enough to spend a lot of time with her, why would you treat her like shit? Make her do things she didn't want to do? If she did go out with another guy, why not forgive her and give her another chance?*

Collin doubted he would ever have a girlfriend. He was just too puffy all over to be considered good looking. But if he did, he knew what he'd do. *I'd treat her real special. Get flowers for her and take her to nice places. We'd walk together, holding hands and shopping or whatever, wherever she wanted.*

Before he tried to make his dream of a girlfriend come true with a good job and some martial arts skills, Collin needed to end another girl's nightmare. A real girl.

Chapter 7

*T*he next school day passed slowly. Collin didn't bother glancing toward Wanda during English or Carmen at lunch. He'd rely on that little brown book to reveal any new clues about Hester's identity. As for the journal itself, he decided keeping it in his backpack was safer than storing it in his locker. For added security, he put the little volume in a crumpled brown paper bag, so if anyone snooped into his backpack, they'd think it was some icky leftover food. Collin didn't have any classes with Herbie, but he usually saw his friend at least once a day between periods. Since they hadn't run into each other yet, he texted Herbie before seventh period Algebra.

U here?
Yes, came late. Allergy attack
Which one this time?
Not sure. Feel OK now
Still on 4 library @ 4?

👍

In Algebra, Ms. Riley hit her students with a ten-question pop quiz that required them to express equations on graph paper. Collin hated working with graph paper. Even so, he managed to give answers for all the questions, hoping maybe seven were correct. He then made an unscheduled stop at his locker to grab a diet-approved snack from his coat pocket. *This diet is going to kill me,* he thought as he swallowed the last bits of a dried mango bar.

Rushing to French, Collin bumped into Blake Emerick—or more likely, Blake bumped into him.

"Sorry," Collin mumbled.

"Don't 'sorry' me, lard ass," Blake snapped. "Next time, I'll break your jaw to help you lose some fat."

"Try it," Collin retorted. Shocking himself.

Blake contorted his pock-marked face into a scowl but apparently couldn't think up a new insult before Collin strode away.

After class, Collin walked the half mile from the high school to the public library. Not so long ago, a walk like this would have left him sweaty and out of breath. Now, however, he came through the library's doors feeling pretty good and relatively dry. As planned, Herbie waited for him by the front desk. His friend pulled an inhaler from his pants pocket, shook it several times, and sucked in a dose. Collin had seen Herbie go through this routine many times, but it worried him anyway. *How will he ever have a normal life when his health is so bad?*

"Are you okay?" asked Collin.

"I am now," said Herbie, stuffing the inhaler back into his pocket. "Got the diary?"

Collin tapped the top of his backpack. "Let's go upstairs and see what else Hester can tell us."

On the library's second floor, the two teens found an unoccupied reading table. Collin opened his backpack and pulled out the journal, still wrapped inside the paper bag.

"Why'd you put it in that?" asked Herbie.

"To hide it from anyone who snooped in my backpack."

"Who'd want to do that?"

"Probably no one, but remember how I got this in the first place."

"Good point."

Collin grabbed hold of the silky bookmark and opened it to the middle where they broke off on Saturday. For six pages or so, she wrote about struggles with schoolwork, worries about her father's health and an application for a Brinkman Foundation scholarship.

> Forget my stupid grades! I've got a good chance to land this prize if my state exam scores are high enough.

"She's right," said Herbie. "Those exams are more important to Brinkman than your GPA."

A few pages later, Red Lion reappeared.

He's taking me back to SC tonight. Worried we might be interrupted at his house.

"Interrupted by who?" Collin wondered.

"Parents, I bet," said Herbie. "Do you want to skip over this?"

Collin pressed his lips together. He really didn't want to pry into Hester's private life, especially this part of her life, and yet if they didn't... "No, some clue might be slipped in all this. Let's keep reading straight through."

Like always, Red Lion seems more like an animal than a man at the start. I almost expect him to start drooling and clawing the ground. He moves toward me, hands outstretched, and the undressing begins. Blouse, bra, jeans, shoes, panties. He's not gentle, but he's careful not to tear anything. His reputation is more important than anything about me.

He gives me a lopsided grin and then begins planting kisses on my ears, my forehead, my cheeks and neck. It's all so gross. His lips are slimy, his palms sweaty and he reeks of cheap cologne. His so-called hugs are the worst things. It's like being pinched by a giant lobster. Yet he never leaves me with a bruise or scratch.

If this guy is so gross, why did she ever go out with him in the first place? Collin wondered. He glanced toward Herbie, who seemed immersed in the sad narrative laid out before them.

Hester's account of her "date" with Red Lion became more lurid and detailed. Interspersed with descriptions of how he assaulted her body came cries for help:

Get me out of this prison! Let me go! I don't deserve this much hell for what I did!

If there are any bed bugs in this place, I hope they get on

Red Lion instead of me. He deserves them!

After the disgusting things she wrote, her final comment felt almost humorous.

Collin had snuck in porn time. He knew mentally how sex worked. This was different. It was real, a real person. Collin never thought a person could be bullied with or about sex. It was a level of hell deeper than any bullying he had suffered. The things Hester described startled him. He would never write down how he felt after someone pushed him around and called him fat. "Why do you suppose she writes about all those awful things Red Lion did?"

"Maybe it's cathartic," Herbie said. "Helps release her fear and frustration."

Pain, too, thought Collin, closing the brown book. "Do you think he really made her do those things?"

"Yes. It fits with this site I started to watch, Ultra X. I stumbled on the site in my emails, got kinda hooked. Like for a few weeks I watched it a few times a day. The things were crazy, like three girls, guys doing the stuff Hester is talking about. Then Dad caught me. He didn't seem mad but put a blocking software on my laptop. Said if I took it off, he'd take the laptop away and make me do schoolwork in the same room as him."

Collin let this sink in for a few seconds. *Herbie hooked on porn? I'd sooner believe Blake got accepted into Mensa.*

"I watched some porn, too, then I felt sad I don't have whatever it takes to get a girlfriend. So I stopped watching; guess that is when I went back to comics. Maybe I need to find something in between."

"Yeah." Herbie relaxed back into his chair. "Do you think we'll ever have sex… someday?"

"Maybe… I mean… who knows? Most of our life is still ahead of us. Maybe when we get to college, we'll be considered cooler than we are now and girls will be more interested in us."

Herbie scowled. "Don't count on it, big man."

The "big man" nickname never hurt, nearly everyone was bigger than Herb, and it was always said with respect. Odd how that actually felt like a connection between them. It was how their friendship was expressed.

Collin nodded, re-opening the felt-covered book. "So far, we haven't seen anything that gives us a new clue as to who Hester is."

The two teens bent their heads over the journal again. A few pages later, Collin's finger darted toward a passage near the top. "Here's something!"

> Just realized I don't have Grandma M's peace locket. Must have left it back at the SC. I hate going back there. Hate the whole place. But that locket is all I have of her now. Must go back and hope the manager found it and hasn't taken it to a pawnshop yet. Speaking of pawnshops, I'd pawn off my own life if I could, but they'd probably only give me five cents for it.

"She's really hard on herself, isn't she?" said Herbie.

"Yes," said Collin. He shrugged. They couldn't do anything about helping her through that unless they figured out who the hell she was. "If she got her locket back, that's how we can identify her. It's what will make the real Hester stand out from the other three."

"But did she get her locket back?"

"Let's find out."

Collin and Herbie resumed their reading. Four pages later, they got their answer.

> Got Grandma M's locket from manager Thursday but chain is broken and top half has a dent. He said maid ran a vacuum cleaner over it, which kind of surprises me because those rooms never look clean.

"So she did get it back!" said Collin. His cry of triumph prompted a scowl from an older woman two tables away.

Herbie seemed unsure. "Do you think she'd still wear it after it got all banged up?"

"Maybe she could get a new chain, and if it's as important to her as she says, she'd probably still wear it even with a dent."

"I guess that's what we have to hope." Herbie flipped the page. "Should we keep reading? There're only about ten pages left."

"Maybe we don't need to. If we can get close enough to each girl, we should be able to tell if she's wearing a locket. I mean, I want to, it just feels not right. But I guess we know so much anyway. I just don't know. Let's just try to find out which of our four girls is the real Hester."

"Lockets can be pretty small, so we'd have to… to…"

"Go right up next to her to make sure." Collin felt a bit excited about this idea.

Herbie shook his head reading Collin's mind. "These girls might not like it if we get *too* close to them."

"It may not be so hard," Collin countered. "If they're not wearing a necklace or anything, there's nothing more to do. If they are, we'll have to play it cool—be clever."

"What do you mean? Like pretend we need directions somewhere?" Herbie shifted in his chair to face an imaginary girl on his right. "Excuse me, Miss, but can you give me directions to the nearest movie theater? If you come with me, I'll buy you some popcorn."

"Come on, Sir Isaac. This is serious."

"Okay, okay. Suggestions?"

"I'll check Wanda during English and Carmen at lunch. Can you do the same for Jane and Leah? Watch them after class in the hallway. Don't get any closer than you have to. See if either one is wearing a necklace, even better if you can see if it is a locket."

Herbie nodded. "Not sure who they are, but I guess I can check their pictures in the yearbook."

Collin put the journal into his backpack, this time without hiding it in the paper bag. "Text me after you inspect each girl. I'll do the same for you after I check out my targets."

"Inspect?" Herbie's caterpillar eyebrows jumped up. "What, are they? Soldiers on parade now?"

"Don't make a big deal out of one word."

Herbie folded his arms across his chest. "You made a big deal when I called them 'suspects.'"

"Okay, fine. Let's go with 'observe,' then." Collin pulled out his phone and texted his sister.

Meet me in front of the library

"Need a ride home Sir Issac?"

"You got your dad's car?"

"No, I took the bus to school and walked here. Ellie's picking me up. I'm sure she won't mind dropping you off."

"Nah. I'll just Uber."

* * *

On the ride home, Eleanor was lost in her own world, staring blankly at the road ahead and mumbling to herself. Her left hand twitched now and then, as if anticipating the ring she hoped would soon be there. Collin wanted to ask her a question but had to be careful about how to ask it. So he started with one he thought was safe and would warm her up.

"What would you like for your birthday, Ellie?"

His sister shot an annoyed glance in his direction. "You asked me that already."

"But you didn't answer, not seriously anyway."

She thought a moment. "How about you clean my room? No, wait, I don't want you in there. Maybe buy me new ear buds? No, you can't afford that. Ask me again in a couple of days. I'll come up with something."

"No you won't. You'll be too busy getting ready for your date with Roger." Collin said that while rolling his eyes. He paused, considered his words carefully. "I think Roger is lucky to have you as a girlfriend. In fact, sometimes I think he doesn't deserve you."

His sister shot him another glance, a perplexed one this time. "What makes you say that?"

"Because you've been going with him for over three years now, and still no ring. If I were Roger, I'd be afraid of losing you to another guy."

Eleanor's eyes burned with indignation. "Roger doesn't need to be afraid of that. He knows I'd never cheat on him."

"Flip it. How would you feel if he found another girlfriend?"

The car lurched forward as Eleanor's foot pressed down harder on the accelerator. "Why would you ask me a question like that?" she snapped. "Why are you suddenly so interested in my relationship with Roger?"

His sister's response didn't surprise him so Collin was ready. He answered quickly. "Because you stress about it so much. At home, at the dinner table, even now in the car. I can hear you saying 'Roger' under your breath."

Eleanor slowed the car down and became calmer at the same time. "I don't know," she said.

"Huh?"

"I don't know how I'd feel if Roger cheated on me, because I can't imagine it ever happening."

"But guys do cheat on their girlfriends… sometimes anyway. I know because I hear about it happening to girls at Bridgeview."

Another glance from Eleanor, a smug one. "That's because boys your age are too immature to be in a committed relationship. They don't really know what they want. They'll have full girlfriends, but then go drooling after the first little hottie who walks by. But Roger's 26. He's ready to settle down… I think. Still…" Eleanor didn't realize she had slowed to below the speed limit. "My friend Midge's boyfriend, Ed, cheated on her. Midge forgave him – once – but when he did it a second time, she dumped him. He tried to win her back with flowers, gifts, even a promise ring but she brushed him off."

"A promise ring? He must've really wanted her back."

"Short term, yes, but not for keeps. Ed would've cheated again. It's a matter of trust. You can't buy back trust, much less love, with gifts and money. If someone doesn't care enough for you to stay faithful, there's no way they'll ever love you. Best to show them out the door and lock it."

Collin nodded thinking this wealth of girl-view information over. What happened between Midge and Ed seemed to be the opposite of Hester and Red Lion. Cheater Ed wanted to get back together with Midge, but she said no. Unfaithful Hester wanted to break up with Red Lion, but he said no and blackmailed her.

Brother and sister remained quiet for the rest of the drive home, but after Eleanor pulled into the driveway, she turned to Collin and said a single word. "Jewelry."

"What?"

"That's what you can get me for my birthday. Some kind of jewelry. Nothing expensive. Maybe earrings or a bracelet."

"Okay."

Chapter 8

Collin just arrived to first-period History class when a text came from Herbie.

Jane's not Hester. Nothing around her neck
You saw her?
Yeah. Her photo's in yearbook. Homeroom next to mine. Watched her in hallway
That helps a lot
Leah's photo not in yearbook. How do we find her?
IDK, must be a way

Disappointment came in second-period English when Wanda didn't show up. *Might be sick,* thought Collin, *or maybe recovering from a long night out with Red Lion.*

Later in the cafeteria, Collin tried to get right behind Carmen in the lunch line. A burly guy whose oversized head rested on his shoulders with no neck in between got ahead of him. As he pushed his tray down the slide, Collin bent forward, backward, and then forward again trying to see Carmen from behind the bear-like student.

"What're you doing, man?" griped a freckle-faced boy next to him. "Practicing your yoga moves?"

"No, I'm more into parkour these days," Collin replied.

"Parkour? Smashed into a wall yet? Fallen on anybody?"

"No, but I keep trying."

The kid laughed as did two or three others behind him. Collin suddenly realized they were paying attention to him, in a good way, then that he hadn't put anything on his tray. Lunch was the one meal where he enjoyed some liberty with his food choices, so he grabbed some green beans and a small plate of spaghetti. He still couldn't see Carmen very well until she took her tray off the slide and moved to the cashier. That's when he saw the silver chain around the back of her neck above the top of her sweater. *Is that the locket?* He still didn't believe Carmen was their Hester – but he had to be sure. That meant getting a closer look at whatever she wore around her neck.

Collin snagged a bowl of cherry gelatin and trudged to the cashier. He noticed Carmen sitting in her usual spot surrounded by other pretty girls. His best chance to see if she wore the locket would come when he walked to his own table. He had to be careful, not make his staring obvious.

He headed toward his table but slowed his pace as he drew close to Carmen and finally came to a full stop. His eyes zeroed in on something hanging from the chain around her neck. *What's that?* He took one more step. Carmen, busy munching on salad and chatting with a friend, hadn't noticed him.

But someone else had.

A thick hand grabbed Collin's shirt from behind, causing him to bobble his tray and send cherry gelatin flying onto the floor. "Are you spying on my girlfriend, you loser?" a gruff voice demanded.

Collin twisted around and found himself staring into the glowering face of the burly student who earlier blocked his view of Carmen in the lunch line.

"I was admiring her necklace," Collin babbled. "That's all."

"Oh really?' Suspicion gushed from the big beast's voice like oil from a wrecked car. He tightened his grip on Collin's arm and dug his fingers into the flesh. Then suddenly he let go as Mr. Scanlan walked toward them.

"What's going on, Harvey?" asked the assistant principal. "Why did you grab this kid and knock his dessert onto the floor?"

"I — uhm—it was a misunderstanding, sir. I thought he might be bothering the girls at this table."

Mr. Scanlan pivoted toward Carmen's table and pointed at Collin. "Is this boy bothering, you?" All four girls sitting there shook their heads.

"I didn't even see him until now," said Carmen.

Mr. Scanlan glared at Harvey and pointed to the mess on the floor. "Get a paper towel and clean this up. Then go back to the lunch line and get... ah..."

"Collin Morris, sir," Collin chimed in.

"Yes, of course. Get him a new dessert and take it to his table, which is… is…"

"Over there." Collin pointed to his table where Fred, Eric and Ronnie gawked at him like five-year-olds staring into a candy store window. Other students from nearby tables also stopped eating and peered at the unfolding drama over a splattered gelatin dessert.

"Yes," Mr. Scanlan continued. "Take a new dessert over to Calvin, then go eat your own lunch. And in the future, let me take care of anyone who's bothering anyone else."

Harvey nodded and then lumbered toward the lunch line. Mr. Scanlan started to walk away but stopped and faced Collin one more time. "You weren't trying to bother anyone, were you, Calvin?"

"No sir," Collin replied, annoyed. *I'm invisible even to teachers.* "I wanted to ask Carmen about her necklace. Thought I might get one like it for my sister. Her birthday is coming up."

Carmen lifted the necklace and showed it to him. Her name, written in silver cursive letters, hung at the end of the chain. A little star sparkled above the C. "One of my aunts gave it to me as a confirmation gift," she explained. "It's nice but not my fav. I only wear it every once in a while. Does that help?"

"Yes, yes it does." Collin felt nervous; he couldn't believe he didn't stammer. "Thanks a lot."

"No prob."

Collin went to his table and took a seat between Ronnie and Eric. Eric sucked in a string of spaghetti; a globule of tomato sauce flew onto Collin's arm.

"Don't be such a slob!" Collin snapped, wiping the sauce off with a napkin.

"Slarry, Doood," Eric mumbled, his mouth already jammed with another forkful of pasta.

Collin had taken only a couple of bites of his own lunch when Harvey shuffled over and plopped a dish of lemon gelatin dessert in front of him. "Thanks. I like cherry better, but lemon's okay, too."

Harvey grunted and stomped away. Ronnie, wide-eyed, watched him go and then leaned toward Collin. "I wouldn't mess with Frymuth, if I were you."

"Well, he shouldn't have grabbed me and ruined my dessert."

"But weren't you staring at his girlfriend?"

"You mean Carmen? Just wanted to see her necklace."

Fred guffawed and poked his head around Eric. "Nice try, man. We know you were scoping out Carmen's hooters."

"Yeah, you're a boob man, aren't you?" leered Eric.

"Sure am," Collin replied. "That's why I eat lunch with the three biggest boobs in the whole school."

Fred, Eric and Ronnie all started talking, but Collin ignored them and continued with his lunch. He had almost finished when a text came from Herbie along with a photo.

Leah is in middle

Collin gripped the phone and held it closer to his face as if he were a poker player. The photo came from Bridgeview's local newspaper and showed the three winners of last year's Peace in Our Time essay contest. Leah, the second-place winner, stood stiffly between two other teenage girls. At first, Collin thought she wasn't especially pretty. Her lanky dark hair, which ran along the sides of her face down over her shoulders, wasn't unattractive—just ordinary. The same was true of her face with its slightly-too-large nose, its slightly-too-crooked smile and its slightly-too-sharp chin. Overall, Leah seemed kind of vulnerable, like someone who might go unnoticed even if she shouted for help. Then he realized he was judging her right now only on how she looked; like so many did to him.

He mentally pushed that out to look again, he had to memorize her and then find her somewhere around school. The more he studied the picture; the more Leah's face did seem attractive to Collin. It took him a moment to figure out why. *It's her eyes!* An inquisitive sparkle danced in those eyes; a gleaming alertness that set her apart from the girls near her. Maybe set her apart from every other girl at Bridgeview High. The unique beauty of Leah's eyes made Collin want to know her, even if she wasn't 'the girl in trouble.'

Below the photo, a cutline gave the titles of the winning essays, including Leah's: "Making World Leaders Fight in Their Own Wars." *Maybe I'll read it later, after we rescue Hester.*

As he continued to soak in Leah's picture, Collin realized he saw her only minutes ago when he tangled with Harvey. She sat among a group of girls at a table next to the one where Carmen sat. *Has she left yet?* Collin rose from his seat just high enough to see Leah still sitting at her table, about 30 feet away. Even at that distance, he saw something hanging around her neck. *I have to find out what that is.*

Before Collin could sit back down, Leah dabbed a napkin to her lips and started stacking up dishes on her tray. There was no time to be subtle or clever. Ignoring his own tray of dirty dishes, Collin jogged toward Leah's table. Two other girls were still eating there, but the seat across from her was empty. As gracefully as his frame allowed, Collin glided in and took it.

"Excuse me, but I happened to notice your —"

"Necklace?" Leah twisted her mouth into a strange little smile that suggested she felt both amused and annoyed by Collin's sudden appearance.

"Yeah. I guess you saw what happened a few minutes ago."

"How could I not?"

A shiver ran up Collin's spine. He realized any girl made him nervous, even when he wasn't asking her for a date. But he was a man on a mission, so he forged ahead.

"Then I guess you know I'm trying to find a necklace to give my sister as a birthday gift."

Leah shrugged. "So? Go online and do a search for necklaces for teenage girls. You'll probably get about a thousand choices."

"My sister, isn't a teenager anymore. She'll be twenty-one."

"Twenty-one?" Leah put a flattened hand over her eyes and moved her head from side to side. "Don't think there's anyone here that old except the teachers. So why ask a girl your age—"

"That's a good idea you had," Collin said, now feeling both foolish and nervous. "It makes a lot more sense to do an online search than to bother people eating their lunch. Thanks, Leah."

Collin rose from the table, but Leah grabbed his arm before he could leave. "How did you know my name? I don't think we've been in a class together, have we?" The eyes Collin found so attractive flashed with suspicion, which he drowned with a quick answer.

"No, but I remember seeing your picture in *The Bridgeview News* when you won that essay contest."

"Huh?"

"You know, the one about Peace in Our Time."

"Oh yeah, did you read it?"

"Well not all of it, but I remember you said world leaders ought to fight in any war they got their country into."

"That's right. You should read the whole thing. It's in the same issue that has my picture."

"Okay, I will."

"It's not the best essay I ever wrote, though. I only got second place."

"You've entered other essay contests?"

"Yeah, I like to write. It helps me when I'm feeling down in the dumps. The last thing I wrote was for the mayor's Good Citizenship Essay Contest."

"How did you do?'

"I won't know until Memorial Day. That's when they'll announce the winners."

She sure sounds like someone who'd keep a journal. Should I ask her if she lost one? No, it might embarrass her if she's Hester or make me look dumb if she isn't. I can't do it in such a public place, way too many eyes around.

Leah picked up her tray and moved away from the table. "You know my name, but I don't know yours. I can't even say you look familiar."

"I'm Collin Morris, and I'm not surprised. I really haven't done much. I've only been in *The Bridgeview News* once back in sixth grade when I got stuck in a barrel and the fire department had to pry me out."

"You got stuck in a barrel?" She laughed.

"Yeah, some kids and I were messing around behind this warehouse and—"

"Maybe you can tell me about it later," Leah said, stepping toward the tray turn-in window. "I've got to go and get ready for Spanish. My group has to be characters in this play and give our lines in Spanish in front of the whole class." Her eyes flashed again but this time with a hint of worry. "Right now I only know about half my lines."

"Good luck with that."

As Leah walked away, Collin continued to talk as if she still stood in front of him. "Sure, I'll tell you about it tomorrow. And thanks for letting me look at your neck—" Collin groaned and mentally kicked himself. *I forgot all about looking at it.* Dejection swept through him along with an overwhelming fear of being the dumbest kid in the world. He trudged back toward his table. Before he got there, a finger flicked against the back of his ear lobe, hard enough to make it feel like a bee sting.

Collin swung around and found Harvey hovering over him.

"You better stay out of my way," the big guy growled as he stomped past him. "Scanlan isn't always gonna be here to save your fat ass."

Collin ignored the unsubtle threat and continued on to his table. He felt too upset with himself to worry about anything Harvey said.

Not until he got home did a new plan take shape in his head. *I know! I'll do what she asked and read the essay she wrote. Then I'll go over and tell her how much I liked it.* Collin opened his laptop and went to the local news archives and typed in his search. In a matter of seconds, the three winning essays, including Leah's, flashed on his screen. He plunged into it as if it held the secret of eternal happiness.

Collin thought the theme of the essay was kind of odd. Leah believed fewer wars would be fought if an international treaty required the leaders of warring nations to fight in the trenches with their soldiers. "Imagine the president manning a machine gun or the British prime minister crawling through barbed wire," she wrote. It was a bizarre thing to imagine since most world leaders were older men who weren't in the best of shape. But as Leah pointed out, leaders in the past often fought in wars and sometimes didn't make it out alive. As she saw it, "presidents and prime ministers shouldn't be sitting in a tent or bunker miles from the action. No, they need to be in the thick of the battle like Henry V at Agincourt or Gustavus Adolphus at Luetzen. If they faced death the same as ordinary soldiers, they may think twice about starting a war that isn't worth anyone's life."

Collin wasn't sure whether he agreed with Leah's argument or not, but in any case, he felt glad he read the essay after noticing the dedication.

> **My grandmother Margaret McAllister worked her whole life to create a more peaceful, caring and compassionate world. I dedicate this essay to her memory.**

Grandma M! Collin powered down and closed his laptop. He leaned back in his chair and tapped his fingers together. No need to wonder who Hester was anymore. She had a real name now – Leah Jennings. But one task remained.

You're next, Red Lion!

Chapter 9

*T*he argument started as soon as Collin set foot into Herbie's bedroom.

"Congratulations on discovering Leah is our Hester," Herbie said. "Tomorrow you can give the diary back to her."

"Not yet. Not until we know who Red Lion is."

"Not your job, big man—or mine either for that matter."

"I'm making it my job. You don't have to help me anymore if you don't want to."

Herbie grabbed a piece of paper off his desk, wadded it up into a ball and threw it at the Einstein poster. It hit the famous scientist's nose before bouncing onto the floor.

Wow, that's about as violent as he ever gets, thought Collin.

Herbie's finger jutted out toward Collin as if he were picking him out of a police line-up.

"You've got to give it back, big man. The longer you hang onto that thing, the more danger you're putting her in."

Collin took a step toward the paper ball and kicked it under Herbie's bed—about as violent as he ever got. "Not until I find out who Red Lion is and stop him."

"Who do you think you are? Some kind of superhero?"

"No, but just because I'm not a superhero doesn't mean I can't help Leah."

Herbie thrust his arms out, palms uplifted, pleading. "You've already helped her. Let the police take it from here."

"Helped? How? The police could stop Red Lion now, if Leah told them what he's doing to her. She doesn't need the journal to do that. But she's not, is she? Something bigger is going on."

"Are you sure?"

"Well… no. But I don't think she made up the stuff she wrote, do you?"

Herbie scratched his chin. "No, but girls do lie about stuff sometimes. You know, to get attention."

"If Leah wanted to make up stories to get attention, she wouldn't write them in a brown journal no one else could see."

"Except you've seen it."

"That's what I don't get. Why give it to me, a total stranger?"

Herbie's finger went up. "Except you're not a total stranger any more. You spoke to her at lunchtime today, didn't you?"

"Yeah."

"That should make it easier to give the diary back to her."

"You mean just hand it to her?"

"Why not? Then ask why she gave it to you in the first place."

"Well, I guess I could, but then I'd never find out who Red Lion is."

"Do you need to know or just want to know?"

Collin sat on the bed. "Like I said. I… I want to help her."

"Fine. Why not give her the thing back and say you'd like to get to know her better? Don't say you've read it… just give it to her. Then start to be her friend."

"What if she asks me how I know it's hers?"

"Lie and say you saw her put it into your backpack."

"She'll know that's a lie. If it were true, I'd already have given it back."

"So tell her the truth. Tell her you figured out the book belonged to her by the classes she mentions and the peace locket, too."

"Then she'll know I lied when I pretended to be looking for a necklace to get for my sister. Plus then she will know for sure I know all her dark secrets."

Herbie made a fist and hammered it on his desktop—a new high in violent behavior for him. "This isn't about you, dude! It's about giving the diary back to the girl who's poured all her secrets into it."

"What about stopping Red Lion from treating Leah like a sex slave?" Collin snapped. He paused for a few seconds, reflecting. "Back on Friday when I called and told you about the journal, you said once we found out who the girl in trouble was, we'd track down Red Lion, too. Or something like that."

Herbie sighed. A more typical reaction from him. "I know, but that was before I read about the things Red Lion was doing." He sighed again, louder. "There's something about this guy that scares me, like really creeps me out."

"No kidding. There're lots of guys at school who're creepy. Take Blake, for example."

Herbie waved a dismissive hand. "No, Red Lion isn't a dumbass jerk like Blake. He's sneaky and smart. Knows how to cover his tracks, which makes him really dangerous. That's probably why Leah hasn't told anyone who he is."

"Hey, we're smart, too," Collin protested. "We found out the journal belongs to Leah without her ever mentioning her name. We can do the same with Red Lion."

"Okay, suppose you do find out who he is. Maybe Leah even tells you who he is. What're you going to do? Challenge him to a fight? Report him to Mr. Scanlan? Call in a SWAT team?"

Collin remained silent for almost a minute. "I'd... I'd stop him, somehow."

Herbie shook his head. "You've been reading too much Scarlet Angel. You want to sweep in and clobber Red Lion, then carry Leah away to your secret hideout and make love to her."

"Well, yes but not right away. I'd ask her to marry me first."

Herbie's eyes widened, his bushy eyebrows running away from each other.

Collin let a little smile creep onto his mouth. "Want to be my best man?" he asked before bursting into full-blown laughter.

"Who else could you pick?" Herbie responded. "Your good buddy Blake?"

Collin stopped laughing. "Fuck Blake and fuck Red Lion, too."

"I agree. Don't go after Red Lion. You don't even know who he is. Let Leah do that."

"But maybe she can't get help from the police without putting herself in danger." Collin paused, deep in thought. "If I don't stop him or at least find out who he is, maybe nobody will."

Herbie folded his arms. "There you go again, sounding like a comic book hero."

Collin's face slumped. "Hero? I'm not even average, I'm a shadow. But still..." Collin tried to sort everything out in his mind. "Let's give it another week. I'm feeling things change a little. I mean for me, which is good. But I know I want to help her. If we still don't know who Red Lion is in a week, I promise I'll give it to Leah."

"And how are we supposed to track this guy down? Stake out Leah's house? We don't even know where she lives, do we?"

"Let's not start with a stake-out. Let's just watch her during the school day. See who she talks to and hangs out with between classes."

Herbie scratched his head. "You mean tail her like a private eye?"

"Yeah, sort of. We did start out joking about being FBI. They are real-life good guys helping people. Let's keep that going. We know almost everywhere she'll be during the day, and it's just for a week. Between the two of us, I think we can do it, if we plan things out."

"Okay, so are we going to have code names?"

* * *

On his way home Collin suddenly realized that as far as Leah's journal was concerned, he could have his cake and eat it too. *It's obvious. Why didn't I think of it sooner?*

He made a quick stop at the Bridgeview Public Library right before it closed its doors for the night.

Chapter 10

The plan was simple. Starting before homeroom and depending on who was closer to her, either Collin or Herbie would follow Leah through the halls as she moved from one class to another. They would take note of the guys she spoke to and see if any of these guys could plausibly have the nickname Red Lion. Herbie led things off, keeping an eye on 'the girl in trouble' from the time she arrived at her locker until she went into her homeroom. Collin then followed her from the end of homeroom to the beginning of second period. Herbie took over to the beginning of fourth period when both Leah and Collin had lunch. While he swallowed the cafeteria's semi-edible meatloaf, Collin watched Leah closely. She ate slowly, occasionally speaking to the girls next to her. The only interruption came when a boy who Collin didn't know came over and started a conversation with Leah, causing her to open her notebook and point to something.

No big deal. Probably just asked about an assignment.

Collin followed Leah to her Spanish class, then didn't see her again until the end of seventh period. That's when she came out of a study hall only a few doors away from the drinking fountain where the mystery began. Collin expected her to walk that way, since her Algebra class was on the second floor and the quickest route there was the central staircase, just beyond where he was standing. But Leah didn't go that way. Instead, she headed in the opposite direction and went up the east staircase, a trip longer than it needed to be. Collin followed until she vanished into Mr. Browning's classroom, making him late for French again. Madame Haas was not pleased.

"*Vous êtes de nouveau en retard, Collin.*"

"*Oui, je suis désolé. J'aidais mon ami.*"

"*Encore?*"

"*Oui.*"

"*Je vous donnerai une dentention si vous êtes de nouveau en retard.*"

"*Je comprends.*" Collin felt no more guilt than the last time he came late. *I told the truth or, well, at least as much as I can right now.*

* * *

After school, Collin met Herbie at his house where they compared notes on who they'd seen Leah talk with during the day. They soon realized Herbie came up empty handed. No clues at all.

"She doesn't even talk to that many girls," complained Herbie. He wadded up a piece of paper he'd been doodling on and hook-shot it toward his wastebasket, missing it by at least a foot. "The only guy she spoke to while I watched her was Larry, and I know for a fact he's been dating Jolene since ninth grade. By now, those two might as well be married."

"Could you tell what they talked about?"

"No, but I doubt it was anything too serious. Leah didn't seem afraid or upset."

"But that's the problem, right? We don't know how an abused girl acts when she's around her abuser, especially if other people are nearby."

Herbie stood, took another piece of scratch paper off his desk, squeezed it into a ball, and jump shot it toward his wastebasket. This time he missed by two feet. "So what did you find out, big man?" Herbie asked, snatching one of the paper balls off the floor. "Any Red Lion suspects from your day?"

"None, and like you, I only saw her talk to a few people – all girls except one, and he was no big deal." Collin plopped onto Herbie's bed and let his head droop. "It must be lonely being an abused kid."

"Well duh," Herbie exclaimed. "You don't have to be a psychologist to know that." He spun around and slam-dunked the wadded-up paper ball into the wastebasket from an inch away.

Collin straightened up. "Do you think she's talked about Red Lion to the school psychologist? You know, what's her name?"

"Dr. Kaufman?" Herbie shrugged. "Not sure, but I'd guess no. If she had, Red Lion might already be in the slammer."

"You think she'd tell Dr. Kaufman his real name?"

"Yeah. Maybe. Why see the shrink if you aren't going to finger your abuser? At the very least, I'd think Leah would show her the di—" Herbie's mouth gaped open like a fish out of water.

"Diary?" Collin got off the bed, picked up the other paper ball and slam dunked it so hard, the wastebasket wobbled from side to side. "Do you know where Dr. Kaufman's office is?"

"It's with the guidance counselors. I saw her name on one of the doors there when I met with Ms. Carson last fall. But I don't think she's in every day."

"What about last Friday?"

Herbie went to his laptop and brought up Bridgeview High School's web page. He tapped over to Staff/Faculty and soon found Dr. Kaufman's profile, which included her appointment schedule. "Yeah, she's there on Mondays, Thursdays, and Friday afternoons."

Collin drummed his fingers on his lip. "If she's with the other teachers and admins, her office is pretty close to the drinking fountain I used when, we think, Leah put the journal in my backpack. What if she meant to give it to Dr. Kaufman?"

"Why didn't she?"

Collin didn't say anything. After a minute, Herbie came over and patted him on the back. "Well, what do you want to do next?"

"Two things. First, we do the same thing tomorrow. Follow Leah from class to class, see who she talks to."

"What's the second thing?"

"We make an appointment with Dr. Kaufman and give her the journal. Maybe Leah never planned to do that, but it's safer than giving it to Lost and Found and… and…"

Herbie looked at his friend and sighed. "And it saves you from having to hand it over to Leah."

Collin nodded sheepishly. *Me a superhero? I'm more like a supercoward.*

Herbie frowned. "You said 'we' should make an appointment with Dr. Kaufman. It won't take two of us to hand the journal over to her."

"We have to do more than that. We have to tell Dr. Kaufman about Leah and what's happening to her."

"Okay, you could still do that without me."

"But we've been in this together from the start," said Collin, exasperated. "If it weren't for you, we might not even know the thing belongs to Leah."

Herbie went to his keyboard and scrolled down on Dr. Kaufman's profile.

Her photo showed her to be a fairly young woman with short brown hair, a confident smile and glasses that seemed too close to the end of her nose. Collin thought she looked very smart, an impression reinforced by the list of her academic credentials.

"A Ph.D. from Cornell," beamed Herbie with admiration. "The Winifred Scoles of her class, I bet. A real brain."

"I hope she has the brains to find out who Red Lion is." Collin's shoulders slumped. "Maybe she won't do any better than we have."

"What makes you say that?"

"She's probably used to dealing with kids who're being neglected at home or starving themselves or getting high on drugs. She may not know how to deal with our problem."

Herbie pointed at his laptop screen. "She says here she'll 'help any student with any problem.' I say give her a try. If we can figure out who Red Lion is, I bet she'll have the clout to throw him out of school, maybe get him arrested."

"Okay."

Herbie scrolled back to Dr. Kaufman's appointment schedule. "Looks like she's pretty busy. There're no openings until the Thursday after next."

"That's way past the one-week limit we agreed on."

Herbie grinned. "Oh, I don't mind giving you an extension." He knew his friend was determined to actually help Leah, just walking by and turning in the personal book wouldn't be enough.

"Does her schedule give the names of the kids who are seeing her?"

"No. The filled-up appointment times are just crossed out. No surprise. I bet a lot of people wouldn't see a shrink if they thought their friends would find out."

"Take the earliest available time."

"It's at 8:45, right in the middle of first period..." Herbie squinted at the screen. "...and there's only room for one name."

"Put my name down. I guess I can do this by myself."

"Oh no, you don't," Herbie said. "You're not going to steal my thunder, big man."

Herbie's fingers danced over the keyboard and when he finished, he swept his hand toward the laptop screen as if presenting a work of art.

"Morris & Kessler?" said Collin in a mocking tone. "Forget being FBI agents. We're more like a standup comedy duo!"

Herbie shook his head. "Dr. Kaufman will realize pretty quickly there's nothing funny about what we tell her."

"Right."

Herbie pressed enter and an "appointment confirmed" message flashed on the screen.

"We're in!"

Chapter 11

School ended an hour early the next day for a teachers' meeting, so Collin and Herbie had less time to spot any Red Lion suspects with Leah. An hour less, an hour more. It didn't matter. They came away the same as the day before—with nothing.

Collin turned to the Scarlet Angel to escape his frustration. Lying in bed, he held the comic book a couple of inches from his nose, as if putting the story this close would allow him to jump into the action.

In this latest edition, *The Saving Voice*, the Scarlet Angel plunged into a mountain cave, believing Vorman held a runaway teen captive there. But he was wrong.

"We both lose this time," an enraged Vorman screamed. "Some evil creature stole the child from me. A creature more powerful than either one of us."

"You're lying, Vorman. This is just another one of your tricks," the angel roared.

"Lying, am I? Maybe this will convince you." The warlock moved aside and waved his claw-like hand at a cage with its door pried open. "Now do you believe me, you worthless, quivering do-gooder?"

The angel stepped back toward the cave's entrance. If Vorman didn't have the runaway, who did?

Collin shoved the comic book under his pillow. *I'm not that different from the Scarlet Angel. He doesn't know who captured the runaway girl, and I don't know who's abusing Leah.*

He got up from his bed and walked to the window. Outside, neighbors were busy with early-spring gardening, while a young kid was squealing doing wheelies on his bike in the middle of the street. Collin didn't see them. Instead he saw Leah's "boyfriend" standing in front of him. This guy stood about Collin's height but with bigger hands and a sturdier, more-muscular build. His face blended the features of Vorman and Blake into an ugly mass of scaly, pimple-scarred flesh and crooked teeth.

The battle began.

Collin started with three quick punches to the phantom adversary's stomach and followed with a head butt to his chin. The villain fought back, slashing with claw-like hands at Collin's face and neck. Collin recoiled but stayed on his feet and drilled the abuser with a fist to his nose. Kicks, punches, head butts and karate chops flew between the combatants. Collin knew he was winning. The abuser's already misshapen face had swollen to the size of a watermelon and blood streamed from gashes that ran from his forehead to his chest. *Time to finish off this dude.* Collin took a step back and swung his leg in a roundhouse kick that crushed the imaginary abuser's head but also hit the all-too-real bedroom wall. The whole room shook as Collin fell to the floor, clutching his foot.

"Colly, what happened up there?" his mother shouted from the first floor. "Are you all right?"

"I'm okay, Mom," he answered. "Just ran into something."

"Well, I'm going to the mall in about five minutes to buy some art supplies. If you haven't gotten your sister a birthday gift yet, you can go with me and find something for her."

"Okay. Be right down. Can I have a doggie biscuit before we go?"

* * *

Collin ended up getting his sister some heart-shaped stud earrings which he gave to her right before she left for her dinner date with Roger. Though he never told her, Collin thought Eleanor was a much-better-than-average looking girl, and tonight, wearing a V-neck fancy dress, she looked downright striking. He hoped his earrings wouldn't be the only jewelry she received tonight; even though she was too young and Roger just wasn't perfect for her.

Collin planned to do nothing more that evening than suffer through some Algebra homework and finish the Scarlet Angel story. A text from Herbie changed all that.

Got a Red Lion suspect
Who?

Eduardo Rojas
The Peruvian exchange student?
Yes
Why him?
He's in Leah's Spanish class
Not much to go on
There's more. Can you come over?
Maybe. Parents home tonight so Dad's car available

When he got to Herbie's room, Collin found his friend leaning back in the captain's chair, laptop open on his desk.

"What's up, Sir Isaac? Why do you think Eduardo is Red Lion?"

"Pull up a chair, big man, and I'll explain."

Collin grabbed a folding chair out of the closet and sat next to Herbie. "Okay, go for it."

"Spanish class is only strike one," Herbie replied. He gestured toward the laptop's screen. "There's strike two."

Collin leaned forward and what he saw made his heart beat faster. Herbie had opened the online sign-up form for one of the school library's study rooms. There were only two names entered for the 3:45 time slot on Monday – Leah and Eduardo. "That does look suspicious," he admitted.

"And if their only contact at school is in the library after the last class, it would explain why we never saw them together when we followed Leah."

Collin drummed his fingers on the desk and stared at the two names, wishing they would fade away. "What do… um… you suppose they do in the study room?"

"What do you think?"

Collin winced. "Oh come on. That would be really stupid. Mrs. Hennessy could have barged in on them. She does that sometimes when she thinks kids aren't studying. And anyway, there's not much room to… to…"

"To have sex? Oh, you'd be surprised."

"No offense, but how would you know?"

"I know how to read, I've watched enough porn, that's how. You'd be shocked where people manage to get it on, even in places as small as an airplane bathroom."

"An airplane bathroom? Those things are like one foot wide."

"A flight attendant wrote an article about all the weird stuff she's had to deal with in her career. She mentioned a young married couple who went at in the bathroom so hard, they fell out and knocked over the soda cart. She said it was the first time there was more turbulence inside the plane than outside."

Collin smiled, even though he didn't think the incident Herbie described was that funny. "I don't know. It's still hard to believe Eduardo is Red Lion. We know Leah started this journal no later than last October, and this guy hasn't even been in the country a year yet. He's not had much time to meet many girls here, much less get into a relationship with one. Much less had time to get something to hold over her head to keep her quiet. And there might be a good reason why he's in that room with Leah. Maybe she's helping him with his English or they're studying together or something innocent like that."

Herbie's bushy eyebrows went up and he stroked his chin. "I guess it's time to show you strike three." His fingers danced across the laptop's keyboard. "You take French, don't you?"

"Yes, French III."

"So you know what the French word for red is."

"Sure, it's *rouge.*"

"Do you happen to know what the Spanish word for red is?"

"No."

"Since Leah takes Spanish, it's a safe bet she knows the word is *rojo* or in the plural, *rojas.*

"Just like Eduardo's last name."

"Exactly. Most of us at Bridgeview High call our visitor from Peru Eduardo Rojas, but Leah may call him Leone Rojas: Red Lion!"

Collin felt himself sinking, almost shriveling, in his chair. "What do we do now?"

Herbie went into his closet. After several seconds of bumping and thumping around, he came out, holding a point-and-shoot camera. "I've got a plan. If Eduardo is not Red Lion, no harm will come to either him or us. If he is…" A sly smile crept over Herbie's mouth. "Let's just say, we'll catch Red Lion red-handed."

Chapter 12

*H*erbie's plan gnawed on Collin the rest of the weekend. *Suppose Eduardo's innocent? Could he get us suspended or expelled for suspecting him? What about Leah? If she's not ready to expose Red Lion yet, she may not like us doing it now. What's going to happen if she and Eduardo are having sex when we barge in? Suppose they're both naked? Won't that make things worse for her instead of better?*

When Collin stepped on the scale Monday morning before breakfast, he saw some good news; his weight dropped eight pounds. *That starvation diet is finally working!* But the questions that harassed and distracted him a day earlier returned in force by the time school started, causing him to forget the name of the astronaut who later became a U.S. Senator. "Mister Morris!" exclaimed Mr. Petrie. "We're not more than ten miles away from an airport named for this man!"

At lunch, Collin wanted to sit next to Leah but chickened out and sat with his usual crowd. He did give her a little wave as he went by, which she returned. Eric, Ronnie and Fred saw that wave.

"Who're you putting the moves on?" asked Fred, a half-eaten roll in his hand.

"No one."

"Come on, I just saw you wave at a girl."

"That doesn't mean I'm putting the moves on her."

"Okay. Who did you wave at?"

"Leah Jennings."

Fred stuffed the rest of the roll into his mouth and chewed away. "Don't know her," he mumbled, while crumbs tumbled off his lips.

"Never heard of her," chimed in Eric.

"Me neither," agreed Ronnie.

"Leah doesn't know how lucky she is, does she?" said Collin then all of them broke out in laughter.

At 3:55, the wannabe FBI agents met outside the library. By then, they figured, Eduardo and Leah would be in the study room, doing whatever they intended to do.

"I'm not sure about this," Collin confided to his friend.

"I'm not either," said Herbie, adjusting the strap of his camera around his neck. "But something has to be done to stop Red Lion. If that's Eduardo, we'll do it now. If it's not, we'll switch to Plan B."

The duo walked into the library. Only three students were in the common area – two at a reading table and one at a computer carrel. Mrs. Hennessy, like a raptor searching for prey, caught sight of them from her perch behind the circulation desk. Collin expected her to question why they were there; instead she nodded toward Herbie and even gave him a little smile. *They'll cut you a lot of slack around here if you're one of the smartest students*, thought Collin.

The teens glided past the reading tables and computer carrels, through the bookshelves and magazine racks, finally stopping at the far corner of the library where the two windowless study rooms were located. The door of one stood open; the closed door of the other suggested it was in use.

"Let's do this," said Herbie. He lifted his camera and moved toward the closed door. Collin followed. As they approached, muffled voices could be heard coming from inside. Collin put his hand on the door knob. He couldn't be sure, but it sounded as if the voices belonged to more than two people. At a nod from Herbie, he turned the knob and flung the door open.

Eduardo and Leah were both there. They sat at a small table across from each other, fully clothed. Two other students – also fully clothed – sat on either side of Leah. *They must have signed up for this room after Leah and Eduardo*, thought Collin. All four had scripts from a play in front of them.

Eduardo, more than a little annoyed, swung around in his seat. "Excuse me, we have this room until 4:15."

Without a second of hesitation, Herbie switched to Plan B. "I know. I'm here to take a photo of this group for the yearbook." Hearing his friend transition so smoothly nearly caused Collin to collapse in relief.

"How did you know we'd be here?" Eduardo asked. "I didn't tell anyone about this meeting outside of our class." Collin noted only a trace of an accent in his English.

"Just a lucky guess. The yearbook staff likes me to take candid photos of students in action. They're usually more realistic."

Eduardo still looked skeptical.

Now it was Herbie's turn to be annoyed – or at least pretend to be. "Come on, what do you think we are? Russian spies? Just let us snap a photo or two, and we'll be gone."

Collin tried to stay in the background throughout this encounter, but Leah caught sight of him. "Hey, Collin, what are you doing here?"

"Hey Leah, I'm… ah…" He groped for an answer, but couldn't come up with one that didn't sound stupid.

Luckily, Herbie supplied one. "My friend's shadowing me this afternoon. He's applied for a position on the yearbook staff so I'm giving him a taste of what a photographer does."

"Okay, go ahead and snap a couple of pictures if you want," said Eduardo. "We need to get back to work."

"Great," said Herbie. "Email Ms. Arthur how you want your names spelled and if your group has its own name. The photos will be better if everyone looks busy. Oh, and no duck faces, please." He took the pictures, thanked the students and closed the door.

Herbie let out an audible *whew* while wiping imaginary sweat from his forehead as they walked as softly as they could out of the library. "That could have been really embarrassing. Luckily Plan B worked to perfection."

"B was Fire. But really, it only kept us out of trouble," said Collin. "We still don't know who Red Lion is."

Chapter 13

Gloom hung over the Morris' dinner table like a thick fog. Collin knew why his dad felt that way. The rejection message he received following his latest job interview explained his despair. Eleanor had been crabby since her date on Saturday with no engagement ring and, more surprising, no Roger, who felt he and El should take a break. Collin thought he kept his own angst well hidden, but his mother must have picked up on it. After dinner, she came into his room.

"What's wrong, Colly – I mean – Collin?"

"Nothing, Mom."

"Come on, something's bothering you. You hardly said a word at dinner. Is it Algebra?"

"No."

"A girl?"

"No. Well, yes, sort of."

"Do you want to tell me about it?"

"Not right now. Maybe later. Let me try to work things out on my own first."

"Okay, you know I'm always ready to listen."

"I know, Mom. Thanks."

"Come here, I want to show you something. It's in the guest room."

The "guest room" is what Mrs. Morris still called the extra bedroom on the second floor even though she'd converted it into an art studio months ago. Collin followed her, noticing as he had many times before that this room resembled Herbie's, but instead of photos and posters the walls had oil paintings. Most of them were still life or landscape, but in the center of the room on an easel was the painting she brought him to see. It was a portrait of his great-grandfather in the crusher cap and flight suit he wore when serving as a navigator on B-17s in World War II. The background included a blue sky dotted with white clouds and a plane coming in for a landing. In the bottom right corner, his mother had put D. Morris. That's how she signed her paintings these days instead of Della, which she thought sounded amateurish.

Collin never had the chance to meet Great Granddad Claude, but he'd heard plenty of stories about the man's wartime adventures. His favorite was the one where Claude piloted his damaged plane back to England after a burst of flack wounded both the pilot and co-pilot. For that act of heroism, he received the Distinguished Flying Cross.

"It looks great, Mom," said Collin. "How did you do it? Great-Granddad Claude's been gone such a long time."

"I used an old picture I found in a shoebox full of old photos."

"I wish he were alive to see this painting," said Collin.

"So do I," said Mrs. Morris. "Your great-grandfather was a true hero."

As Collin walked back to his room, he decided he wanted to spend some time with another hero. This one wasn't real, had never been real, but inspired Collin anyway. He felt he needed a little inspiration right about now; but didn't want to be seen reading a comic at his age. Closing the door behind him, he dashed to his bed and reached under the pillow for the half-read issue of The Scarlet Angel. This story began with a prized student, Lola Schmid, running away from the Bavaria School of Music to escape the advances of a lecherous voice teacher. Unfortunately, the naïve young girl fell in with the evil Vorman, who pretended to be a Hollywood talent scout. Just before the warlock could sell Lola into slavery, a second villain broke into her cage and escaped with her to parts unknown and for reasons unknown.

"Come!" urged Vorman, extending a clawed hand. "Let's work together to bring the girl back to us. Our combined powers will be no match for whatever creature stole her."

"Us?" cried the angel. "There is no 'us.' You only want the girl back to sell her as a slave to some rich oligarch. I am the only one who truly wants to save her. And save her I will."

With Vorman hurling curses at him, the Scarlet Angel sprang into the air. With no danger nearby, Collin's hero could fly, his red jacket acting as a kind of parasail, but that power would vanish once he confronted whatever villain had kidnapped Lola. Forcing him to fight face-to-face and keep himself and the girl alive by using his wits and his sword.

The Scarlet Angel searched tirelessly for the twice-stolen young singer, but it wasn't easy. While flying through the Fichtel Mountains, he suffered a leg injury when a gust of wind hurled him against a rocky ridge. His wound was bad enough to need the care of an old doctor who lived in a little German village.

"You'd better get some rest before you continue your journey," the doctor advised. "They should be able to put you up for the night at Black Knight Inn."

The angel took the doctor's advice, but resumed his search on foot the next day, using his celestial sword to support his wounded leg. Following clues, apparently sent from heaven, he drew closer to whoever held Lola. These clues, as in previous issues, appeared on natural objects like trees or ponds, and always took the form of riddles. The angel was always able to solve the riddles. Collin thought this was a bit unrealistic, but it never made him lose interest. This time, the final clue came in an unusual way. While Scarlet Angel hiked through a dense forest, a sudden windstorm tore the leaves off a huge tree and sent them spiraling to the ground. When they landed, the leaves wrote out these words:

> Scarlet Angel, be not mistook
> Leave the knight and take the rook
> On mountain near, you'll need to leap
> To find Lola in the deepest keep.

As soon as the angel finished reading the clue, the leaves blew away, but he knew what they meant. "Lola's being held prisoner in the castle on top of Mount Kohlberg. I must leave the Black Knight Inn at once and go there." Off he went.

So now he knows where the girl is, but who is holding her prisoner?

"Collin, are you doing your homework?" his mom shouted from the first floor.

"Yep, definitely," he replied, unconvincingly.

Collin tossed the comic book aside and shuffled toward his writing desk. Lola's rescue would have to wait, but it wasn't as if that was in doubt; the Scarlet Angel always triumphed in the end. He might get punched, kicked, clubbed, slashed, hit with rocks or thrown into a wall. He might follow the wrong path and get lost for a while, but in the end, he rescued the kidnapped children and brought them home. *Real life isn't that way at all.* At some level, he always knew that, but the quest to save Leah and stop Red Lion shoved that fact into his face.

After six Algebra problems, two chapters of American History and one final murder in *MacBeth*, Collin returned to the Scarlet Angel. By now, ten o'clock closed in, but he wanted to finish…

When night fell, Scarlet Angel made his way up Mount Kohlberg, his injured leg slowing his progress. Sure enough, he found Lola chained inside the keep of the castle at the mountain's summit. Several feet away from her, a huge tarp covered an unknown object. While the angel pondered how to free the girl, a shadowy figure came up from behind and whacked him on the head. *No surprise*, thought Collin. In nearly every other Scarlet Angel story, the hero ended up at the mercy of the villain at some point. The identity of the villain, however, surprised him. It was the kindly old village doctor who mended the angel's leg after his accident. Someone he trusted – until now.

"Dr. Retarius!" a now-shackled Scarlet Angel yelled. "What are you doing? Release us at once!"

"I'm sorry, young man, but I can't," said the doctor, a wrinkled man whose wild white hair and lab coat made him look like a cross between a Yeti and Herbie's favorite scientist. "You and the girl must sacrifice your lives for the sake of science."

"Sacrifice? What're you talking about?"

"I'm an old man who's nearing death and it isn't fair," lamented the doctor. "I have so much to give the world, so much knowledge, so much power and inspiration, but all that will be lost if I die."

"You're supposed to be a healer not a killer, doctor," the angel retorted. "Sacrificing us won't stop you from dying." Now, as he often did, the angel tried to reason with the villain, but that never worked.

"Oh yes, it will," the doctor said. He put his hand on the tarp and yanked it off, revealing a complex, bewildering apparatus with wires, glass tubes and flashing lights surrounding a huge bottle of bubbling liquid. Under the bottle, a rack-like bed stretched out with straps. "Behold, my rejuvenating machine. Once I transfer the girl's youth into my body, I shall live at least another 50 years."

"And what happens to me?" asked a terror-stricken Lola.

Dr. Retarius' face sagged. "I'm afraid you will perish, my dear, but you will have the honor of giving your life for the cause of science."

Lola screamed. "Let me go! You have no right to do this to me."

The mad doctor ignored her and walked toward his machine. Lola slumped as far as her chains allowed and wept, but her scream had given Scarlet Angel an idea. "Lola," he said. "You're a singer, right?"

"Yes, a soprano," she said through sobs.

"Hit some high notes and sing them as loud as you can. Look right at the machine as you sing."

"Huh?"

"Just do it and hold the notes until you run out of breath."

"Okay."

Lola let out a series of ever-rising high notes that resembled a shriek more than a song. When she ran out of breath, she repeated the procedure.

Dr Retarius, meanwhile, now held a syringe and moved toward Lola with the needle pointed toward her. Menacing. "Giving us one final song, my dear?" he cackled. "Goodness, you seem rather off key. But go ahead and —"

Suddenly, the big bottle at the center of the rejuvenating machine shattered, showering the mad doctor with a thick dark-blue liquid. "Arrrrrrrrghhhhhh," he screamed, trying vainly to wipe off the liquid, which in a matter of seconds turned him first into a skeleton, then a pile of bones and finally a mound of dust.

The Scarlet Angel pulled free from his shackles. He flew Lola back to her music school where they discovered the sinister voice teacher was now in jail. Lola fell asleep in her dormitory bed and remembered nothing the next day beyond a terrible nightmare.

Collin put *The Saving Voice* onto his bookshelf with the other finished issues and returned to his homework. Later, as he lay in bed, he thought about the story. More than anything, he liked the way his hero used his brain more than his muscles to defeat villains and rescue kids. *Of course, none of it's real. If I ever find out who Red Lion is, what will I use to stop him? My mental brilliance? My fighting skill? My athletic ability? I don't have any of those things!*

Collin drifted off to sleep, feeling defeated in a fight that hadn't yet started by an enemy he didn't even know.

Chapter 14

The next day after school, the two teenage sleuths headed to Herbie's bedroom where they searched the latest Bridgeview High yearbook for any boy's name with 'red' or 'lion' in it or a name similar to those words. They ignored the graduated seniors and focused on guys in the three lower classes who were sophomores, juniors and seniors today. They didn't have any photos of the current freshmen class, but shrugged that off, certain no junior girl would ever get involved with a freshman boy, much less let herself be abused by one.

"This is a waste of time," griped Collin, when they hadn't found any suspects by the time they finished with the junior class. "We're never going to find Red Lion this way."

"Do you know a better way?" asked Herbie.

"No, but how do we know the name Red Lion is connected to the guy's real name?"

"We don't."

"And that's why I think we're wasting our time. For all we know, Red Lion refers to his car, his hair color, some kind of clothing he wears or even a tattoo."

Herbie leaned back in his captain's chair and rubbed his chin. "How many guys at school have tattoos?"

"Jake is the only one, I think."

"Lomax has one, too. On his forearm. It's some kind of bird and it's mostly green and blue. I haven't seen Jake's up close."

"Me neither."

"Maybe one of us should."

Collin didn't relish that idea. Jake was at least 19 and hadn't graduated with his classmates because of bad grades or poor attendance. He owned a motorcycle decorated with lightning bolt decals and often came to school wearing a leather jacket. Some accused him of belonging to a gang, which he denied. Jake had no reputation as a bully, but even so, he wasn't someone you'd mess with – or get close to if you didn't have to.

"Let's finish with the yearbook first," said Collin. "Maybe we'll come across some suspicious names in the senior class."

Herbie smiled. "Sure. Jake probably isn't Red Lion anyway because I can't imagine a smart girl like Leah going out with Jake."

The two teens turned pages, scrutinized names and debated who should or should not be a suspect. They dismissed Janet Redman, since Leah used male pronouns to refer to her abuser, and on they puzzled. Finally, only one suspect emerged – David Lionel, a popular senior who quarterbacked the Bridgeview Rams' football team. He was in Leah's Algebra class, making him even more suspicious, although Collin had never seen the two of them together.

"Isn't he going out with Trish Delvecchio?" asked Herbie.

"He broke up with her over a year ago. Don't think I've seen him with any girl lately, including Leah."

"We know whoever Red Lion is, he doesn't meet up with her during the school day, so it could be him. And remember what Leah said about Red Lion getting geared up for the football game against Westport? That's just what you'd expect from our starting quarterback."

"Yeah, but how do we find out for sure? Following Leah didn't do us any good and following David probably won't either."

Herbie got up from his captain's chair and leaned against the wall next to the Einstein poster. "Noooo, but hacking his cell phone will."

"Hack his phone?" Collin felt a stab of hope and fear. "Isn't that illegal?"

Herbie glanced at Einstein, as if seeking the scientist's approval, then toward Collin. In a strange tone he said, "You're only half right, big man."

"Half right? What do you mean?"

"Come over tomorrow after dinner and I'll show you. Oh, and bring ten dollars, too."

Chapter 15

SpyNow. That was the name of the app that allowed someone to view the cell phone activity of another person without them knowing it. The boys only wanted to view David's texts and phone calls, but SpyNow gave them the power to do much more than that.

"Look at this!" exclaimed Herbie, peering at the online ad, describing SpyNow's abilities. "It lets you see all texts, even if they've been deleted. It shows the target's social media activity, their photos and videos, e-mails, websites he's visited and all the apps they've installed. You can even activate the cell's microphone and listen to what the target's saying."

Collin leaned over Herbie's back and scanned the ad. "It's kind of scary in a way. Like something the CIA would use."

"Hell, man, the CIA probably invented it." Herbie scrolled to the bottom of the ad. "There're only two things we need to do. We have to pay a twenty-dollar license fee and find out what David's phone number is."

"So that's why you had me bring ten dollars."

"Right. I've got a $25 MasterPay gift card we can use to buy the license. If you give me your ten dollars, it's a 50-50 deal."

"Sounds like a plan to me. What about getting this dude's number?" Collin asked. "I don't know anyone who could give it to us."

"Me neither, but there may still be a way to get it."

"How?"

Herbie put his fingertips together, creating a little pyramid with his hands. "With all my allergies, I've gone to the nurse's office more than most kids."

"I'd say you're number one in that category."

"There's no gold medal for that. Anyway, Ms. Jamison keeps a clipboard on her wall with the names of students who routinely come to her for care. Next to each name are two phone numbers. The first is for one of the kid's parents; the second is for the kid's cell. I'm on it, of course, and so is David Lionel."

"Wonder why?"

"I didn't know until I saw him limping into Ms. Jamison's office a couple of months ago. Turns out he pulled a hamstring in the last game of the season. It didn't heal right, so he needed surgery earlier this year. I guess he goes to Ms. Jamison for painkillers or physical therapy or something."

"It doesn't sound like he could push some girl around. All she'd have to do is kick him in the leg and he'd turn into jelly."

"Don't be so sure, big man. I've sat next to this guy in the nurse's office. He's totally ripped. Over six feet and has more muscles than you and I put together."

"So, I guess the plan is for you to look at Ms. Jamison's frequent-patient list and get David's number off of it, right?"

A clenched-teeth grin forced its way onto Herbie's face. "Yeah, except you'll have to be the one who gets the number, cause I have two different doctors to see tomorrow and might not make it to school at all."

"Couldn't you go on Friday?"

Herbie grimaced. "I suppose so, but I'd rather not."

"Why? You're a regular in her office anyway."

"That's the problem. I'm too regular. I saw her once this week and twice the week before. All false alarms. I just thought an attack was starting when it really wasn't. Ms. Jamison got kind of pissed at me. Said I was becoming a hypochondriac and wasting her time. Told me not to come see her unless my symptoms could be confirmed by a teacher." Herbie shook his head. "I don't want to see what happens if I go in with another false alarm."

"Oh," Collin said, "but there's no reason for me to see Ms. Jamison either."

"I'm sure with your vivid imagination, you can come up with one."

Collin scowled. "Thanks for your vote of confidence."

* * *

The next day, right after first period, Collin went to the nurse's office instead of English. The office's little waiting room had three seats, one of them occupied by Susie Eisenberg. When Collin sat next to her, Susie twisted her face in horror.

"Ewwww, gross! What happened to you?" She scooted to the far side of her seat.

"They're just zits that burst open last night," Collin answered. "I want to get something from Ms. Jamison so they don't get infected."

"It looks like they already are," said Susie, her face transitioning from horror to concern.

Collin had only three small zits, all on his forehead — and they had, in fact, burst open last night… because he scratched them relentlessly for at least five minutes before going to bed, making them wider and deeper. In the morning, all three areas were flaming red. One scabbed over while the other two became little pus-filled mounds. Careful placement of his hair and hands allowed the wounds to escape his mother's attention at breakfast, and later from his classmates on the school bus and in homeroom. On the way to see the nurse, he rubbed all three zits again, so that by the time he arrived, blood and pus trickled down to his eyebrows.

Ms. Jamison, a petite blonde woman who looked fresh out of college, emerged from her examining room and scowled at him. "What on earth did you do to yourself?"

"They're zits that got infected."

"I can see that. Were you picking at them?"

"Maybe a little."

"I'd say maybe a lot. I'll give you something in a minute." She motioned for Susie to come into the exam room. Susie got up and looked at Collin, making a not-quite-silent *yecch* sound before following the nurse. Now alone in the waiting room, Collin stretched out his legs and considered his next move. According to Herbie, the clipboard with the phone numbers hung on the wall of the exam room with a clock and the nurse's framed diploma on either side of it. *How can I look at the clipboard without arousing Ms. Jamison's suspicion?* He'd have to think of something on the spot.

After five minutes, Susie came out, crinkling her nose at him in disgust before leaving. "Your turn now," said the nurse. "I'll put a warm compress on those zits and then some anti-bacterial cream. After that, the most important thing will be for you to leave them alone."

"Yes, ma'am," said Collin, following her into the room.

Ms. Jamison motioned him toward the bed that occupied almost a third of the small but neatly arranged room. Before sitting down Collin scanned the walls. One held a Junk Food Facts poster and a sign that said "Stay Calm, I'm a Nurse." He spotted the diploma, the clock, and the open space where the clipboard should have hung. Except it didn't. *Where is it?*

He felt the nurse's oversized white coat brush against his leg. "Look this way, please," she said.

Collin complied and soon felt the soothing warmth of the compress on his forehead. Ms. Jamison held the compress in place for several seconds while Collin darted his eyes around the room.

Miss Jamison gently took his hand and lifted it up to the compress. "Hold this in place for a couple of minutes," she instructed then turned around. Collin watched her open the cabinet and reach in and that's when he saw it, on the counter next to the sink. *It's now or never.*

Collin got up from the bed, still holding the compress to his forehead, and began to shuffle toward the counter.

"Wait! I've still got to put the cream on you," the nurse said.

"I'm not leaving. Just want to stretch and get a crick out of my back."

"Do you want me to check on that, too?"

"No," said Collin. "It should be gone in a few seconds."

"Well, keep the compress on your head."

Collin bent over the counter pretending to use it for balance while stretching a leg out behind him; the clipboard was right beneath him, close enough to touch. Like Herbie said, it appeared to list the names of students and their phone numbers, but he couldn't read them since the clipboard was upside down. *Now what do I do?*

"Is the crick gone?" asked Ms. Jamison.

"Almost."

"Well, keep standing if you want, but don't move so I can put some salve on those zits."

The nurse pulled open a drawer and took out a little tube of salve. She put some on a cotton ball and turned his head to the side to dab it on Collin's forehead. At the same time, Collin shifted his eyes toward the counter. He noticed the top of the clipboard hung a couple of inches over the side of the counter. Squinting, he thought he recognized some of the upside-down names, but the numbers were too weird looking for him to decipher from this angle. He inclined his head toward the counter, causing Ms. Jamison to almost drop the cotton ball.

"Please don't move your head!" she snapped.

"Sorry."

When she finished putting on the salve, Ms. Jamison tossed the cotton ball into a trashcan and stared him in the eye.

Oh gosh, I wonder if she's figured out what I'm up to.

"No more picking at these zits," she ordered, handing him the tube of salve. "When you get home, do the same thing I've done here. Put a warm wash cloth across your forehead and then dab some more of this ointment on each zit. When you finish, don't put a band-aid on them. They'll heal faster if they're exposed to the air."

"I understand," Collin replied, but the only thing he understood was he would soon have to leave without getting David Lionel's phone number. *I've got one last chance.*

Ms. Jamison went to her desk and began typing on her keyboard. Collin bent over again and scooted sideways toward the counter again.

"Is your back still bothering you?" the nurse said, looking up. "Maybe I should get –"

Collin lurched forward, flinging his arms toward the counter. One hand grabbed the side of the sink, the other struck the bottom of the clipboard with such force that the thing flew into the air, spinning like a football.

The nurse gasped and jumped up from her desk, as the clipboard hit the wall below the posters.

"Oh, I'm so sorry," Collin blubbered. When Ms. Jamison started to rise from her desk, he rushed to where the clipboard lay, face-up, on the floor. Grabbing it, he stared at the names and numbers that were now easy to read and turned his back to the nurse.

> Jenny Walcott 545-8810/545-4735
> Herbie Kessler 577-3491/545-9814
> Paul Franklin 552-4679/552-6251
> Terri Baskin 552-8003/552-7178
> David Lionel 552-7515/545-1863

He focused on David's numbers. It would be easy to remember the first three numbers – many local numbers started with them – but what about the last four? Something seemed familiar about those numbers. They reminded him of a date. Yes –July 1863! The year of the Battle of Gettysburg and the Gettysburg Address.

"Gettysburg, Gettysburg, Gettysburg." Colin spoke the historic name out loud, imbedding it in his memory, as he handed the clipboard to Ms. Jamison.

The nurse gave him a puzzled look. "Gettysburg? You have a history test coming up or something?"

"Oh, no. It's... um... just one of my favorite vacation spots. I think about it sometimes when I'm a little nervous. All those incredible monuments, and the visitor center is amazing."

"I went there once with my family years ago. Too much sorrow and death for me." She paused. "Why would you be nervous here? All you had were some infected pimples."

Collin could feel sweat on his palms and the back of his neck. Now that he had David Lionel's phone number, he just wanted to get out – before Ms. Jamison became suspicious. *Why not tell her the truth, sort of?*

"Actually, it's not the zits that worry me. It's just there's this girl I really like and I want to ask her out, but I think she might already have a boyfriend."

Ms. Jamison laughed. "Oh is that all?" She gave him a get-out-of-here wave of the hand. "Go ask her out, for heaven's sake. Maybe she'll say no, but then again, she might say yes. You'll never know if you don't try."

"But her boyfriend is –"

"Who cares who her boyfriend is? For all you know, she's ready to dump him."

That's for sure.

"Again, you won't know if you don't try."

Maybe she should be an advice columnist instead of a nurse. "Okay, I'll give her a call tonight."

"That's the spirit!"

A minute later, Collin walked out of the nurse's office with a tube of salve in his hand and a phone number in his head.

As he headed toward his next class, he passed David Lionel apparently on his way to the nurse's office himself. *Is he limping?* Collin couldn't tell, but it didn't matter. *If David is Red Lion, he'll have more to worry about than an aching leg.*

Chapter 16

*T*hey zeroed in on David's list of recent calls. Collin read off the names from Herbie's laptop. "Brad, Neil, John C, Bridgeview Pharmacy, Greg, Brad again, Neil again, Briggs Clothing, Tony, John A, Village Barber Shop, John A again, Bridgeview Pharmacy again, Joyce …"

Herbie's caterpillar eyebrows went up. "Joyce?"

"Probably Joyce Ward," answered Collin, clicking on the i button. "He called her at 11:45 yesterday – during lunch, I'd guess – and they only talked for a minute. Joyce is a math tutor, so it probably had something to do with school. Let's keep going."

Sucking in some air, Collin started the sing/song listing again. "Dr. Rosen, Neil again, Sunset Bowling Alley, Brad again, L, Brian—"

Herbie's eyebrows went even higher this time. "L? That's all?"

"Yeah, no full name."

"Like it was a secret. When was the call?"

"Nine last night… for 38 minutes."

"Sounds like they had a lot to say. About what I wonder?"

"Maybe his text messages will give us a clue." Collin switched to the list of David's recent text messages and read them off, one by one. "Mom, Coach T, Brad, Mom again, Neil, number with no ID, and… there! L! This morning!"

Herbie craned his neck toward the screen. "What did they say?"

Collin brought the message exchange up; both teens stared at it, wide-eyed.

David: C u tonight?
L: Yes
David: We'll go to Seacrest. Only safe place
L: What time?

David: 8

L: C u then

"Looks like we might have found our man," Herbie whispered.

Collin nodded. Both felt more awe right now than triumph. They did it, by themselves.

"What do you want to do? Spy on them?"

"More than that." Collin closed the laptop and pushed it toward Herbie. "Here's what I think we should do…"

* * *

Like all of Collin's plans, this one was simple enough, but it caused Herbie to rub his chin at least a dozen times. "It's risky, that's for sure, especially if we get caught."

"If we succeed, we'll bring Red Lion down and end Leah's nightmare for good."

"How are we getting to the Seacrest?"

"Have to borrow my dad's car."

"Are you going to tell him what we're doing?"

"Not exactly. But I'll come up with something that's sort of true." *I hope.*

* * *

At dinner, Collin's dad had something on his mind. First, he drummed his fingers on the table, then he pressed them against his temples, and finally he clenched his hands into fists and bumped them against each other. After a minute or so, he repeated the sequence. Meanwhile, his lasagna sat in front of him, half eaten.

"Something wrong, Dad?" asked Collin.

Mr. Morris smiled. "Actually, it's something good – maybe. I've got a second interview tomorrow morning with Universal Dynamics Land Systems. They're considering me as a team project manager."

"That's great, Dad," Eleanor said. "Your unemployment days might be ending soon."

"Yes, except…"

Mr. Morris looked at his wife. She reached over and put her hand on top of his. "You'll do fine, dear," she said. "I'll help you, if you want to do a rehearsal."

"A rehearsal?" Eleanor asked, totally confused. "You mean like for a play?"

Mr. Morris chuckled. "Not a play, sweetie, a speech. They want me to do a 20-minute presentation in front of the executive vice president and several other bigwigs at this place. And public speaking has never been easy for me." He turned to Mrs. Morris. "Remember that oral book report I gave in senior English on *Animal Farm?*"

Mrs. Morris winced.

"I stammered through the whole thing and forgot the author's name."

"You were much younger then," said Mrs. Morris.

"Yeah, but I don't think I've improved with age."

"Do you know what you're going to say?" asked Eleanor.

"I've got a few notes jotted down, but I need to flesh them out and rehearse, just like your mom said." He shook his head. "Even though that might not help."

Collin saw the opening and jumped in. "Say, Dad, if you're staying home tonight, can I borrow the car?"

"What do you need it for?" asked his mother.

"I want to hang out with Herbie."

"It's not that far to his house. Couldn't you walk if the weather's nice?"

"Well, that would be okay except we might—"

"You can have it, son. The keys are in my coat pocket. Don't be out too late. I know I liked to just drive around sometime. Go easy on the gas."

"Thanks, Dad." *And someday, Leah might thank you, too.*

Chapter 17

When Collin picked him up that evening, Herbie was ready and eager to carry out the night's mission. He bounded into the car and put a small carrying case at his feet while he buckled himself in. "Got the binoculars?" Herbie asked.

"Check," said Collin. "Got your camera with the telescopic lens?"

"You mean my Canon EOS Rebel t7 24.1MP SSLR camera?"

"If it has a telescopic lens, then that's the one I mean."

"Right here," Herbie said, tapping the case at his feet.

"Then we're ready as we can be."

That was probably true; Collin still felt nervous. The plan itself didn't make him too nervous. It involved parking near but not at the Seacrest and then photographing Leah and the quarterback as they hooked up before going into one of the motel rooms. His jitters came from what to do with the photos afterward. *Give them to the police? If they just showed David and Leah together at the motel, that would humiliate Leah without necessarily getting David in trouble. Give them to Dr. Kaufman or Mr. Scanlan? Since the photos weren't taken on school property, their hands might be tied. Show them to David and threaten to expose him if he didn't leave Leah alone? Then we might be the ones in trouble with the law for blackmail.* In the end, they decided on simply deciding later; one step at a time.

Neither Collin nor Herbie said much during the drive to their stakeout spot. Herbie took his camera out of its case and tinkered with the lens. Collin turned on the radio, keeping the volume low, but flicked it off when they reached the edge of town where the Seacrest sat next to a strip mall with a coffee shop, nail salon and other small businesses, all closed at this hour.

The Seacrest Motel had seen better days. Even with darkness closing in, Collin saw warped shingles clinging to the motel's roof and dark splotches along its outer walls where the paint had peeled off. A dingy sign out front with the motel's name provided some illumination, although the lights behind the c and the t were burned out. The only other nearby lighting came from the office, located in the middle of the 16 units. Three vehicles, two cars and a pick-up truck were in the gravel parking lot. None of them were David's. Collin parked his own car in front of the coffee shop, the closest business to the motel; just the two parking areas separated the buildings. Both he and Herbie stayed inside and took turns peering at the place through the pair of binoculars Eleanor once used for birdwatching.

"No sign of our suspect," whispered Herbie as he moved the binoculars back and forth.

Collin checked his watch. "It's 7:56, still four minutes to go."

"I sure hope the police don't see us," Herbie stated. "What do we say if they do?"

"Hadn't really thought of that," Collin confessed. "Maybe we say our GPS is broken and we're lost."

"That's lame," said Herbie, handing him the binoculars. "Especially when they look at your registration and realize you live fifteen minutes away."

"Well, you think of something then. I just don't—" Collin stopped talking as a man wearing a fedora and jacket exited a motel room and got into one of the parked cars. A few seconds later, a woman wearing a shawl and beret came out of the same room and got into the car with the man. They drove away. Collin knew what went on behind the closed doors of the Seacrest. It made him sick to his stomach to think of Leah and her slimy boyfriend "doing it" at this place. Somehow, someway, he had to get her out of this mess and away from this dump forever.

Collin lowered the binoculars and was about to hand them to Herbie when a car glided into the Seacrest's parking lot. He brought the binoculars back up to his eyes, but didn't really need them. David's Camaro was a familiar sight around Bridgeview High, and now it was less than a football field away. "It's him!"

Both teens stared as the vehicle crunched through the lot and parked close to the Seacrest's office. The driver's side door opened; David got out. He pulled his wallet from the back pocket of his jeans and went into the office. Collin and Herbie shifted their gaze back to the Camaro –

which was empty.

"Where's Leah?" Collin asked without expecting an answer.

"Maybe she's already here."

"Doubt it. That pick-up truck doesn't look like something she'd drive."

"Maybe she'll come in an Uber."

"Possible, I guess." But Collin doubted that, too. *Why wouldn't they just drive over together?*

David came out of the office, twirling a key. He leaned against the hood of his car and focused on the entrance of the parking lot.

"Looks like he's expecting Leah any minute now," said Herbie.

"He's expecting someone." Collin opened the door and stepped out of the car.

"Where are you going?"

"To get a closer look. Are you coming with me?"

Herbie opened the passenger door, but hesitated. "Suppose he sees us?"

"Then we'll have to introduce ourselves, won't we?"

The two teens crept toward the motel, crossing a small patch of weeds and wildflowers before reaching the edge of the motel parking lot. A rusty dumpster with a cracked lid offered the only place to hide. They scurried over next to it and crouched.

Three minutes passed. David grew impatient, tapping his foot and glancing at his watch. Then a beige sedan pulled into the motel parking lot, came up next to the Camaro and stopped. David straightened up as someone got out of the newly arrived car.

"Is it Leah?" whispered Herbie, leaning over Collin's shoulder.

"Don't know," Collin whispered back. "David's car is blocking my view."

The voice that greeted David sounded unmistakably female and its tone seemed friendly, even affectionate.

I've got to move closer and see who it is.

"What are you doing?" gasped Herbie, as Collin slunk out from behind the dumpster. There wasn't time to explain. Bending over, as though bullets were flying over his head, Collin eased his way toward the Camaro. The closer he got, the more he heard what David and the young female were saying.

"We can't keep doing this," she said. "Someone at school is going to find out."

"As long as you're in that goddamn broom closet you call an apartment with your sister, where else can we go?"

Leah lives with her parents, not her sister. Wait, does she even have a sister? Something isn't right.

"Don't your mom and dad go out some nights?" she said.

"Yeah, but we've got neighbors who are super nosy. They'd find out what we're up to."

There was a crunching sound on the gravel as David and his companion moved away from their cars toward one of the motel rooms. Out of the corner of his eye, Collin saw Herbie, still by the dumpster, shaking his head and gesturing wildly for him to return. *He must see who's with David,* thought Collin. *Maybe it really isn't Leah.* That thought brought him comfort because whoever was with the Bridgeview High quarterback definitely wanted to share his company. Still bent over, he began to backtrack toward the dumpster. He had gotten maybe ten feet when the heel of his right foot hit an empty beer bottle, sending it clinking over the gravel.

"What's that?" shouted David. "Is someone over there?"

The quarterback clinched his hands into fists and dashed back toward his car getting ready to barrel around it into the shadows toward Collin. A girl—no, woman—came up behind and grabbed his arm. Collin couldn't believe what he was seeing. It was Ms. Lenore Jamison, Bridgeview High's reliable school nurse.

"Who the hell are you and why are you spying on us?" yelled David. The guy's voice carried unmistakable anger but also a note of fear.

"I… I… I'm sorry," stammered Collin. "It's my mistake."

"You got that right, dude," snapped David, pulling away from Ms. Jamison's grasp and closing in on Collin. The quarterback's fists shook, but whether from fear or rage, Collin couldn't tell.

"Wait, Dave," said the nurse. "I know this student. Let me handle this." She moved around her student/boyfriend and planted herself directly in front of Collin. "What are you doing here, Collin?"

"We came here looking for—"

"We?"

Collin gulped and turned around toward the dumpster. "Come on out, Herbie."

His friend shuffled out over the gravel. He came up next to Collin and gave a sheepish wave to Ms. Jamison.

"Why, it's my favorite patient," said Ms. Jamison. "Okay, why are you two here?"

"We thought another couple might be coming to this place tonight," Collin explained. "And we think the girl is being brought here against her will."

"What were you going to do?" Ms. Jamison suddenly looked astonished as she realized what they planned. "Rescue her?"

"Maybe. At least we wanted to find out who her asshole boyfriend is so we could get him in trouble."

"And you thought this… mean… boyfriend was Dave?"

"Possibly."

The nurse's face brightened, as if a light bulb turned on over her head. "I'm guessing your trip to my office this morning had more to do with your rescue mission than it did with your zits."

"Yeah, we needed to get David's phone number. That's the real reason I came to see you today."

"Oh…" the nurse nodded knowingly. "And that's why you knocked the clipboard on the floor. So you could find out David's cell number." Her eyes shifted toward Herbie. "I'll bet your friend here is the one who told you where it would be."

"Yes, ma'am." The confession squeezed out of Collin's dry mouth as Herbie frowned in embarrassment. He felt as though he had shrunk to the size of an ant. And yet, something in Ms. Jamison's voice indicated she wasn't very angry.

"I see," said Ms. Jamison. "Who is the girl you're trying to save?"

Collin looked down at his feet. "We'd kind of like to keep her identity a secret."

"I can understand that." She paused for a second, taking a deep breath, as if trying to figure out the words she needed to say. "Now here's something I want you to understand. Dave and I…" she put a hand on his chest "… are in a committed relationship. We are both adults, and he's no longer a student at our school."

Collin looked up. "You mean he already graduated?"

"He sure did, at the end of the last grading period." The nurse beamed at the quarterback, who glared at Collin and Herbie the way a hungry wolf might look at a flock of sheep.

"The point is," she continued, "there's nothing illegal here, but people at our school still might not like what we're doing, might not think it's appropriate. So, we'd like you to keep our relationship a secret. I assume you can do that along with the identity of the girl you're trying to help?"

"Oh, sure, sure," babbled Collin. "We wouldn't want you to get in trouble."

"Yeah," Herbie chimed in. "You're a great nurse; we wouldn't want you to get fired or anything."

"I'm glad you feel that way." The nurse turned to the quarterback. "Come on, sweetie. Let's go. I think we can trust these boys to keep our secret."

"I hope they know what will happen to them if they don't," said David, giving the boys one final glare.

Chapter 18

A half hour later in Herbie's room, Collin watched his friend tapping on his keyboard. "SpyNow is put to sleep," Herbie said. "Our cell phone hacking days are over."

"They should never have started," said Collin.

"I beg to differ. David was a legitimate suspect. We had to check him out."

"We did a lot more than check him out. We scared the hell out of him and Ms. Jamison, too." Collin let his head droop. "Can you believe that?! How will I ever look that woman in the eye?"

"Crazy, crazy for sure, but I think as long as we keep their secret to ourselves, they'll both be okay." Herbie walked over to the Einstein poster and stared at it a moment. "Remember how I said everyone's life is like an iceberg? Wow, is our school the same. The classes, the teachers, the learning that's supposed to be going on. That's just the surface. Underneath, so much more is happening. For all we know, David Lionel isn't the only student having sex with a staff member."

"Well, David's graduated, I guess, and yet…" Collin thought about his morning visit to the nurse's office. "Wait, if he graduated, why is his name still on that phone list and why did I see him in school after I finished with Ms. Jamison?"

"Good questions," said Herbie. "We still have his phone number. You could call and see if he'll tell you why." Herbie snickered.

"No thanks. I really don't care. I just want to find out who Red Lion is."

"Which brings us back to our last suspect."

"You mean Jake Clancy?"

"One of us should at least take a closer look at his tattoo."

"One of us meaning me?"

"Why not you?"

"Because your eyes are as good as mine, and I did the last risky thing."

"I'm the total nerd. That was closer than I like to get to any action. Let's flip for it." Herbie snatched a coin off his dresser and tossed it into the air. "Call it, big man."

"Tails!"

Herbie grabbed the coin before it hit the floor and slapped it on his wrist, leaving his hand over it. After a few seconds, he peeked underneath with squinted eyes, then broke out in a smile.

"You're elected, big man."

* * *

Collin didn't have any classes with Jake, but the two of them ate lunch during the same period and then went to the same study hall right afterward. *How am I going to get a good look at his tattoo?* he wondered, as he rode the bus to school the next day. *Should I sit next to him at lunch? No, he might not like that, and the Three Stooges would be all over me about why I didn't sit with them. Study hall maybe? No assigned seats; I don't usually sit anywhere near him. Might look odd if I did now.* He started to pull a comic book out of his backpack but decided to leave it there, realizing he wouldn't get any answers from a make-believe character. *Maybe this isn't as hard as it seems. I'm looking for a red lion. I won't have to get too close to see if his tattoo is red.*

When lunch came a few hours later, Collin scanned the cafeteria and spotted Jake at a corner table, stooped over a plate of turkey slices and mashed potatoes with room on one side of him to walk close; it was an opportunity. He decided not to pretend to be getting more food or throwing something away; he would just get close enough to see the color of the tattoo, turn around, and go back to his own table. He doubted anyone would notice, but if they did, he'd tell the truth. *I just wanted to see Jake's tattoo.* He just wouldn't say why.

Leaving his tray behind, Collin got up and walked toward Jake's table. Luckily, Eric was absent and Fred and Ronnie were playing games on their cells. No hesitation, no backward glances, he walked to within ten feet of where Jake sat, with his right arm – the one with the tattoo – lying across the table. Collin couldn't tell what the tattoo was supposed to be, but its color was obvious — red. *Need a closer look.* He took another step and then another. Now he could see the image on Jake's arm had eyes, a nose, and a soft curved mouth. *Not a lion. A girl with flowing red hair.* A scroll over her head spelled out her name: Clara.

Collin didn't need anything more. *Another dead end. Jake isn't Red Lion.* He swung around to go back to his table but kept his eyes on Jake's tattoo for a second longer… and plowed into someone's massive torso.

"Get out of my way!" roared Harvey, shoving him aside.

Maybe he won't remember who I am, thought Collin, tensing his muscles.

"You again, grub-chub? Didn't I warn you about bugging me?" He grabbed Collin's shoulder. "Do you know what I could do to your fat ass right here and now?" Harvey made a quick scan of the cafeteria and grinned. "Especially with Scanlan gone."

"Leave him alone, Frymuth," said Jake, turning around in his seat. "He didn't mean to run into you. He just wanted to get a look at my tattoo."

The grin vanished from Harvey's face, but he kept his grip on Collin's shoulder. "Then he's bugging you. I'll still pound him."

"I'll decide who's bugging me," Jake replied. "And right now, you're bugging me more than he is. So let him go and get lost."

Harvey's hand fell from Collin's shoulder. "If you say so," he mumbled then shuffled away.

For a moment, Collin froze, not sure what to say or do.

"Well, do you want to see my tattoo or not?" asked Jake.

"Sure," said Collin and sat down next to him. Jake stretched out his arm across the table, allowing Collin to see how colorful and detailed the tattoo was. The girl's fire-red hair swirled downward from Jake's elbow all the way to his wrist where the tips touched each other. A small white flower peeked out of the hair above one blue eye. At the edge of the other eye, a teardrop hung, ready to stream across the pink cheek below. The girl's mouth was also red, but darker than the hair. The lips were slightly parted, as if she were about to say something. Collin had already seen the scroll above the girl's head with her name. Now he noticed the two little hearts, one red and one white, that bracketed the scroll.

"Who's Clara?" Collin asked. "Your girlfriend?"

"No, she was my sister."

"Oh. I see." Collin hesitated for a second, then realized Jake probably wanted to tell him what happened to Clara. "Did you lose her somehow?"

"Breast cancer."

"That's awful. My great aunt had breast cancer, too, but they caught it in time and saved her life."

"Clara might have survived, too, if she hadn't already gotten MS before the cancer."

"Your sister had MS *and* breast cancer?"

"Yeah, the MS started when she was 18, right after graduating from high school." Jake stared into space as if speaking to someone only he could see. "First, she started having double vision and numbness in her legs. Next came dizzy spells and muscle tremors. Finally slurred speech and uncontrolled muscle contractions. In less than a year, she went from being a cross-country star to an invalid in a wheelchair."

"I don't know much about MS," said Collin. "Aren't there treatments for it?"

"Oh, yes," said Jake, still staring into space. "She tried them all: infusion, steroids, even had bees sting her along her arms and legs. It worked for a little while. Clara could even take a few steps with a walker. Then two years ago, she was diagnosed with stage four breast cancer. They might have found it sooner but the treatments for her MS masked the symptoms of the cancer. In her weakened condition, she could only undergo radiation one time – and that wasn't enough. She died last October. Just 22 years old."

"I'm sorry," said Collin. "That's just so unfair. To get cancer after getting MS."

Jake finally turned his gaze toward Collin. "It's called life and it never has been fair and never will."

"Thanks for letting me see your tattoo," said Collin.

"No problem. The more people who see it, the more Clara will be remembered."

Collin stood up, reached out and put his hand on Jake's shoulder then walked away. A month ago he would never have even sat near someone like Jake, he would have been terrified to speak to him, and now he had just reached out to give some guy-support. And he hadn't been punched for it.

Collin returned to his seat where his half-eaten lunch waited.

"What were you doing over there with Jake?" asked Fred.

"Learning that life sucks sometimes," said Collin.

"Hell, I could've told you that. Just now when I was about to get a new high score on Asteroid Invaders the charge on my phone crashed."

A sarcastic response came onto Collin's lips, but he stifled it. "Yeah, that does suck." *Like so many other things around here.*

* * *

On his way home from school, Collin texted Herbie.

Jake not Red Lion
Did you check tattoo?
Yes, it's his dead sister
Sad
Just like our chances of helping Leah

Chapter 19

*T*hat evening, Collin finished his homework right after dinner and went to bed early. In the shadows of sleep, a figure appeared and came toward him. Collin recognized who it was immediately from that dark-red jacket and a blue bandana around his neck. "Scarlet Angel! Where did you come from?"

"From your imagination, of course," the angel replied. "Where else would a make-believe character come from?"

"Yeah. Anyway, I hope you can help me with something."

"Doubt that I can, but go ahead and try me."

"I need to find out who Red Lion is and stop him from abusing Leah."

"I don't know who Red Lion is; even if I did, I couldn't stop him from hurting Leah."

"You couldn't?"

"Of course not. I'm not real and my adventures, which you love reading about, aren't real either. You know that." The angel put his hands on his hips and stared at Collin with steel-gray eyes. "Think about your great-grandfather for a moment. He didn't know what was going to happen when he took control of that damaged B-17. Maybe he'd run out of fuel. Maybe a wing would fall off. He and the other men on that plane couldn't be sure of surviving until he landed the plane at their air base. With me, everything that happens is scripted ahead of time by the artist who draws me. Every move I take, every word I speak, every clue I find, every kid I rescue – it's all settled before I appear in the first panel."

"But you've had some close calls, even been injured a few times."

The angel chuckled. "Well, it wouldn't be very interesting to people like you if I just rescued kids without any worry or trouble. It's the conflict I have with Vorman and other villains that make my stories fun to read. But it's not as if they ever have a chance of beating me."

"Yeah. You always win in the end."

"That's because my stories are for entertainment, for escape. You read them to have fun. To think about the *What Ifs*. You can't use my stories as a guide for capturing Red Lion or saving Leah, because you live in the real world. In the real world, good guys can lose and bad guys sometimes get away with their crimes."

"I guess I always knew that. But shouldn't I still try to track down Red Lion? If I don't, who will?"

"Maybe no one."

"That's what I can't stand. Just letting Red Lion go on with his abuse."

"Okay, keep looking for him, if you want, but don't expect there to be a connection between Leah's name for him and his real name or with his physical appearance. He may not even be in any of her classes."

"How do I find him?"

"Your best bet is to get to know Leah better. Talk with her more at lunch or even ask her for a date. The more comfortable she feels with you, the more she will begin to trust you with secrets – like the identity of Red Lion."

"Okay. But suppose Leah won't go on a date with me? I mean, that's why Red Lion is pissed with her. She went out with another guy."

"So what? She might say no. Then again, she might say yes. You'll never know if you don't try. And sometimes a rejection can turn into a friendship."

"The school nurse said the same thing."

"It's true no matter who says it. If you do find out who Red Lion is, be ready to fight him with your wits rather than your fists. You know Leah wants to break up with him. You may be the best chance for her to do that." The Scarlet Angel began to fade away. "Maybe even the last chance."

The dream faded... into dreamless sleep.

Chapter 20

*W*hen Collin woke up the next morning, his dream remained fresh in his mind. It felt like a good bye in a way, as well as his own subconscious giving him some hard truths. He really was too old to be reading comics and taking them as seriously as he did. *I have to really grow up, and that means accepting things as they are.* After getting dressed, he opened the middle drawer of his desk and reached inside. His fingers brushed past the journal, which lay beneath a puzzle book, but kept going until they bumped into a small stack of papers at the bottom. Collin pulled out a single piece of paper from the middle of this stack. He read the writing, folded it up and squeezed it into his wallet. In some way he didn't entirely understand, this piece of paper tied into the advice he dreamed to himself.

Later, while mowing the lawn, Collin thought more about the dream. *My common sense bringing me down to earth. I guess it won't hurt to try to get to know Leah better even if it doesn't lead me to Red Lion. I do know I care about justice. Right to my soul. That's why knowing she is being abused hits me so hard. That's why finding clues felt so fun. I really may be cut out to be an FBI agent.*

The rest of the weekend drifted by uneventfully until Sunday night when another dream creeped into Collin's sleep. It began with Collin standing at the darkened end of a corridor in his high school. At the opposite end, a shaft of light fell on something he couldn't recognize until it began to grow larger. A compact body, sturdy legs and shaggy mane; there could be no doubt. *A lion!* The creature regarded him with the cold hungry eyes of a predator and then moved toward him at a saunter that quickly turned into a full-on charge.

Collin ran like his life depended on it, because within the dim, narrow world of this dream, that's exactly what was at stake. He ran past classrooms, lockers, offices, drinking fountains and doors to nowhere, never daring to look back. Rounding a corner, he took only three or four more steps before a metal fence snapped across his path, bringing his escape to an abrupt and agonizing halt. The fence was actually a retractable security gate that had flashed out of a wall. Collin turned around and found the lion, jaws open and teeth bared, only a few feet away. As it leaped toward him with claws outstretched, it turned a deep blood red from the tip of its nose to the tuft of its tail.

Collin woke startled, sweaty and frustrated. He knew an all-too-real person was behind this dream lion. A predator who had Leah at his mercy.

On the bus to school Collin slumped in his seat and gazed out the window. While his eyes took in the homes and neatly mowed lawns that glided by, his mind grappled with the so-far unanswerable question. *Whoever the Red Lion guy is, he seems to be invisible during the school day. Maybe he goes to a different school, but then what about Leah's journal saying he wanted the Rams football team to clobber Westport? I have to figure this out.*

One thing did make sense, though. He'd have to return the journal to Leah someday soon. That meant giving it to Dr. Kaufman to give to her, or putting it right in Leah's hands. The first choice seemed cowardly, but the second seemed unpredictable, even dangerous.

The driver opened the door. Before Collin stepped into the open air he saw Blake sauntering away from the drop-off zone. If he got off now, he'd end up right next to the ugly brute, just about the last place on earth he wanted to be. To avoid that calamity, he shuffled behind the driver's seat and pretended to search for something in his backpack, all the while keeping track of Blake.

When Blake was halfway to the west entrance, Collin exited the bus, still keeping the bully in sight. Blake looked the way he usually did. Buzz haircut, rumpled shirt, canvas pants and camo backpack. For some reason, he carried a notebook today. Even from 40 or 50 feet away, it stood out because of its bright color. Its bright *blood-red* color.

When did Blake get that? Collin wondered. He didn't know, but one thing he did know. While there were other red notebooks being carried around, none belonged to anyone as awful as Blake. *Could he be Red Lion?* A red notebook wasn't much to go on. Still, he and Leah had a study hall together, so they might have met there. *And maybe… just maybe Blake isn't as dumb as he seems.* The more Collin thought about Blake as a human being *or maybe a sub-human being*, the likelihood his tormentor was also Leah's abuser increased. Collin couldn't imagine why Leah would ever have dated Blake in the first place but that didn't matter. Blake was now the prime suspect. At lunchtime, Collin sent a text to Herbie:

I think Blake might be Red Lion
Why?
Blake's red notebook = Red Lion
That's all?
He's a mean dick and they have same study hall
Never saw him with Leah
Watching him anyway
Don't get too close He'll hit you
Don't worry

Collin was lucky enough not to be in any classes with Blake, but he sometimes saw the asshat when they left Algebra and study hall at the same time. The same one Leah was in. Maybe he'd see something that would confirm his suspicion.

When the bell ending seventh period sounded, Collin snatched his backpack and moved to the door as quickly as possible. Once in the hallway, Collin bolted to the study hall's door and then sidled up next to a row of lockers, hoping to go unnoticed. The students flowed out one by one with a few amorous pairs sprinkled in between. Among the couples was Carmen and Harvey, her hulking wannabe boyfriend, who followed her like a guard dog.

Collin stiffened when he saw Leah. She looked the way she always did. Vulnerable but alert. Curious but purposeful. A girl you might overlook until you gazed into those sparkling eyes. Then came Blake. His backpack hung lopsided over his shoulders, he carried his books in both hands as if they were weapons. Though his face scowled as it usually did, Blake seemed distracted. Maybe lost in a daydream, assuming his brain could conjure one up.

The bully got lost in the crowd for a moment and then reappeared farther down the hall. Next to Leah. His face angry. Apparently saying something. Collin was too far away to hear, but judging from the expression on Leah's face it wasn't nice. Leah seemed to shrink as she pulled her books close to her chest. She said something back, her lips barely moving.

She's scared. Just how a victim would feel with her abuser. He'd seen enough.

Collin charged away from the lockers and headed down the hall. No longer feeling like a bully's victim, he prepared to become a bully buster. Jostling his way past meandering students, sometimes bumping into them, Collin caught up to Blake at the bottom of the east staircase. Leah wasn't with him now, but the slimy creep no doubt planned to prey on her later.

It all seemed so clear.

Collin reached out and grabbed Blake's shoulder. The bully swung around, his scowling face changing to a sneering smile when he recognized who grabbed him.

"Well, look who's here," said Blake. "What's the big idea of putting your paws on me, fat ass? Think you're good enough to hang out with me?"

"No," Collin shot back. "And neither does Leah."

"Leah?" Blake let his books and backpack fall to the floor. "What the hell are you talking about?"

"You know what I'm talking about. Leah doesn't want to be your girlfriend anymore, so stop demanding she have sex with you just because she went out with some other guy."

Blake's eyes bulged out of his skull. "What? You think I've got the hots for Jennings? I wouldn't be caught dead with that dog. But you know something, Morris? You and her'd make a great pair. Fat Collin and Skinny Leah. Trouble is, though, after you screwed her, they'd need the jaws of life to pry her out of your bed."

Then Blake laughed – a long, rancid laugh with his mouth wide open and his tongue wiggling inside like an oversized worm. Then, somehow, Collin's right hand formed a fist and sprang toward Blake's head. It connected with the bully's nose, clapping his mouth shut and sending him reeling backward until he hit the staircase's handrail. Pain, shock and rage passed in succession over Blake's face right before he lurched forward and threw a punch of his own, which caught Collin under the left eye and sent him backward two or three steps, stumbling yet still standing.

"Fight! Fight!" Someone shouted.

Collin ignored the gathering crowd and approached his adversary again. This time he threw a succession of punches at Blake, some missing, some connecting. For his part, Blake kicked Collin in the shin, sending a wave of pain shooting up his leg. When Blake brought his foot back for another kick, Collin lowered his shoulder and plowed into Blake's midsection. A grunt spewed out of the bully as Collin pushed ahead, again knocking him into the handrail. Both of them then fell to the floor, clawing at each other, rolling over the feet of onlookers. Above them, a security camera took it all in, but neither combatant cared.

Suddenly someone pushed through the crowd, seized both boys by their collars, and jerked them to their feet. "What do you clowns think you're doing?" bellowed Mr. Scanlan.

"He started it," wailed Blake, pointing at Collin. "I just defended myself."

"Oh yeah?" snapped Collin. "Since when do you have to kick someone in the shins to defend yourself?"

"You're the fat ass who –"

"Shut up, both of you," exclaimed Mr. Scanlan. "I don't really care which one of you started it. You were both fighting in the halls. You've got some punishment coming. Let's go to my office and decide what it'll be."

Mr. Scanlan let go of their collars but stayed close behind them while they walked to his office. Collin moved slowly. He ran a hand over his shirt, brushing off some dirt and catching a finger on the torn flap of his lapel pocket. Raising the hand to his face, he felt a welt coming up under his eye. *I must look awful. Mom and Dad are going to go nuts.* Having never caused any trouble before, he didn't know what to expect. At one point, he glanced over at Blake. His clothes were even dirtier than Collin's and a stream of blood came out of his nose. *I did that? Well, he had it coming, for Leah and for me.*

Once Collin and Blake were within a few feet of the assistant principal's office, Mr. Scanlan moved ahead of them and opened the door. "There are two chairs in front of my desk. Blake take the one on the right, Corwin… or… ah…"

"It's Collin."

"Yes, Collin, take the one on the left."

Blake dropped himself into the designated chair and stared at the floor, his face expressionless. While they may have been equally guilty, Collin suspected Blake's record of bad behavior put him in greater danger of a serious punishment, maybe even a suspension.

Mr. Scanlan circled around the seated teens and went to his desk. But the assistant principal didn't sit down. Instead he leaned against the side of the desk, his eyes darting back and forth between Collin and Blake while his fingers drummed impatiently on the desk's surface. After 30 long seconds, the man fixed his gaze on Blake.

"Stand up, Emerick," Mr. Scanlan barked.

Blake rose from his seat; his head down and his eyes still focused on the floor.

"How many times have you been in my office this year?" Mr. Scanlan snapped. "Four? Five?"

Blake raised his head slightly, but didn't answer.

Mr. Scanlan reached into a drawer and pulled out a folder. "Let's see..." and he read off a list of days, times and detention hours Blake received for bad behavior.

Collin tuned out Mr. Scanlan's voice and wrinkled his nose. There seemed to be a sweet scent in the air, like cotton candy. It might have come from an air freshener or a too-heavy splash of cologne on the assistant principal's face. *There **are** times when this high school is like a circus. Maybe it's no surprise it can smell like one, too.*

While this office had an unusual sweet smell, it didn't look much different from what Collin expected. There were photos, plaques, a framed Rams football jersey on the wall, shelves full of books and a fully-loaded inbox on the desk beside a computer monitor and keyboard. At the front of the desk was a brass nameplate. Behind the nameplate was a coffee cup filled with pens, and a sharp-pointed letter opener that could have doubled as a weapon. There were artistic touches, too: on the bookshelves, a bust of Napoleon and a ship in a bottle; on the desk, a pyramid made out of mirrors, a model of a one-room schoolhouse and a...

Collin went numb, his body feeling as if it had rubbed against a glacier. *No, it can't be what it looks like.*

Mr. Scanlan's voice suddenly rang in his ears again. "What is it with you, anyway, Emerick? Do you like getting into trouble? Does that make you a tough guy or some kind of rebel?"

Blake's face twisted into a mask of despair. "It wasn't my fault this time," he whined. "Morris is the one who started the fight. I was just minding my own business. He came over and blamed me for picking on this ugly girl."

"Ugly girl?"

"Well, I think she's ugly, but he must like her. I told him I didn't do anything to her, but he punched me in the nose anyway."

"Stand up, Collin," Mr. Scanlan ordered, putting down the folder. "Is what Blake said true?"

Collin stood, his eyes still fixed on Mr. Scanlan's desk. He opened his mouth but no words came out.

"Well, speak up," Mr. Scanlan continued. "I don't want to miss anything you're about to say."

Collin was too shocked, too scared and too confused to think of any words, much less speak them. He closed his eyes as if doing so would make the object disappear, like a mirage. But when he opened them, that little statue was still there.

Delicate, maybe hand carved, mounted on a granite: a red lion.

Chapter 21

Collin planned to call Herbie as soon as he got home, but less than a minute after walking through his front door, Herbie called.

"I heard you got into a fight with Blake," said Herbie. "Was it about Leah?"

"Yeah. He yelled at her after leaving study hall, so I went after him."

"And kicked his ass from what I hear."

"Well sort of, but kind of got my own ass kicked, too. Also got four hours of detention, so the next person who kicks my ass will be my dad."

"Did you find out if Blake is Red Lion?"

"Yeah, and it's not him."

"Didn't think so."

"But I know who is."

"You do?"

"Yeah. Are you sitting down?"

"I'm actually lying in bed with my laptop, why does that matter?"

"Because when you hear who Red Lion is, you just might faint."

"Huh? Who is it?"

"Mr. Scanlan."

At least twenty seconds passed before Herbie spoke again. "You mean our assistant principal?"

"What other Mr. Scanlan do we know?"

"Why do you think it's him?"

"Because when Blake and I were in his office getting chewed out for fighting, I saw a little statute of a red lion on his desk."

"That's odd for sure, but maybe it's just a coin—"

"It's no coincidence, Sir Isaac. *Think!* We've been looking for a Bridgeview student, but for all the times we've followed Leah, we've never seen her hanging out with any guy. And that's because Red Lion is not just *any* guy; he's the second most powerful person at our school."

"Is that little statue all you're going on?"

"Actually, no. Remember what the journal said about Red Lion reeking of cheap cologne? Scanlan had so much of it on, you'd have thought he was selling cotton candy. But the lion statue is the big thing. Who else would have something like that? In that weird color?"

"Wait a minute. Let me check something."

Collin heard the sound of fingers tapping on a laptop. A few seconds of silence followed.

"The Red Lions is the nickname of Southwestern Pennsylvania College. I bet that's where Scanlan got his degree, and he keeps that statue as a memento of his college days."

"And if it is him, Leah definitely saw that statue when Scanlan brought her to his office to..." Collin let his voice trail off, not wanting to finish what he began to say.

"Let me check on something else," said Herbie. More tapping on keys was followed by a pause of about three minutes before Herbie spoke again. "I've been checking the minutes of the State Board of Education. My uncle used to work for them, and he told me once that sometimes at their meetings they revoke the licenses of educators who've committed a serious crime."

"Like what?"

"Like drunk driving and domestic violence but sometimes sex crimes, too. Just listen to this." Herbie cleared his throat as if preparing to deliver a lengthy speech. "From last September, Jerome Wallace, Elwood local school district, permanent revocation of a five-year professional teaching license for an inappropriate sexual relationship with a fifteen-year-old female student. From January, Alex Bowman, Masefield city school district, permanent revocation of a four-year resident teaching license for an inappropriate sexual relationship with a seventeen-year-old female student. And last month, Franklin Post, an art teacher in Lewis Circle for doing it with *two* high school girls."

"I remember hearing about Post. Didn't he start off by having those girls pose nude for his own paintings?"

"Yeah, and he didn't stop there."

"Okay, I get it. Male teachers sometimes try to hop in the sack with their female students. But one thing still doesn't make sense."

"What do you mean?"

"Mr. Scanlan isn't a teacher. He doesn't have any classes. He only sees students if they're in trouble or something, so how did he get the chance to hit on a girl?"

"Well, there must be girls who get in trouble sometimes. Hey, remember that fight between Marla and Jordan? I'm sure they ended up in his office."

"I'm sure they did, too, but they've had it in for each other since fifth grade. Leah's not going to get into a fight like that."

"How can you say that? You don't know her that well."

"Well, I know everything that's in her journal and there's nowhere she mentions having a fight or even an argument with another girl."

"But the journal is just one part of who she is. It's maybe not even the most important part."

"You're right. I need to know more about her. I can start doing that when I take her out."

Collin heard the snap of a laptop being shut followed by the thump of feet hitting the floor. "Take her out? You mean on a date?"

"Yep! You were right when you said I didn't know Leah that well. What better way to change that than by taking her on a date?"

"If you're right about Mr. Scanlan being Red Lion, then he's—"

"I don't care what he does. If Mr. Scanlan is Red Lion, then it's time I figure out how to get him caged."

Chapter 22

*T*he following day, Collin sat in the cafeteria, one hand holding a page from a newspaper while the other held forkful of coleslaw. His eyes jumped back and forth between an article in the newspaper and Leah, eating at her usual spot, a few tables away. She wore a light-blue blouse, a black skirt, and little boots with fur around the top. The only noticeable piece of jewelry was a locket that hung on a chain around her neck. *The one that belonged to her grandmother, the one she nearly lost in that seedy motel where she and…*

Collin shifted his attention back to the newspaper. A headline ran across the top: Comic Art Exhibit Comes to Columbus. The article below, which Collin had read several times already, gave the details.

Collin decided this exhibition gave him an ideal opportunity to ask Leah for a date because a lot of the displays and vendors dealt with the writing and art so she may like that. It would put him in a place where he felt comfortable, even confident. And, uncultured oafs like Blake wouldn't be caught dead at this kind of event. *Suppose Leah doesn't like comic art?* He'd have to take that risk, but it wasn't as if that would ruin everything. He could still take her to see the classical and modern works of art in other parts of the museum where the event was being held. Being a creative person, Leah would likely appreciate a day looking at other artists' work.

Collin shoved the coleslaw into his mouth, dropped his fork and got up from his seat.

"Hey, where you going, dude?" asked Fred, looking up from his cellphone.

"Just over there." Collin pointed to Leah's table.

"What? You don't like us anymore?" Eric joked.

"I'll be back," Collin replied. "I just got to ask Leah something."

Eric smirked. "Well, while you're over there, why not ask Carmen for a date?" He jerked his head toward Carmen who, as usual, sat at the table next to Leah's. Today, she had a skinny red-headed guy sitting next to her, yakking into her ear.

"Nah. She's not my type. But if you want, I'll tell her you wanna take her out, but don't have the balls to ask."

Horror gripped Eric's face. "Don't you dare!"

Collin turned his eyes toward Leah again. She'd finished her lunch and now had her nose in a book. *This is the time.*

"See ya later, guys." Collin said, pushing his chair in and heading toward Leah. He glanced over his shoulder and saw Eric watching with wide eyes, no doubt fearful he would make good on the Carmen threat.

Collin moved slowly, trying to be as cool as an average-looking teenager could be. He circled behind Leah, paused a couple of seconds and then sat next to her.

"Hey, Leah. How's it going?" he asked.

Leah's head jerked up from the book. "Oh, hey, Collin. I'm okay. Did you ever find a necklace for your sister?"

"Nah, I ended up getting her some earrings. The necklaces were too expensive or were too cheap looking."

"Well, earrings are a nice gift, too."

"Yeah, she seemed to like them."

"I'm glad."

"Me, too."

Leah smiled but when several seconds passed without Collin saying anything more, she returned to her book.

Collin swallowed hard, trying to get the dryness out of his throat. He pressed his fingertips together. Finally, he spoke. "Hey, how would you like to go with me to the art museum this weekend?"

"Might be nice. I haven't been there in a long time."

"It's got a special exhibit on comic art right now. But if that doesn't interest you…"

"Does it interest you?"

"Ah, well, yes it does."

"Because you're in the school's Graphic Novel Club, aren't you?"

Collin's mouth dropped. "Yeah, I am. How did you know that?"

Leah smiled. "Oh, I've been asking around about you."

Collin was dumbfounded. The idea that a girl might be attracted to him, might want to know more about him, didn't fit into his understanding of who he was. For a moment he couldn't think of anything to say. Then something flashed in his mind. *Maybe she's sees me as someone who can rescue her from Mr. Scanlan. If so, I can't let her down.*

"How about I pick you up on Saturday, say around noon?" he finally said.

"That will probably work. I live at 357 Westwood. Do you want me to write that down for you?"

I'm more likely to forget my own address than yours, thought Collin. *But just to be safe...* "Sure, just in case."

Leah pulled a pen and notepad from her backpack, then wrote down her address on the top sheet. "My phone number's there also," she said with a slick smile. "Just in case."

"Thanks," Collin said, taking the sheet from her and doing a quick study of her handwriting. If he had any remaining doubts they were immediately squashed—it matched the journal exactly.

Leah took her phone out. "Do you want to give me yours?"

"What?"

"Your phone number. Can I have it?"

"Sure." He read it off and she typed it into her contact list. "One other thing," he asked, "would it be okay if I started to sit with –"

Shouts and sounds of chairs scraping on the floor suddenly filled the air. At the next table, Harvey had a headlock on the skinny red-headed kid dragging him to the floor. "Let go of me, you sack of shit," yelled his latest victim, arms flailing. Next to the combatants, Carmen remained seated, her head turned slightly toward them, nose wrinkled in disgust. Harvey threw two punches into the red-headed kid's stomach, but before he could throw a third, a hand grabbed his arm and yanked him off the kid.

"At it again, are we, Harvey?" Mr. Scanlan bellowed.

Harvey waved a finger at the red-headed kid, who slowly rose from the floor. "Don't blame me. I just wanted to protect—"

"Shut up!" snapped Mr. Scanlan. The assistant principal paused and appeared to take a deep breath before continuing. "I'm the protector here, not you. Call me the guardian, the watchdog, Mr. Iron Fist. I don't care. Just understand when it comes to keeping girls away from guys who could hurt them, that's my job. When it comes to making our school a safe and happy place, that's also my job. People who forget that will soon be very sorry. And people who think they can do my job better than I will be even sorrier."

Collin felt a tremor climb up his spine and his stomach did a somersault. Although Mr. Scanlan's words were supposedly meant for Harvey, the assistant principal was staring straight at him.

***

At dinner, Collin told his parents about his date to the art museum on Saturday. The questions rained like money. Finally the practical parent ending the babbling.

"If you're going to the museum," his dad stated loudly to cut everyone else off, "I suppose you'll want to borrow the car."

"Yes, for a few hours in the afternoon."

"Will you be finished serving your detention by then?"

Collin nodded. "Friday's my last day."

His father let a little smile creep onto his face. The day before, he had chewed his son out for getting into a fight, yet Collin sensed his dad had mixed feelings about it. *He's probably glad I finally fought back against a bully.*

"Collin got detention?" asked Eleanor, surprised. "Why?"

"Got into a fight," said Collin.

"I guess that explains the little bruise under your eye and why we're having dinner a half hour late tonight." Eleanor leaned over toward her brother. "Who did you fight with? Did you—"

"This girl, Leah," his mother interrupted. "Does she live near us?"

"Couple miles away on Westwood Street."

Eleanor sniffed. "She must be a brave girl to trust your driving."

"My driving's fine," Collin retorted. "Who knows? Maybe on the way to the museum, we'll see Roger with a new girlfriend." As soon as those last words were out of his mouth, Collin knew he'd gone too far.

"Collin!" His mother snapped. "That was mean! Apologize to your sister."

"I'm sorry, El, I didn't mean it. Roger was a sleazeball for leaving you."

Eleanor waved a dismissive hand. "I accept your apology," she said, her lip quivering. "I'm totally over Roger now anyway."

Ten minutes later in his room, Collin was shaking as he told Herbie about Mr. Scanlan's stare.

A long pause came before Herbie spoke. "I can see why that might freak you out, but I don't think you need to worry."

"What do you mean I don't need to worry? Scanlan must know I'm onto him and then —"

"No, he doesn't. Don't spiral. He probably thinks you're just interested in Leah. Maybe he figures you were asking her for a date and wanted to see how she'd react. He wants her all for himself."

"I did ask her for a date. She said yes!"

"Congratulations. You did it big man. That is so cool I'm so happy for y—" Herbie sucked in some breath. "But so what? Guys ask girls out on dates everywhere in school, including the cafeteria. How can Mr. Scanlan find anything strange about that? He doesn't know you have Leah's journal. Hell, he may not even know it exists."

Collin took a deep breath and at the same time noticed his hand no longer trembled. He marveled at how his friend's cool logic could settle his nerves.

"Where are you going on the date?" Herbie asked.

"The art museum. There's a special exhibit on comic art."

"Sounds like fun. You know, you could give the journal back to her when you take her home."

Collin bristled. "We already decided to give it to Dr. Kaufman and let her handle it... remember?"

"Sure I remember. It was just a suggestion. This might be better for her, will keep her secret."

"Let's stick with our plan."

"Got it, but are you ever going to tell her you're the one who found the journal?"

"Yeah... someday... but this date isn't the time to do that."

"Okay, but if you're going to start dating Leah, you need to answer a question before things go too far."

"I know. When am I going to tell Leah —"

"No."

Exasperated, Collin rolled his eyes. "What, then?"

"Do you want to be her rescuer or her boyfriend?"

Collin fell silent, unsure how to respond.

"Well, whatever you decide," Herbie continued, "just remember you aren't the Scarlet Angel."

"Thanks for reminding me."

They ended their call, but Collin continued to hold the phone up to his mouth. After a few seconds – though Herbie was no longer there – Collin said, "Why can't I be both?"

* * *

*H*erbie's words were in his head as he went to sleep; and as usual, his imagination grabbed them and ran.

Mr. Scanlan's office appeared out of the darkness, huge and cavernous. In the middle, the assistant principal sat in a throne-like chair behind a desk that resembled a judge's bench. Seeing Collin, he smiled and motioned for him to approach.

"Come to rescue your true love, have you?" the man taunted. "Well, you've come to the right place. First let me show you my other guest."

Mr. Scanlan rose from his chair – all ten feet of him. "I'm the protector here," he bellowed, "the guardian, the watchdog, Mr. Iron Fist. People who forget that will be sorry. People like him." The giant Scanlan waved a hand to his right. From out of nowhere, a cage appeared. Inside, Herbie peered out, face bloated, hands clawing for an inhaler just beyond his reach.

Collin tried to move toward his friend, but found himself paralyzed, unable to take a single step.

"Trying to be a hero?" said giant Scanlan, who seemed to have grown another five feet. "Go ahead."

Collin suddenly lurched forward, the paralysis gone. He rushed toward Herbie, hoping to free his friend or at least push the inhaler closer. But both the cage and Herbie vanished before he could reach them. The assistant principal sneered.

"Not quite fast enough are you? What a shame! Maybe you'll have better luck with her."

Mr. Scanlan waved a hand to his left and another cage appeared, this one with Leah in it. The only part of her Collin could see clearly was her face, eyes squeezed shut, tears streaking down her cheeks, mouth opened in a soundless cry.

Again, Collin tried to move to make a rescue, but though not paralyzed, his steps came in slow motion as if huge weights were tied to his arms and legs. *I sure wish the Scarlet Angel was – No! He's not real, but I am.* Suddenly Collin's arms and legs felt normal, even stronger than normal. He found himself clad in a trench coat and wearing a fedora. *I'm really an FBI agent.*

From her cage, Leah reached her hands out. "*Help me!*" she pleaded. "*Get me out of here.*"

Without a word, Collin raced toward the bars and grabbing the door, flung it open. Scanlan disappeared and Leah, still in the cage, gazed up at him, face alight with gratitude and admiration.

* * *

Collin woke up, not disoriented, he felt sharp. He stopped a dream from becoming a nightmare. He was taking hold of his life. He never would have thought he might have to confront the assistant principal, but this was what life was throwing at him.

He went to his desk. Flinging open the middle drawer, he tossed away the crossword puzzle book and brushed his fingers back and forth across the journal's cover. Sighing with the knowledge he had to decide what to do about it very soon, he pulled it out and lay it on his desk. There, a moonbeam fell on the small book, giving it a soft glow like some mystical treasure.

A treasure that was bringing danger and inspiration.

Chapter 23

*T*he next day, Collin had trouble concentrating during morning classes. He almost dozed off during Mr. Petrie's PowerPoint presentation on the Vietnam War and didn't volunteer to answer any questions Mrs. Rowland asked about the opening chapters of *The Great Gatsby*. In gym, he made sure to get quickly eliminated in the three games of dodgeball so he could stand on the side and zone out. At lunch, he thought about eating with Leah, but that idea died when Eduardo sat next to her. They had a Spanish textbook opened between their lunch trays, so Collin wasn't worried about losing her as a date. Still, he wondered if the exchange student might be the guy Leah dated, triggering her guilt and Mr. Scanlan's wrath.

In study hall, Collin pulled out the latest edition of *The Ram Courier*. The headline blared "Prom Preparations Accelerate." A few weeks ago, Collin would have ignored the article that followed, but now he read it word-for-word.

> Saddle up your horses, juniors and seniors, and get ready for a ride back into the Old West... That's where you'll be going for this year's prom! Saturday, May 14, our gymnasium will be transformed into Tombstone, Arizona (or something like that). A dinner will be served in the gym, starting at 6:00pm with the help of cowboy and cowgirl celebrities – otherwise known as loyal faculty members. Local DJ Danny Beard will spin music for dancing, which will follow at 7:00. Tickets are $20 a couple and can be purchased online at the high school's website or outside the auditorium during lunch periods. Don't be left in the dust! Avoid the last-minute stampede! Get your tickets today.

If my date with Leah this Saturday goes okay maybe I'll ask her to the prom. Never thought I'd have someone to go with. And maybe after school's out, we could do some other things together, stuff she likes to do. I need to find out what that stuff is.

Later, his Earth Science class went outside to study some rock formations near the school. Collin lost interest quickly and wandered away from the group.

"Collin, these rocks have been waiting 300 million years for you to study them," his irritated teacher said. "Please don't keep them waiting any longer."

"Sorry," Collin replied stopping himself from adding, *if they've been waiting that long, what difference will another minute make?* He didn't want to get any more detention. Especially for some snark-mouth reason. That would only add to his father's problems.

On his way to French class near the end of the day, he received a text from Leah.

May have to cancel for Saturday
Why?
May need to help with my dad
What happe—

Collin deleted the question before finishing it. *I already know the answer.* Instead he asked...

Can I help?
Thanks, no. Will fill you in at lunch tomorrow

Chapter 24

Collin didn't bother going to his regular table when he came out of the cafeteria line the next day. Instead, he went straight to Leah's table and sat next to her.

"Hi, Leah."

"Hey, Collin."

"So, how's your dad?"

Leah took a drink of water and then turned toward Collin. "He had a major stroke last August. It came out of nowhere. He was doing a crossword puzzle at the kitchen table, and then the pencil rolled out of his hand. My mom asked him if something was wrong, but he just sat there staring into space for a few seconds and then fell on the floor."

Oh yeah, she wrote about that. "My Great Uncle George died from a stroke," Collin replied sadly. "At least your dad survived." As soon as he spoke those words, Collin realized how insensitive they were. *What a stupid thing to say.*

Leah didn't seem offended. "Yeah, he survived," she continued. "But the stroke left him paralyzed on his right side and with blurry vision. He spent over a month in the hospital and then went to rehab for three months. We brought him home in a wheelchair for Thanksgiving. Even with our neighbors helping us, my mom and I couldn't handle it for more than a day."

"I would have helped you, if I'd known you then," Collin said meekly, feeling a flush of humility.

Leah gave him a funny look, a frown combined with a smile. "It was a lot more than just pushing a wheelchair. He needed help eating, dressing, even using the bathroom. For the last five months, my dad's been in an assisted-living place that also does rehab. He's made some progress. Can eat using a spoon and drink through a straw now. He can even get out of his wheelchair if he uses a walker. We may be bringing him home on Saturday, if his physical therapist says it's okay, and if so… I won't be able to go with you to the museum."

"I understand," said Collin.

"The PT is supposed to tell us tonight if he is or not, so I'll let you know as soon as I know."

Collin nodded, realizing he was selfish to wish her dad's homecoming was delayed by one day — but wishing it anyway. At least it wasn't what he first thought, that Red Lion threatened her if she spent any time with him.

Later that evening, a phone call from Leah fulfilled Collin's wishes.

"Dad had a small relapse," she said. "He won't be coming home for at least a week."

"I'm sorry," said Collin, which in a way, he was. "So we're on for Saturday?"

"We are. I gave you my address, didn't I?"

"Yes, 357 Westwood. How about I get you at noon on Saturday?"

"Can we make it a little later, say more like one? I promised to help my mom with some chores in the morning."

"No problem. See you at lunch tomorrow?"

"Not sure. I'm meeting with my Algebra teacher right after third period. There's just so much about that subject I don't understand."

"That makes two of us," laughed Collin. He felt so normal right now. He couldn't believe he was about to have his first date.

Chapter 25

Collin pulled his family Malibu into the Jennings' driveway three minutes before one on Saturday. He took a moment to study the two-story white-brick house. It had a large picture window with flowers growing along the walkway. More flowers grew in a small garden that surrounded a redbud tree in the middle of the front yard. A larger tree grew between the Jennings' place and the house on the right.

Collin got out of the car and walked toward the front door. Before he got there, it burst open and Leah appeared. "Hi Collin," she said. "Come on in."

"You have some pretty flowers here," Collin said, pointing toward the ones beneath the redbud. "Did you plant them?"

"Yes, with help from my mom and our next-door neighbor."

The Jennings' living room looked like most others with one exception. A stair-lift chair had been installed, something Mr. Jennings would apparently need once he did come home.

Leah's mother walked in from a back room. She was about the same age as his own mother, with short brown hair and a pleasant smile. But the dark circles around her eyes attested to the stress she'd been under.

"I was sorry to hear about your husband's stroke," Collin said with full sincerity. "And about his relapse," he added at least half sincerely.

"It may not be as bad as we thought," said Mrs. Jennings. "Leah's dad might come home tonight if we can work things out with the rehab facility."

"Do you need me to bring Leah back at any particular time?"

"Not to help with her dad, but she promised... to help our neighbor Gerry with some yard work before dinner."

Leah scrunched up her lips as if she'd bitten into a lemon. "Mom, I don't think he really—"

"You promised," Mrs. Jennings repeated, narrowing her eyes and pressing her lips together as if she didn't care if her daughter didn't want anything to do with this chore.

"I don't think it will take that long to go through the comic art display," Collin said. "If I bring her back by 3:30, will that be soon enough to help your neighbor?"

"I think so," said Mrs. Jennings.

"Let's go," said Leah and gave his arm a little tug as if trying to leave before being reminded of another thing she was expected to do.

On the way to the museum, Collin and Leah small talked about the same things they did at lunch. But in the back of Collin's mind, a question gnawed on him. *Could this neighbor give us the answer to who Leah cheated with? The way Mrs. Jennings talked about him, Gerry is an adult. Maybe Leah got involved with another adult man or maybe someone in Gerry's family, like a son, got between Leah and Scanlan and made her feel guilty. There were at least two initials in the journal he and Herbie couldn't identify. Maybe they belonged to someone right next door to the girl in trouble.* He pushed his imaginative thoughts away; he could use them later as an FBI agent trying to solve crimes. Right now he was on his very first real date! He needed to enjoy every second of it.

The Columbus Museum of Art was housed in an ancient two-story concrete-and-limestone building with three large pillars at the entrance. Once parked and inside, Collin pulled $20 out of his wallet.

"I can pay for myself, if you want me to," said Leah, putting a hand on her purse.

"No way," said Collin. "This is my treat. Maybe sometime you...." Collin halted and stared at his own hand. Without realizing it, he had reached over and put his hand on top of Leah's, as if to stop her from getting out her money. He left it there for a few seconds before moving it away.

I touched a girl and she didn't mind at all! he thought.

Leah smiled. "Okay, I'll let you treat me... this time."

Inside the museum, a sign for the comic exhibit directed them to the main gallery. There, two parallel rows of kiosks stretched across the floor. Leah stepped up to the kiosk closest to the gallery entrance and gasped.

"What a weirdo!" she exclaimed.

Collin came up next to her and laughed. "That's Mr. Obadiah Oldbuck.

He's one of the first comic book characters ever created."

"How long ago was that?"

"Around 1835 in Switzerland. A caricature artist named Rodolphe Topfler created him. Obadiah went to London then finally made it to America in 1842 as a supplement to a New York newspaper."

Leah pointed at a label next to the image of Mr. Oldbuck. "That's just about what it says here verbatim."

"Topfler drew his characters on a special kind of paper that gave him more freedom than standard lithography would have."

"You're right," Leah said, continuing to read the label. "It was called autography." She shifted her gaze back to Obadiah. "I wonder where Topfler got the idea for such a funny-looking guy."

"Obadiah looks funny but his adventures weren't. He gets into fights and has to use disguises to escape. He falls in love but has to deal with a nasty rival. He becomes so unhappy, he tries to commit suicide but doesn't succeed."

"How depressing!"

Collin glanced at the next kiosk and grinned. "I think you'll like this next guy a lot more." He put his hand on Leah's back and gently guided her along. Touching a girl, even lightly, was exhilarating and best of all – Leah didn't seem to mind.

"Well, this guy is a lot cuter than Obadiah," Leah exclaimed, as she inspected the character featured in the second kiosk. "But what an outfit!"

"It's another oldie, the Yellow Kid."

"Is that a nightgown he's wearing?"

"Yeah, it's the only thing he ever wears."

"And there's something written on it."

"I think the kid is supposed to be speaking those words."

Leah read the label next to the kiosk. "Hey, listen to this. For a while, there were two people drawing the Yellow Kid in two different newspapers."

"I know. Richard Outcault, the guy who drew the kid, started off drawing for *The New York World*. But then William Randolph Hearst offered him a higher salary if he'd come work for *The New York Journal American*. Outcault took the offer but never got a copyright for the Yellow Kid, so another artist named George Luks kept drawing the cartoon for *The New York World*. But his version of the kid wasn't as popular as

Outcault's. The first full-fledged comic book in the U.S. was actually a collection of the comic strips Outcault drew for Hearst's paper."

Leah stared at him then smiled. "I don't even need to bother reading the labels. I'll just ask you."

"Well, I don't know *everything* about comics."

"Are you sure about that?" She laughed.

Collin felt his face redden. *I must sound like a big know-it-all. But that laugh, I'd do anything to make her laugh like that every day.* "Let's see what else they have here."

The next few kiosks focused on the Golden Age of comic books. There were cels featuring all the well-known superheroes who made their first appearances between 1938 and 1956. Kiosks highlighting the next decades of comics carried them deeper into the large room.

"Comic book history is a little bit like human history," said Leah. "With all these different eras it went through."

"Yep. I'd say comic book history and human history are almost the same thing," Collin added.

They didn't spend too much time at the kiosk on underground comic books which Leah thought were creepy. The displays on foreign comics held her interest.

"Get this," Leah said, pointing to a series of characters with names like Nelvana and Brok Windsor. "It says Canadian artists created these superheroes because the government wouldn't let American comic books come across the border during World War II."

"Yeah, they had some kind of law that didn't allow non-essential products to be imported, and unfortunately comic books weren't considered to be that important."

"Why do you say 'unfortunately'"?

"Comics make people happy, especially kids. They give you hope that things will turn out okay in the future even if bad things are happening now. And if a war is going on, what could be more important than hope?"

Leah stared at him, her eyes slightly squinting and her mouth barely open. It was as if she were seeing something she'd never seen before and didn't know what to make of it. Finally, she broke into a broad grin. "I don't believe you."

"What?" He was totally confused.

"I don't believe it when you say you don't know everything about comics. I think you do."

Before Collin could utter another denial, Leah shifted her attention to a section on manga. "It says here that manga is often used as a teaching tool in Japanese schools."

"Now that's something I didn't know," said Collin. "See? I'm not that much of an expert."

Leah patted his arm and then moved to a section on European comic characters. *I could sure get used to feeling her touch me.*

Leah turned her attention to another series of strange-looking characters. "Blacksad, Thorgal, Corto Maltese – I've never even heard of these guys," she said.

"Neither have I," admitted Collin. He pointed to a cel showing little blue creatures on a grassy hillside. "I recognize them."

"Oh my gosh, it's the Smurfs!" Leah exclaimed. "I never knew they came from another country."

"Belgium." Collin read the label next to the cel. "Smurfs is actually a word their creator Peyo invented when he was eating with another cartoonist and couldn't remember the French word for salt. When Peyo asked his friend to pass the 'smurf,' his friend replied, 'when you are done smurfing, smurf it back.'"

Leah laughed, her eyes widening and her lips expanding into a soft crescent. "Well, let's smurf our way to the next kiosk."

"Okay, Smurfette."

The theme of the next kiosk—Minority Superheroes and Social Relevance—gave Collin the chance to introduce Leah to the Scarlet Angel. Mentioning that right now it was his favorite.

"What do you like about him?" Leah asked.

"Lots of things. For one, he shows that even if you start off being a jerk you still have the chance to become a good person. For another, he's brave. He's not that much stronger than the bad guys he's fighting, so it's never easy for him to accomplish his mission."

"And what is the Scarlet Angel's mission?"

Collin paused. *How is she going to react when I tell her? But what else can I do but be honest?*

"He rescues kids – mostly girls – who've been kidnapped and turned into slaves, usually sex slaves."

"Really?"

"Yes, his main enemy is a warlock named Vorman, but sometimes the villains are people you'd never suspect."

"Like who?"

"Businessmen, scientists, doctors... even... teachers."

Leah stayed silent for a moment and then moved on to the other characters in the display.

Collin watched her closely for any sign – a scowl, a shiver, gritted teeth – that indicated discomfort but saw nothing of the kind.

The last display focused on cutting-edge artists and innovators. There were photos and bios of Jackie Ormes, Lily Renee, Matt Baker, Fran Hopper, Will Eisner, Osamu Tezuka, Stan Lee, George Herriman, Jerry Siegel, Joe Shuster and a host of other artists, some even Collin didn't know.

"Wow, she had an incredible life," Leah exclaimed after finishing Lily Renee's bio. "She escaped the Holocaust and then got hired as an artist at Fiction House to replace a male artist who'd gone off to fight in World War II. She illustrated everything from *The Werewolf Hunter* to *Elsie the Cow*."

"Yeah, I'm glad they included her. She and a lot of other women artists have been overlooked for too long."

"Would you ever want to draw a comic book character?"

Collin drew back. "Me? I can hardly draw stick figures much less a complete character. I'm more the guy that imagines the storyline, maybe I'm too imaginative. And besides, any comic you read these days is usually drawn by a team of artists."

"What do you mean?"

"Well, first there's the artist, who lays down the panels on each page and draws the actual artwork. Then there's the inker who finishes the artwork and makes it ready for printing and the colorist who... well they add the color. And the writer, who develops the dialogue, and the letterer, who puts in the captions and speech balloons."

Leah shook her head. "I would never have guessed making a comic book would be so complicated." The soft crescent smile returned to her lips. "Luckily, I have an expert who can explain it all to me."

With those words, she reached out and squeezed his hand.

As he felt the warmth of her fingers seep into his flesh, Collin remembered Herbie's question:

Do you want to be her rescuer or her boyfriend?

Chapter 26

After leaving the comic book display, the two spent several minutes strolling past other rooms in the museum, but aside from some Impressionist paintings, nothing held their interest for long.

"I'm sorry," said Leah. "Guess I'm not that much of an art lover."

"Me neither," Collin replied. "If this comic book exhibit wasn't here, I'd probably never come." He paused. The question that pushed its way into his mind seemed disingenuous, dishonest even, and yet he couldn't help asking it.

"I know you like to write. Is there anything you've written that you'd let me read?"

Collin held his breath, expecting a flush of fear, shock or suspicion to run across Leah's face. That never came. "Well, you've read my essay for the Peace in Our Time contest, but I've written a few others too. You could read those, if you'd like."

"I'd like to." Collin pointed to the museum's Starry Night Café just a few steps away. "Let's get a snack in there."

"Okay!" Leah beamed a smile at him, and a crazy thought struck him like a glove across the face: *Is she enjoying this date as much as I am?*

Collin bought a lemon tart along with a cup of green tea for Leah.

"Not a tea drinker?" she asked.

"Iced tea's okay, not the hot stuff," Collin replied, as he filled a glass with water.

"Well, this tart's too big for me to eat by myself. I'll split it down the middle so we can share it."

A little bit off my diet but... "Sounds good."

Once they sat down, Leah ran a knife down the center of the tart and then started describing the essays she'd written for different contests. Some of the ideas she advocated in her writing, such as building microscopic robots to fight cancer cells, seemed a little far-fetched to Collin.

"You really think scientists could build robots that small?" he asked sipping water.

"Absolutely!" Leah answered, her eyes gleaming. "They've already created a robot that's just one-fifth of a millimeter long."

Collin put his glass down harder than he thought. "One-fifth of a millimeter? Can you even see it without a microscope?"

"Just barely."

"How's it work?"

"The floor of the robot has tiny electrodes. They create an electrical charge that causes the robot to move like an inchworm."

"Incredible!" Collin wasn't exaggerating. "But a robot would have to get much smaller than that to fight a cancer cell."

"That's exactly what I said in my essay! Then I pointed out that scientists in Germany are close to building a molecular-sized nanobot."

"Nanobots! This is sounding like a storyline." He leaned forward, eager to hear her explanation.

"Yes, they constructed a heat-powered motor using a single vibrating atom trapped inside a nano-sized cone of electromagnetic radiation. The funny thing is it works a lot like a car engine – expanding, cooling, contracting, then heating."

"Wow! That's great!" Collin didn't entirely understand what Leah talked about, but he felt captivated by her enthusiasm and energy. When she talked about her writing, her bright eyes glowed even more, and a broad smile beamed out toward him. At the same time, her fingers were demonstrating the flow of an electrical charge or the motion of an inchworm.

Collin finished his water and leaned back into his chair. "I don't do much writing myself except for school. I did think my essay for that State College Entrance Exam we took last fall was pretty good."

"What did you write about?"

"Well, they gave us three or four choices. I wrote about the most-interesting place I ever visited."

"Where? Some foreign country?"

He didn't know it, but it was time for his eyes to sparkle. "The attic of my grandmother's old house."

Leah folded her hands under her chin. She looked so cute. "What made that so interesting?"

"It was more like a museum than an attic."

"What did your private museum have in it?"

"A stack of old photo albums in one corner. Some went back to the 1930s."

"That *is* cool."

"There were pictures of my parents on their wedding day, pictures of my grandparents dancing at a nightclub, pictures of Uncle Jeff playing football and one of my grandfather standing next to his old DeSoto."

"His DeSoto? Is that a car?"

"Yeah, they stopped making them a long time ago. Anyway, the best pictures were ones my grandpa took at Yosemite. Photos of waterfalls, rivers and giant trees that were so awesome you could make postcards out of them."

Leah leaned forward a little, still keeping her hands under her chin. "What else is in this attic museum?"

"There's a trunk full of old clothes. Some were eaten up by moths but a lot you could still wear now. Oh, and there are toys and gadgets – a hula hoop, a transistor radio, model airplanes, a 45-record player and a globe you can spin around. And comic books, piles of them. My grandma didn't know who they belonged to, so she let me take them home. There were detective comics, science fiction comics, superhero comics. I read them all. I guess that is why I still read comics."

"Is that how you got started becoming an expert?"

Collin felt himself blushing. "Come on. I'm not really an *expert*."

Leah laughed. "Oh, yes you are."

"There were regular books in the attic, too. Books they don't print any more like Tom Swift, the Bobbsey Twins, Nancy Drew –"

"Oh, they're still publishing Nancy Drew mysteries. I got some for my birthday a few years ago."

"Really?" Collin's blush deepened and he felt foolish, but Leah's interest didn't waver.

"Yeah! Go on," she urged.

"Okay, but I could go on for an hour telling you about everything in there. Stop me when you get bored. Old bikes with horns, games like Easy Money and Parcheesi, a telescope by the window that could let you see

Mars and Jupiter on a clear night."

"Awesome! I can see why you wrote about that attic. Do you still have some of those things?"

Collin's head drooped. "Only the photo albums and some of the comic books. All the rest was given away or thrown out after my grandma died." He brought his head up and looked at Leah. "What did you write about for that essay question?"

Leah shrugged. "Oh, nothing as interesting as that attic museum. My total test score was pretty good, though. I just hope it's good enough for a scholarship."

"Where do you want to go to college?"

"Kenyon. It's got one of the best creative writing programs in the country. But there's no way my family can afford it if I don't get a scholarship." She glanced at her watch and Collin felt his heart sink a little. *She wants to go home now. Guess she's tired of listening to me yak about dumb things.*

Leah reached across the table and took his hand. "I've got to get back home pretty soon to help a neighbor with a chore."

"Yeah, I remember."

"This is the most fun I've had in a long time! You'll have to let me treat you to something next time."

A little gasp escaped from Collin's mouth. "You don't have to do that – unless you want to."

"I want to." Leah's eyes made it easy for Collin to believe her.

They carried their dishes to a busing station and headed to the parking lot. Once outside, Collin felt Leah's hand touch his back. *Uh oh. Is something wrong with my belt? Are my pants sagging?* When he realized what she was doing, he could scarcely believe it. *Oh my God, she's putting her arm around my waist.* He had thought about holding her hand on the way to the car, but this was better.

Even before they reached the Malibu, a crazy thought pushed its way into Collin's mind. *Maybe Leah isn't the journal writer after all. She seems so happy, so untroubled, so – well – normal. Maybe it's an act but I don't think so. A lot of things point to her; we've been wrong before even after careful analysis. Maybe we overlooked another girl who owned a necklace like Leah's and had the same classes and same handwriting. And what about Leah's date with me today? If Mr. Scanlan was already angry with her for cheating with another guy, why would she add to her troubles by cheating again with me?*

Collin opened the car door for Leah and then went to the driver's side. As he settled behind the steering wheel, he decided that for now, it didn't matter whether or not Leah was the girl in trouble. He'd go ahead with the next step of his plan.

As he pulled out of the museum parking lot and drove back to Leah's house, Collin felt something he never felt before, at least not with girls: Confidence. A justified belief – not a hopeless one – there would be a next time with Leah; maybe a lot of next times, if he stayed cool and used his head. Then, the thought that maybe Leah wasn't the journal writer gnawed at him again. *But if Leah isn't the one in trouble, then who –*

"You okay, Collin?" Leah asked. "You've been pretty quiet since we left." The tenseness in her voice suggested she was genuinely concerned about him and not just trying to make small talk.

"I'm okay. I was thinking about something coming up at school pretty soon."

"A big test or term paper?"

"No, nothing like that. I was thinking how great it would be if you could go with me to the junior/senior prom."

Collin expected Leah to hesitate, to say she would have to check her calendar and get back to him – but she answered immediately. "I'd love to go with you. When exactly is it?"

"It's a couple of Saturdays from now. May 14th I think. The dance will be in the gym and before that there'll be a big dinner in a make-believe Old West town."

Leah laughed. "How romantic. Guess we'll need to wear cowboy boots and spurs."

"Yes!" said Collin, adding his laughter to hers, hoping it drowned out the sound of his rapidly beating heart.

They small talked about teachers, TV shows and siblings – Leah had an older brother in the Air Force – until they arrived at her house on Westwood. With the garage door closed and no vehicles in the driveway, Collin suspected no one was home. When he started to get out of the car, Leah gave her head a gentle shake.

"That's okay," she said. "You don't have to take me to the door."

"But I want to. It doesn't look like anyone is home. It's good manners to walk you up to the house and make sure you get inside."

"I have a key, so it doesn't matter." Leah pulled a brass key from her purse and held it up for Collin to see. At the same time, her eyes darted around first toward the house next door, then toward her house, then back to next door.

For some reason, she doesn't want me to get out of the car with her. Okay, I won't. Don't want to upset her.

But he didn't want to give up completely. "Then let me at least watch you from my car until I'm sure you're safe inside."

"Sure, thanks, that would be nice. See you at school!"

"Yeah, see you at —"

Suddenly, Leah leaned across her seat, put a hand on his shoulder, and planted a firm yet delicate kiss on his lips. A flutter danced through his stomach. He started to put his arm around her shoulders, but then, without another word, she scooted out and scurried across the driveway toward her front door. She opened it but glanced toward her neighbor's home one more time before disappearing inside.

Collin eased his car down the driveway and into the street. He headed for home, passing several houses, but stopped and pulled over to the curb while still on Westwood. His feelings were too jumbled, too confused for him to make any sense of them or to concentrate on the road. *I have a prom date. One I like! She likes me too. SHE kissed me.* That goodbye kiss still tingled on his lips. Collin concentrated on just taking deep, slow breaths.

Soon his brain was working again. Leah's rush to get out of the car was strange. And she kept looking toward her neighbor's house; double strange. Did it have something to do with the chore she promised to help with? She seemed more nervous than washing dishes or mowing a lawn would warrant.

Collin shifted the car into drive. Then into reverse. He crept backward on Westwood just enough so that he could look at that neighbor's house. The door to the neighbor's house opened and a man in jeans and a blue shirt walked out. In one hand, he carried a pair of hedge clippers, in the other, a black trash bag. A baseball cap hid the man's eyes, but Collin could see the rest of his face well enough. In recent days, he'd seen that face often and in different situations but until now, always at school.

My God. Leah's neighbor is Mr. Scanlan.

Chapter 27

*T*he sound Herbie made was hard to describe – something between a gasp and a laugh. "You're not serious," he said after gaining some composure.

"Totally."

"No way Mr. Scanlan is Leah's neighbor."

"Swear to God."

"How'd you find that out? Did she invite him over for milk and cookies?"

"Almost."

Herbie let out another gasp-laugh. "What do you mean by that, big man?"

"On the way back from the art museum, Leah said she had to help her neighbor with a chore. Then, after I dropped her off, I saw Scanlan come out of the house next to hers."

"A chore?" Collin could almost hear his friend gritting his teeth. "You don't suppose he was going –"

"Scanlan had some hedge clippers in his hand, so I guess the chore was some kind of yard work. At least, I hope that's all it was. Oh, another thing, before I dropped her off, I asked her to prom. She said yes!" Collin braced himself for another lecture on trust and responsibility.

"YOU? Going to the prom? That is outrageous! But congratulations. I hope both of you have a great time."

"Wow, thanks. I thought you were going to chew me a new one again."

"What would be the point of that? It's not as if I'm an expert on girls or sex or anything like that. But the future is a little clearer."

"It is?"

"Just being this girl's rescuer isn't enough. You want to be her boyfriend, too."

Collin paused. He knew from the tone of Herbie's voice that something worried his friend. "Is there something wrong with that?"

"Wrong, as in morally wrong? No. But think of all this girl's been through. Somehow, she got into a relationship with an older man, who happens to be our assistant principal. Maybe, since they're neighbors, they were just friends at first. But then Mr. Scanlan wanted more. Romance, sex, control. Again, maybe because he's the *assistant principal*, Leah felt she couldn't refuse, but her journal proves she didn't want the relationship to go there. So then —"

"Then Leah went out with some other guy," Collin interjected. "Mr. Scanlan found out about it and now is more demanding, more controlling than ever."

"Yeah, that's the picture I get, too. My point is, I'm not sure Leah will find it easy to go from Mr. Scanlan to… you."

"I won't be like him. You read about the awful things he does! He's worse than an animal. I'll be a good boyfriend. I'll care about her feelings. She won't have to do anything she doesn't want to. Compared to him, I'll be a saint."

"You won't be able to undo the damage Scanlan's done, at least not right away. Leah needs to heal. She'll probably need counseling and other kinds of support."

A wave of despair ran through Collin's gut. "I… I'll give her that support." *I have no idea how.*

"Okay. But you may have to be her friend long before you're her boyfriend, if you catch my drift."

"I do."

Herbie remained silent for a moment.

Something else is bothering him, Collin thought.

"Did you meet Leah's parents?"

"Yeah, her mother anyway. Her dad is at a rehab facility right now."

"You'd think Leah's parents would realize something's going on between their daughter and their neighbor. Maybe if your husband nearly dies from a stroke, you don't notice other things happening to your family."

"They probably trust Mr. Scanlan just like we did until we read the journal."

"Maybe, but don't you think after a while they'd get suspicious? If Leah and our assistant principal are in some kind of relationship, they must be spending a lot of time together and not just mowing the lawn. Which brings me to another question. Why, if they're neighbors, do they bother getting it on at some cockroach haven like the Seacrest?"

"I don't know, but I think the only one 'getting it on' is Scanlan. There's nothing in that journal that shows Leah having a good time. The opposite, really. She wants to get away from him – for good."

"Why doesn't she?"

"We've asked that question plenty of times and answered it, too, haven't we? He is blackmailing her with something, or threatening to post pics or something that is really bad."

"Yeah. So what are you going to do now, before the prom, I mean?"

"For one thing, starting Monday, I'm going to be eating lunch at a different table."

Herbie laughed. "Those clowns you eat with will be heartbroken."

"They'll survive."

Chapter 28

*M*onday Leah didn't come to school, so Collin wound up eating with Eric, Fred and Ronnie just as he had over 100 times already.

He wondered where she was as he stared dejectedly at his half-eaten turkey corn dog, suddenly not hungry. He pulled out his phone and brought up Leah's number.

You ok?
Yes. Had doctor's appt. Will be in class by 1

Collin put his phone down and tried to fight off the fear that jabbed at his gut. *What kind of doctor? Oh, God, could she be pregnant?* He couldn't ask her that, but he still wanted to know.

Not serious I hope
Nah. Routine check-up with skin doctor dw
Cool. Eat with you tomorrow?
Sure

Collin returned to his lunch. He'd finished off his corn dog and started on diced peaches when a paper "football" bounced next to his plate.

"No good!" exclaimed Fred.

"Yes, it was!" Ronnie snapped back. "It hit the crossbar but still went over. Right, Collin?"

Collin scowled. "I don't know. Can't you just kick it again?"

"I guess that would be okay," said Fred with a sneer. "After all, Ronnie-boy needs all the help he can get."

Ronnie puffed out his chest like a gorilla. "At least I got a date to prom."

Eric, who'd been fiddling with his phone, lifted his head. "You're going to the prom? With who?"

"Janie V."

"I didn't know Janie was that desperate," said Fred, his sneer staying in place.

Ronnie half rose from his chair. "Desperate? I'm a catch! What about you dill-weed? You're so lame you couldn't get your own mother to go with you."

It's like we're back in seventh grade. Collin snatched the little triangle of paper and tossed it back between the two. "Just keep playing football and forget about the prom."

Eric made some unclassifiable noise then said, "I want to hear about Ronnie's date."

Ronnie sank down into his seat, stuck out his lip, and put his hands behind his head as if his self-confidence was soaring. "It's no biggie. Janie's one of the sophomores in my Environmental Science class. She's not the hottest girl, but she's not too bad either. So after class one day, I got her phone number and last night I asked her to the prom. She said yes. End of story."

"Bet you wish you had a car now, don't you?" asked Eric. "That would really impress Janie."

"Sure, but I don't need one for the prom. Janie and I are gonna go with Russ and Kelsey. Her dad is dropping us off and picking us up."

"Probably chaperoning you, too," added Fred, who still seemed ready to pick a fight.

"Well, there might be a few parents chaperoning but not Janie's. If it's like last year's prom, Mr. Scanlan will be the head chaperone."

Collin, who'd only been half listening, jerked his head toward Ronnie. "How do you know all this? You didn't go last year."

"Nah, but my cousin went, at least for a while. Mr. Scanlan kicked him out after he tried to spike the punch with little shots of vodka."

"Scanlan kicked him out? That's all?" Eric wiped a napkin around his mouth while he spoke. "That dude's lucky he didn't get suspended."

"Oh, he did," said Ronnie. "Also got 80 hours of community service and the guy who bought the vodka for him got a year's probation."

By now, Fred had cooled down enough to resume his football game with Ronnie. Collin finished his lunch and headed toward study hall. Eating with the Three Stooges was rarely an enlightening experience, but this time it gave Collin something to think about.

* * *

That thought which burrowed into Collin's mind during lunch deepened its roots through the afternoon and evening, and came to fruition by the time he went to Herbie's house after dinner.

Up in his friend's bedroom, Collin leaned against the dresser, trying to be as nonchalant as possible before making his request. "I want you to go with me to the prom."

Herbie chuckled. "Hey, man, I like you as a friend but I'm not wired that way, you know?"

"Oh ha-ha-ha. You know that is not what I mean."

"I thought you were going with Leah, so I actually don't know what you mean. Explain please."

"I want you to come, too. With us."

"Huh? I don't think Leah needs two dates for the prom. Or do you want me to replace you halfway through the night?"

"Stop playing dumb, Herbie. You know what I mean."

"Really, I don't."

"I want you to ask someone and come with Leah and me. Like a double date."

Herbie didn't say anything for the next ten seconds, but his face contorted in bewilderment, as if he'd been asked to tackle an unsolvable math problem. "Why?" he finally asked.

"For one thing, I'll feel more comfortable having you there. If I run out of things to talk about, you can jump in and keep the conversation going. If I start to say something dumb, you can stop me before I put my whole foot in my mouth."

"So you want me to sort of be your guardian angel on this date?"

"Well, no, I wouldn't put it that way."

"It doesn't matter since I'm not going anyway."

"Why not?"

"It's obvious isn't it, big man? Who is supposed to be my date?"

Collin took a deep breath before speaking. "Um… maybe Winifred Scoles."

"No way. I'm too dumb for her and too uncool for any other girl."

"Don't be so hard on yourself, Sir Isaac. I think Winifred would love to go out with you. In fact, I'm almost certain if you asked her, she'd say yes."

Herbie gave a little snort. "What makes you think so?"

"Because you're the only guy in school who's even close to her level of intelligence. If you want, I could introduce you."

"You know her?"

"A little. She's been in the Graphic Novel Club with me since freshman year. I've talked with her some after meetings. It wouldn't be hard to introduce you to her."

"You wouldn't need to introduce us."

A wave of hope surged through Collin's heart. "That's great! Is she in your Physics class?"

"No, AP Computer Science."

"If you already know her, that should make it easy to ask her to the prom. So what's the prob?"

Herbie's face looked anguished. Collin sensed that asking why would only add to his friend's discomfort. Like a good friend, Herbie figured Collin wanted an explanation, so he forged ahead. "Back in ninth grade, Winifred and I did a joint science project with another student—"

"Let me guess, you totally aced it?"

Herbie shot him a look, holding up a hand like a traffic cop. "Hold up, let me finish. So, this other kid's dad was a professor at OSU—animal science, specializing in sheep. Naturally, we decided to study sheep lungs for the project. We put together this killer display with photos breaking down all the parts and how they worked. We even had microscopes set up so you could see the tissue up close, like right down to the alveoli. But the coolest part? A live demo showing how sheep lungs actually worked."

"You built a model of sheep lungs? In ninth grade?"

"Better than just a model. We had an actual set of flesh-and-blood sheep lungs sent straight to our classroom from the university."

"Wicked!"

"It was my job to conduct the demonstration. I used an old bicycle pump to show how the lungs inflated and deflated whenever a sheep breathed in and out."

"Sounds like a good idea."

Herbie sighed. "It would have been a good idea... if I hadn't pumped too much air into the lungs."

"Uh oh!"

"Uh oh is right. I pumped in so much air, the lungs exploded. Everywhere."

"Just how 'everywhere' was it?" Collin snickered, enjoying a rare story of Herbie not being perfect.

"As 'everywhere' as you can get. Blood and pieces of sheep lung all over the floor, the ceiling, the desks, the windows, the lab equipment..."

"The students?"

"Especially the students, and especially Winifred. She had so many splotches of blood on her face and clothes it looked like a slasher flick."

"I remember you telling me about that accident in biology class, I didn't know it was that bad."

"I didn't give you all the details back then. No one else in our class was supposed to mention it. But other students found out anyway, as they always do when something crazy happens. Our parents found out, too, so my dad ended up paying about a grand to clean the room and cover laundry bills. And that wasn't the worst of it."

"Don't stop now! What?"

"I don't know if Mr. Fairly was mad at me or whether he didn't think the project was that good, but anyway, we got a B-. For Winifred, that was like a flunking grade. She's never spoken to me since, just gives me a cold stare if we happen to pass each other between classes."

"But that... um... accident was two years ago. It's ancient history. I doubt she still holds that against you."

"Wanna bet?"

"No, I want you and Winifred to go to prom with Leah and me. So ask her out and then you will know for sure if she's a super grudge holder."

Herbie threw up his hands and stomped across the room. He snatched a paper clip off his desk and flicked it toward Collin. "What is it with you? Since when did it become so important for us to double date for the prom?"

"Since I found out Scanlan will be there, too."

Herbie's exasperation vanished. "As a chaperone?"

"Probably *head* chaperone."

"I can see why you're concerned, but why would it make any difference if I'm with you?"

"For one thing, you'd be another set of eyes on him. If he did anything to hurt Leah or me, you'd be a witness."

"There'll be a ton of other students and parents there. If Scanlan got nasty, they'd all be witnesses, too. The guy may be evil but he isn't stupid. He's not going to try anything that puts his ass in a sling in public."

"Scanlan's sneaky. He may get at Leah in a way that isn't obvious to anyone not watching him closely."

Herbie's eyebrows came together, giving him a bushy unibrow. "Do you think he'll try to do anything to you?"

"Maybe, maybe not. No matter what he does, I need to go into the prom with confidence. I need to feel that I'm not a helpless klutz."

"And if I'm with you... you'll somehow miraculously have this confidence?"

"No miracle to it. I always feel confident when I'm with you. You're the one I can always count on to have my back. That's been true since we were kids. Climbing a tree, searching for a lost dog, figuring out some impossible math problem, you being there with me made a lot of difference."

"Likewise, big man. There've been at least a couple of times when you probably saved my life."

"True, I remember calling 911 when you had some kind of allergic reaction after eating a s'more." Collin shook his head. "Who'd ever believe a guy could be allergic to marshmallows?"

"It was the corn syrup in them."

"Didn't the same thing happen a few days later when we went to get ice cream?"

"Strawberry flavoring that time. But nothing beats that day in fourth grade when we were walking home from school, and Kyle Bailey came up behind me as I was about to use my inhaler."

"Oh yeah," Collin said, nodding. "The sleazeball called you a third-rate wannabe then pushed you in the back, didn't he?"

"Right. Knocked my inhaler into a sewer. There I was, wheezing and gasping for breath, while you reached in and pulled it out."

"Lucky it hadn't been raining or that inhaler might have ended up in a much grosser place."

There was a moment of silence. "I guess I owe it to you."

"Owe me what?"

"Double dating with you at the prom. But what if Winifred doesn't want to go with me? I doubt I'm any girl's idea of a hot date."

"I don't think Winifred wants a hot date. My guess is she'd just want to have a good time with a guy who's smart and interested in the same things she is."

"I already told you about the bad vibes between us. I may be the last guy in the world she'd want to go out with."

"You won't know if you don't try. I'm pulling the friend card. I don't ask for much. I'm asking for this. For all the years we've had each other's back."

Herbie drummed his fingers on his lips. If the human brain made noise when it thought, Herbie's could have been heard for three blocks. He stopped the finger drumming and turned toward Collin. "Let's compromise."

"Compromise? How?"

"You see Winifred at Graphic Novel Club meetings, right?"

"Right."

"Next time you see her, ask her if she'd go to the prom with me."

"Aw, come on. What do you think I am? Some kind of matchmaker?"

Herbie plucked a not-so-clean T-shirt from under his bed and wrapped it around his head as if it were a scarf. "Matchmaker, matchmaker, make me a match. Find me a find. Catch me a catch."

"Cut the comedy, Sir Isaac. I'm serious."

"I am, too. A few minutes ago, you were ready to introduce us if we didn't know each other. What I'm asking now isn't much different."

"Except that—"

"Listen, big man. I've embarrassed myself in front of Winifred once already. Before I risk it again, I want to be sure she doesn't still hate me." Herbie let the T-shirt fall to the floor. "Let me add another thing. It's hard to believe Winifred or any other girl would want to go on a date with me. But I'd at least like to know she'd be willing to tolerate me this once."

Collin nodded. "Okay, Sir Isaac. You're on."

Chapter 29

The next school day started off fine—until third-period gym. During a scrimmage, Collin took off after a stray basketball. Mid-sprint, his foot snagged, and down he went. Nothing unusual—except this time, his gym shorts betrayed him. They slid down to his knees, giving the entire class a perfect view of his red, white and blue boxers.

"Yo, check out Collie!" Kyle hollered, pointing. "Stars and stripes, baby!"

"Gotta respect the patriotism," Clint Rutherford chimed in, snapping a mock salute as the other guys howled.

Collin scrambled to his feet, face burning, and yanked his shorts back up.

"Hey, ever hear of a jockstrap?" Clint sneered. "Oh wait, you're not a jock. Guess you could at least get shorts that fit."

Before Collin could retort, a sharp whistle blast cut through the chaos. "All right, that's enough!" Coach Alexander barked. "Outside. Quarter mile. Now."

As the guys filed out to the track, still snickering, Collin folded the waistband of his boxers over his shorts to keep them in place.

That's when an odd thought struck him. *Clint's right. I do need new shorts.* These had been a snug fit at the beginning of the school year. He knew he'd lost some weight, but didn't realize it would mean buying new clothes. *So many good things are happening to me now,* he thought, as he strode onto the track. When he completed the quarter mile, another surprise was suddenly evident. Though he gasped and panted as usual, two of his classmates finished behind him. Later, after showering, he got onto the scale outside Coach Alexander's office and learned why his shorts no longer fit. *I've lost 17 pounds!*

At lunch, Collin ignored the Three Stooges and placed his tray down on the table next to Leah's and smiled. "Mind if I join you?"

Leah returned the smile. "Hoping you would."

Collin eased himself into the seat next to her and compared their respective food selections. "I see you went with the black bean salad and squash instead of the turkey sub and potato wedges."

"Yeah, during my vegetarian days, I got to liking salads and cooked vegetables for lunch. I still like to eat them if the meat choices look yucky."

Collin held up his sub. "Would you call this yucky?"

"Not really. It was the Italian wraps next to the subs that made me decide on veggies today."

Collin nodded. "The wraps did look kind of bad. Sort of like… like…"

"Something that oozed out of a petri dish and multiplied?"

"Right!" Collin threw back his head and laughed. *Wow, she's hilarious.* Once more, the thought that nagged him after their date at the art gallery returned. *Leah seems so happy, so normal. It seems impossible she could be in an abusive relationship with Mr. Scanlan or anyone else.*

While they ate, the new couple chatted about teachers, tests and other things at school. At one point, Collin looked back to the table where he used to eat. Ronnie sat a few feet away from his normal spot, playing paper football with a guy Collin didn't know. Eric wasn't there at all. Fred, however, gazed right back at Collin. His face could have belonged to a little kid who dropped his ice cream cone. A pang of guilt hit Collin in the chest before he looked back at his new lunch companion, her soft eyes causing the guilt to vanish.

"Have you rented your tux yet?" asked Leah around a bite of squash.

"My tux?"

"Of course. You'll need one for that date we have coming up. It's a formal event, you know."

"I'll get on it as soon as I get home. Promise." Collin took a final bite out of his sub and wiped a napkin across his lips. "What about you? Do you know what you'll be wearing?"

"Yep. An A-line dress with spaghetti straps and ocean blue beading."

Collin's eyes widened. "I'm not sure what that is, but I'm sure you'll look great in it."

Leah laughed at that as she stood up. Before she could pick up her tray, Collin placed his hand gently over her wrist. "I need to ask you something before you go."

"Yes?"

"Would you mind if we went to the prom with another couple?"

"I guess not." Leah sat back down. "Who?"

"My friend Herbie Kessler."

"Oh, yeah. The yearbook photographer. Who's he taking?"

"Winifred Scoles – I hope."

"Hasn't he asked her yet?"

"Herbie's kind of shy, so I'm helping him with that."

"So you're going to ask Winifred out for Herbie? Kind of be his ambassador?"

Collin nodded, saying, "I'm not sure what I'm going to do… exactly…"

Leah patted his hand. "It's okay. I trust whatever you do will work out."

I wish I trusted myself that much.

They took their trays to the turn-in window and then headed out into the main corridor. They walked side by side until they came to the door of Leah's next class. Collin wanted to say something to reassure Leah she wouldn't be going to the prom with a total klutz.

"I can't wait to see you in your blue ocean spaghetti… um I mean your… blue A dress with ocean beads … *Jesus…* In your beautiful formal gown."

Leah giggled. "Close enough, Collin. Just be sure to order your tux tonight. The last thing I want is to go to the prom by myself."

Considering who will be there, it's the last thing I want, too.

The regular school day ended as it always did with French III. Then came the Graphic Novel Club meeting. The members were going to analyze, discuss and debate the role conspiracy theories play in Nick Drnaso's *Sabrina*. Then, with help from Mrs. O'Brien, the club's faculty advisor, they had a scheduled Zoom with a local graphic artist. Winifred Scoles took part in all the meeting activities and afterward had a friendly chat with Collin. He didn't exactly do what Herbie asked, but a plan emerged anyway.

Chapter 30

Collin set the scene carefully. Two chairs pulled up to his desk. Open Algebra II textbook on the desk. Pencil and graph paper next to the textbook. Most important of all was the crumpled-up T-shirt draped over his PC monitor.

When he came through Collin's bedroom door at 7:15, Herbie made no attempt to hide his irritation.

"What's this Algebra homework problem you couldn't show me over Facetime?"

"I have to graph an equation. You know I'm no good at that." Collin held up a piece of graph paper with crooked pencil marks and dark smudges where fake erase marks had been made. "See? I tried."

Herbie shook his head, his irritation undiminished. "You've made a mess of it, but I've helped you with graphing problems before over our laptops. I'm not feeling good. Why did you have to drag me over here for this one?"

"Because it's more complicated than those other problems."

"In what way?"

"I can't explain it myself. There's a diagram on my laptop that will show you what's involved."

Herbie put his finger under the edge of the T-shirt and lifted it about an inch. "What's this? A new way to keep your screen clean?"

"Nah, I just got frustrated and threw it there," said Collin holding back a snicker. "You know me. I got to act everything out."

"Yeah, I do know you. I almost feel like telling you to exit stage right, but you better stay here and learn something."

"I think we're both about to learn something."

"What's that mean?"

Collin pointed at the shirt on the laptop. With one jerk of his hand,

Herbie pulled it off. On the now-exposed screen there were no diagrams, no equations, nothing mathematical at all. Just the smiling face of a freckle-faced girl with red bangs, dimpled cheeks… and a smile that was as confident as it was pretty. "Hi Herbie," she said. "Collin said you wanted to ask me something. Here I am."

Herbie dropped the T-shirt, but otherwise remained motionless for ten long seconds. Then his mouth moved just enough for a single word to squeeze out. "Winifred."

***

*T*he look Herbie flashed in his direction made Collin's stomach drop. The flared nostrils and snarling mouth made his friend's usually innocent face look wild and vengeful, if only for a couple of seconds. *Maybe I went too far with this surprise.*

"Yeah, it's me," said Winifred, regaining Herbie's attention. "What's up?"

"Funny you should ask," Herbie replied. "I was wondering the same thing since Collin told me he needed help with an algebra problem, which I believed because Collin is kind of, you know – dumb. Turns out he had something else planned."

"We did talk a little after our club meeting. He asked me if I hated you and when I told him no, he said you wanted to ask me something."

Herbie closed his eyes, clutched his hands and pulled his shoulders up. He looked like someone about to bungee jump for the first time. "Would you like to go to the prom with me?"

"Yes, I would."

Herbie opened one eye and then the other. "You said yes?"

"Yes, I said yes. Does that surprise you?"

"Actually, it does."

"Why?"

Herbie swallowed hard and his head fell, his chin resting on his chest. "I didn't think you liked me."

"Why would you ever think that?"

Herbie gulped again but brought his head up. "Well, every time you pass me in the hall, you have this awful expression on your face."

"Huh?"

"You give me this icy stare like you wish I would disappear into thin air."

"I only look at you that way because of the expression on *your* face."

"*My* face?"

"Yeah, you look at me like you're a zombie ready to eat my brains."

"I never knew that." Herbie gulped a third time. "But what about that awful accident back in AP Biology when I put too much air into the sheep lungs? And... well... you know the rest. I ruined your clothes and kept you from getting an A. I figured you were still angry about that."

"Mom got the blood stains out of my skirt, but my blouse was ruined. Didn't bother me too much. I bought a better one with the money your dad gave to Mr. Fairly."

"But what about... um... the grade we got?"

"The B-? That's the grade we got for the project, but I still got an A in the course." Winifred laughed. "In a way, I should thank you. I was coasting along in that class, but after getting the B-, I couldn't take an A for granted. Your sheep lung accident forced me to spend more time studying so I ended up learning a lot more than I would have otherwise."

Herbie glanced over at Collin again. The hostility he flashed toward his friend vanished. Now he nodded gently, perhaps in appreciation, perhaps in understanding.

"Have to get back to my homework now," Winifred continued. "I'm in the middle of watching a video of the Kennedy/Nixon debate and then I have to write a report explaining who I think won."

"I hear you," said Herbie. "And I need to talk to Collin right now... and not about Algebra."

* * *

Herbie powered off the PC, his eyes focused on the empty screen. A heavy silence hung in the air. Collin sure as hell wasn't going to be the one to break it. He'd never seen Herbie that angry, and even though it ended right, Collin felt he'd crossed a line and needed to let Herbie take the lead here.

Herbie suddenly jumped up and clenched his hands into fists.

"You lied to me, big man! Should punch you in the mouth!" The fists unclenched. "Or maybe thank you. I'm not sure which one you deserve more."

"Wouldn't punching me cause an asthma attack?" They grinned at each other.

"Could probably get away with just one."

"Okay, but I kind of doubt you'd stop with one."

The fists re-clenched. "I just don't like being lied to!" The grins faded as Herbie worked himself up.

"I know, but I couldn't think of anything else with how the situation played out. It was the best thing to do!"

"What do you mean?" The clenched fists started to turn red. "I asked you to set things up with Winifred. You didn't do that!"

"Yes I did! Just not the way you expected."

"But she didn't know I was going to ask her—"

"Come on, man. Do you really think what you said surprised her? She answered in a half a second."

The fists unclenched.

"She figured out what you were going to ask. No doubt."

The hands fell to Herbie's sides. "I suppose so."

"And this worked better than me just setting everything up for you. This way, you heard straight from the source that Winifred doesn't hold any grudge against you."

"Yeah, and now I know the reason she gives me an unfriendly look in the halls is because apparently I'm doing the same to her."

"Right!"

Herbie rubbed his fingers over his chin. "So… what do I do next?"

"What I did after school. You make an appointment at Men Forward to get fitted for a tuxedo. I'm going there Saturday at ten. Maybe you can get fitted at about the same time."

"Okay."

"On the day of prom, we'll get wrist corsages for Leah and Winifred. You'll want to find out what color Winifred's dress is, so the color of the flowers complement it."

"Got it. Anything else?"

"Not about prom, but it so happens I do need help with a few algebra problems on page 175."

Herbie handed the Algebra textbook over to his friend. "Which ones?"

Collin smiled sheepishly. "All of them."

Herbie nodded. "Well, big man, this may take us awhile, but at least I know you're not lying to me now."

* * *

The next day while heading to English class, Collin received a text from Leah.

Got surprise 4 u
☺ **When can I get it?**
Lunch

A couple of hours later, Collin sat next to Leah, as he had yesterday and planned to do from now on.

"Look at this," she said, holding up her cell. The screen showed a beautiful flowing blue dress with thin straps.

"So that's an A-line dress with spaghetti straps and ocean blue beading?"

Leah nodded.

"You'll look fantastic. Can't wait to see you in it."

"It needs a couple of alterations, but it will be ready in time." Leah put her phone away. "You've ordered your tux, right?"

"Yeah, Herbie and I are going to be fitted Saturday."

Leah's lovely eyes rounded a little. "Oh, so he got around to asking Winifred, did he? Or maybe you asked for him?"

Collin forced a little smile out. "Let's just say I gave him the push he needed."

"It's nice of you to help him out."

Leah took a bite of salad and seemed lost in thought for a few seconds. "A few days ago," she finally said, "you mentioned you'd have helped with my dad if you'd known me when he had his stroke." She look shyly at him and said quietly, "You can help with him now, if you still want to."

The excitement that ran through Collin made him bump his lunch tray hard enough to spill some tomato soup. "Of course, I still want to. How can I help?"

"My mom and I have to get my dad to an appointment with his physical therapist tomorrow afternoon. Trouble is his stair-lift chair broke down and can't be fixed before Saturday morning. He's in his bedroom upstairs right now. I don't think my mom and I can get him to the first floor by ourselves."

"I'll be glad to help get your dad downstairs. When do you need me?"

"His appointment is at 4:30, so you'd need to come to our house right after school."

"I'll be there. And I'll come back to help him back up if you need to get him to bed afterward."

Collin took a risk making that promise since he didn't know if his dad's car would be available, but it didn't matter. *I'll rent a car if I have to.*

Chapter 31

Collin arrived at 357 Westwood a few minutes before four o'clock the next day, and after a quick hug and hello from Leah, found himself climbing the stairs to the second floor. Once at the top, Leah guided him into the master bedroom where her mother sat on a love seat next to a tired-looking man wearing a blue denim shirt and khaki pants. The man's salt-and-pepper hair was neatly combed, but the right side of his face sagged as if it were starting to melt, while the eye above was only half open.

"Dad," said Leah, "this is my friend, Collin Morris. He's going to help get you down the stairs and into the car."

"It's nice to meet you, Mr. Jennings," Collin said. He started to bring his hand up for a handshake but stopped, realizing Leah's father might not be able to reciprocate.

Mr. Jennings nodded slightly and then spoke, his words coming slowly but distinctly. "So... you're... the guy taking... my daughter... to the prom... next week."

"Yes, sir. I'm the lucky guy."

"I agree," Mr. Jennings continued. "You are... lucky."

"Brad, we need to get going," said Mrs. Jennings, rising from the love seat.

Collin reached a hand down to help Mr. Jennings get to his feet, but he brushed it aside. "Don't need anyone's help... getting up," he complained.

"Sorry," said Collin, backing away a few steps.

Once Leah's father was standing, Mrs. Jennings brought a walker over which he used to edge his way out of the bedroom and over to the top of the staircase. Once there, Leah and Collin came up on his left and right one step below him, and steadied him while he made a slow descent toward the first floor. Meanwhile, Mrs. Jennings held onto the back of his belt to prevent him from pitching forward. About halfway down, they passed the broken stair-lift chair, leaning cock-eyed off its rail.

Two or three steps from the bottom, Mrs. Jennings went back upstairs and brought the walker down. "I'll bring the car out into the driveway," she said, rejoining Collin and Leah by the front door. "Can you get him outside by yourselves?"

Both teens nodded. At the same time, Mr. Jennings spouted off indignantly. "Of course they can… take care of… me. I'm not… a three-year… old."

I like this guy, thought Collin. *Still feisty despite a stroke. Someone who doesn't give up easily. I hope Leah inherited some of that feistiness. She'll need it if she ever hopes to get away from Scanlan.*

Outside, again using the walker, Mr. Jennings made his way toward the car, which was as close to the house as his wife could get it without running over the lawn. Leah and Collin continued to give her father support under both arms, which was a good thing, since a crack in the walkway nearly caused him to lose his grip on the walker and fall. Eventually, however, Mr. Jennings was safely in the backseat.

"Do you want me to go with you and help get him to the physical therapist's office?"

"No thanks," said Leah. "The PT has people who can help us do that."

"Text me when he's finished and I can meet you back here."

"I'll be here to help them, so they won't need you, Collin," said a harsh male voice behind him.

Collin swung around and found himself staring into the cold threatening eyes of Mr. Scanlan. The assistant principal stood just a few feet away with his hands on his hips and his chest puffed out. He gave the impression of a man spoiling for a fight. *I may have to fight him someday,* thought Collin. *But not yet. Right now, I need to use my brain.*

"Oh, hi there, Mr. Scanlan," said Collin. "Do you live nearby?" He posed the question in the most-innocent voice he could muster.

"Next door. So they won't need to bother you."

Collin looked first at Leah, who sat stiffly in the backseat next to her father, her face pale and expressionless. Then, he shifted his gaze to Mrs. Jennings, who rolled down her window. "That would be great, Gerry," she said to Mr. Scanlan. "I'll text you when we leave the PT and you can help us get Brad back into the house. We're going to keep him on the first floor for now, so you won't have to deal with the staircase like poor

Collin did." She looked over her shoulder at Collin and smiled. "I guess you know Gerry from school, don't you?"

"Yes, I do know Mr. Scanlan," said Collin, emphasizing the mister. "I was in his office only a few days ago."

"Collin's taking Leah to the prom, Gerry. Isn't that nice?"

"Really? I'll be there, too."

"That's what I heard," said Collin. "A chaperone, right?"

"Head Chaperone," Mr. Scanlan corrected.

"Ah, yes," said Collin, not taking the bait. "The perfect job for Mr. Iron Fist."

Mr. Scanlan's eyes became even colder and more threatening, if that was possible.

Mrs. Jennings, perhaps sensing the rising tension, jumped in. "We've got to be going or we'll be late for Brad's appointment. Thanks so much for helping us, Collin, but Gerr—er—Mr. Scanlan's right. It will be easier for him to help us once we're back home."

"I'm here to help anytime you need me," said Collin. He shifted his eyes toward Mr. Scanlan, but the assistant principal was already headed back to his house.

Mrs. Jennings pulled her car out onto the street. Before she drove away, Collin caught sight of Leah in the backseat, her face as pale and blank as it was when Mr. Scanlan came over to offer his help.

* * *

The woman Collin spoke to at the rental place told him they'd need to know his weight to fit him for his tuxedo. So on Saturday morning, he bounded out of bed to the bathroom, tossed off his briefs and stepped on the scale. The numbers at his feet flashed on and climbed, finally stopping on 219 -- a loss of 21 pounds since the start of his diet in February. *I'm never going to be a fit-and-trim hunk, but my days of being a fat loser are just about over.* As he stepped off the scale, he modified that conclusion a bit. *Maybe a dependable average guy? Maybe I can use that as an FBI agent and be a dependable average crime-solver..*

At 9:45, Collin picked up Herbie. On the way, he talked about his latest encounter with Mr. Scanlan.

"Her dad's in pretty bad shape," Collin explained. "Even with three of us helping him, he could barely make it down the steps and to the car. And that's when our assistant principal showed up and said he'd help Mr. Jennings when they got back."

"I guess he wasn't too happy to see you," said Herbie.

"If looks could kill, I'd have been chopped into about a thousand pieces."

"Lucky her mom was right there."

"Yeah, but her mom kind of made things worse by saying I'd be taking Leah to the prom."

"He was going to find out about you and Leah anyway."

"The question is what's he going to do to Leah? Now he has time to plan how to punish her. He didn't like it when she went out with some other guy the first time. What's he going to do now that she's going out with me?"

"Not only that, but what's he going to do to you?"

Collin didn't know the answer to that question – and didn't want to.

At Men Forward, a woman who carried a yellow tape measure in her teeth fitted Collin and Herbie for tuxedos at the same time. Collin enjoyed watching his friend stand straight and firm as the woman bounced around them, taking measurements. They both tried on a few tuxes. Collin picked a black notch-lapel suit with a blue bowtie and matching pocket square. Because of Herbie's small size, only two tuxes were available to him. He opted for a dark-gray satin-edged notch-lapel tux over the white satin-edged peak-lapel one. After admiring themselves from different angles in the full-length mirrors, the two teens made arrangements to pick up the tuxes on the day before the prom and headed out to lunch.

"Do you still need to stay on that diet?" asked Herbie. "It looks like you've already lost a lot of weight."

"Don't know," answered Collin. "I've still got two or three pounds to lose before I'm officially no longer obese. I'm seeing the doctor Monday after school. He'll let me know if it's okay to start eating like a normal person. I have a little more freedom at lunch, anyway."

While they waited for their food, Herbie kept looking toward the front of the restaurant where a small stage jutted out. On it, were a piano and a set of drums. "Guess they have live music at night here," he said.

"Yeah, looks that way."

A flush of worry came over Herbie's face. "They'll have band music at the prom, too, won't they?"

"Yeah. Either a band or I think I heard about a DJ."

The worry on Herbie's face deepened. "That means they'll expect us to dance."

"Only if we want to."

"We'll look like nerds if we don't."

"We are nerds, you mostly. I don't totally fit in anywhere. But that doesn't mean we can't be dancing nerds."

"Except I don't know how to dance."

"No big deal. Just shake your hips, and throw your arms up like you're trying to hold up the ceiling."

"That's all?"

"And shuffle your feet now and then, so you're not standing in the same place all the time. On the close dances, just put your arms around her back and let her rest her head on your shoulder. Then just lean to each side."

Herbie brought a finger up to his mouth and bit on it. "What if Winifred doesn't want to have any close dances with me?"

Collin slapped a hand on the table to snap his friend out of it. "Come on, Sir Isaac! Winifred wouldn't have agreed to go with you if she didn't want to slow dance."

When their lunches arrived, Collin wasted no time starting in on his burger with no fries, but Herbie didn't seem interested in eating now. He sat slumped in his chair, spoon in hand, face still gripped with worry.

I need to get his mind off dancing. Collin brought his sandwich up to his mouth but paused before taking another bite. "The prom will be your first date ever, won't it?"

"Well, it will probably be my first complete date," Herbie said.

"Complete date? *Oh* spill those deets man, what have you been hiding?"

Herbie stirred his soup and then took a sip. "Remember that blind date I had about a year ago with the daughter of my dad's client?"

"Oh yeah, you never told me what happened. I just assumed she canceled on you or something."

"I wish she had canceled."

"She ghosted you?"

"Worse."

"Say something racist?"

"No."

Collin put his burger down. "Did she have some jealous boyfriend who tried to pick a fight?"

"Even that would have been better than what happened." Herbie sipped another spoonful of soup and then slouched a little, his eyes shifting toward the floor.

"I'd heard Pauline loved opera, so I got two tickets to *Pagliacci*, which was playing at the Gemstone Theater. My dad paid for a taxi to take us to dinner at Fielding's, which is only a couple of blocks from the theater. Things seemed to be going fine for a while. I found out she plans to be a civil engineer and work on finding an alternative to fossil fuels."

"Sounds like a perfect match for you. So what went wrong?"

"Well, on the taxi drive to the restaurant I accidentally called her Paula."

"Oh well, you'd just met her so it wasn't so --"

"Then at dinner I called her Paulette, not once but twice."

"Oof!"

"The second time I did that she gave me the side eye and said she had to go to the powder room." Herbie paused to take two more sips of soup.

"And?"

"And I never saw her again. I guess instead of going to the powder room, she got a taxi and went home."

"Just because you messed up her name?"

"Messed up her name three times." Herbie shook his head. "I felt like an idiot, sitting there alone, staring at the empty seat across from me. Maybe it was my imagination, but I thought people at the other tables were laughing at me like I was some sort of clown. So I got up and went to the opera by myself, and wouldn't you know? It was about some clown who gets dumped by his wife."

"Winifred won't dump you."

"Hope not," said Herbie. "At least I won't forget her name." He took another spoonful of soup and frowned. "Of course, I might be so nervous, I'll forget my own name and yours, too."

"In that case, maybe we should wear name tags along with our tuxes."

"Good idea, Calvin."

***

Collin ate lunch with Leah on Monday and Tuesday. Sometimes Mr. Scanlan would walk nearby, still, he didn't seem to pay them more attention than anyone else. On Wednesday, a text came from Leah just minutes before Collin headed to the cafeteria.

Have to take make-up test - miss lunch Sorry
Good luck! I'll miss you
Miss you too 😞

With Leah absent, Collin scanned the cafeteria for other tables where he might eat. The sports team tables were totally out of the question, as were the people-to-avoid-at-any-cost tables with gaggles of bullies, wise guys, troublemakers and angry rebels. All the other tables had varying combinations of clowns, oddballs and ordinary guys like him. *Might as well go back to the Three Stooges.* But when he put his tray down at his old eating spot, he noticed someone was missing.

"Where's Ronnie?" Collin asked, after he seated himself next to Eric.

"Probably in some corner by himself," answered Eric. "He's gotten too emo for us lately."

"Why?"

"Cause Janie isn't going to the prom with him after all."

Collin made noise that was a cross between humor and feeling sorry for his friend. "Did she get a better offer?"

Fred sucked in a strand of spaghetti before leaning over the table. "No, it's really weird. Janie got into some deep shit."

"What kind of shit?"

"Not sure I believe him," Eric sniffed. "According to Ronnie, Janie got caught stealing from another girl's gym locker. Part of her punishment is not being allowed to go to prom."

Collin didn't know Janie well, but stealing didn't seem like something she'd do. "Who... who caught her?" he continued.

"Must've been Ms. Hankins," said Eric, referring to the girls' Phys. Ed. teacher. "There's allegedly a video of Janie trying to break into this locker."

Collin scowled. "That doesn't make any sense. There aren't any security cameras in the locker rooms."

"Not in the boys' but how can you be sure about the girls'?" Eric asked with a smirk.

"Get real, dude," Collin said. "They'd put a security camera in our locker room way before they even think about doing the same with the girls' area. That's trouble waiting to happen."

Eric shrugged. "I don't know. Maybe Ms. Hankins took the video with her phone. Who else would take it?"

Neither Collin nor Fred answered that question, and before long, all three were well into eating. With only a few minutes to go before the lunch period ended, Ronnie bounded over to them. Maybe he'd been brooding somewhere by himself, but now he had a huge smile and held his phone aloft as if it were an Olympic medal.

"Great news!" he shouted.

"What?" asked Eric. "You get another date to the prom?"

"I don't have to get another date," Ronnie beamed. "Janie just texted. She's going with me after all."

"Really?" Fred did look happy for his friend. "You mean they're not gonna punish her for trying to steal from another student?"

Ronnie dropped himself onto the bench next to Collin and shook his head. "No, no. She wasn't trying to steal anything. Mr. Scanlan looked at that video and realized there'd been a misunderstanding. No harm, no foul. So everything's cool."

Collin dropped his fork onto his plate and gripped the sides of his tray. *Everything is not cool, especially for Janie who might just be the next girl in trouble.*

Chapter 32

*T*hat evening, seconds after swallowing his last bite of dinner, Collin called Herbie while still going up the stairs. "We've got to do more than just turn Leah's journal over to Dr. Kaufman tomorrow," he said. "We've got to have her stop Scanlan, too."

"Good idea, but she'll probably need Leah to—"

"It's not just about Leah anymore."

"What do you mean?"

"I mean he's planning to go after Janie Vilditch once Leah leaves."

"How do you know?"

Collin told Herbie about the conversation at his cafeteria table earlier that day.

"I got to admit it sounds suspicious," said Herbie. "But how can you be sure?"

Collin sighed. "I'm not. I'm not sure about anything anymore except Scanlan needs to be stopped or he'll keep finding ways to get girls under his power so he can have sex with them. He could be planning to blackmail Janie about stealing when he makes his move on her."

"Why should we be the ones who stop him?"

"Because you and I are the only ones who know what he's doing—"

"Leah certainly knows."

"…and right now we're the only ones who can stop him."

There was a pause and Collin felt sure his friend was pressing his fingertips to his head. He did that whenever Collin seemed particularly thick about some homework problem. "Listen, big man, this is real life, we're almost adults, but we're still are not going to win against an assistant principal. You can't pretend you're the Scarlet Angel or any other superhero."

"I know, but I do have one trait that all heroes have."

"What could that be?"

"I'm ready to take risks to save someone who can't save themself."

"So what are you going to do?"

"Tomorrow at our appointment with Dr. Kaufman, I'm going to do more than just identify Scanlan as Leah's abuser: I'm going to ask her to take action against him."

"Even if she believes what you say about Scanlan, she might not want to do that."

"I don't think she can get Scanlan arrested by herself, not without Leah's help. But I bet she can keep him away from the prom. That will show him his days as an abuser are numbered. I'll tell Kaufman about the video on Janie, too. He'll be the one sweating and worrying instead of Leah."

"I guess it won't hurt to ask."

"There's also another plus if Scanlan is not at the prom."

"What's that?"

"We'll have a lot more fun."

Herbie couldn't help but grin.

Chapter 33

A no-nonsense professional. That was Collin's first impression of Dr. Kaufman when he and Herbie stepped into her office Thursday morning. Her navy-blue blazer and white blouse fit her perfectly, her short brown hair was neatly styled and her soft, inquisitive eyes beamed out behind glasses. Everything about Dr. Kaufman's beige-carpeted office, from the carefully organized desk to the precisely spaced pictures on the wall, made it clear she took her job seriously. When she saw Collin and Herbie, she remained seated but extended a well-manicured hand to them.

"I'm Suzanne Kaufman," she said as she shook first Collin's hand and then Herbie's. "Please sit down," she added, motioning them toward two matching chairs in front of her desk. "As soon as I saw 'Morris and Kessler' on my schedule, I realized there'd be two of you showing up."

"Yes, ma'am," said Collin. "There wasn't any way for both of us to sign up for this appointment online."

"And I need to change that. With more young people coming out and getting into open relationships, I should have something set up for students like the two of you at the same time."

Collin and Herbie exchanged nervous glances. "Um… we're not gay, Dr. Kaufman. We're here for another reason."

"Oh," the psychologist said, slapping a hand over her mouth as if keep words back or hiding a smile. "I'm sorry for jumping to conclusions. So why are you here?"

Collin had tucked the journal behind him, between his shirt and pants. Now he brought it out and handed it to Dr. Kaufman.

"What do we have here?" she asked.

"A diary or journal or something."

"Yours?"

"No." Collin hesitated. "Someone else's."

"Do you know whose?"

When Collin hesitated again, Herbie jumped in. "Leah Jennings."

Dr. Kaufman opened the journal. She took a minute to scan through it before going back to the beginning, her questions resuming after she moved beyond the first page. "How did you end up with Leah's journal? Did you find it somewhere?"

"No ma'am," Collin answered. "It sort of found me."

Dr. Kaufman put the journal down and fixed her eyes on Collin. "You're going to have to explain that. Knowing someone's deepest thoughts is serious."

Collin told the story of finding the brown book in his backpack after school without ever seeing Leah. "My best guess is she put it in there while I bent over a drinking fountain, so I never saw her."

The psychologist continued to read the journal, and after a minute or two, she put it down again. "So far, I haven't seen any full names in here. Just initials or the first letter of a last name. How do you know it's Leah's?"

Now it was Herbie's turn again. He explained their strategy of identifying girls on the class rosters who were taking the same courses with the same teachers as the writer.

"Interesting," said Dr. Kaufman. "You and Collin became modern-day detectives. But I'd think your method could only take you so far."

"You're right. We got down to four girls as possible targets."

"So we had to find other clues in the journal," said Collin, jumping in. "Further in, the girl talks about a peace locket she got from her grandmother. It turned out Leah was the one who had a locket with the peace sign on it."

"You saw Leah wearing this locket?" asked Dr. Kaufman.

"Yes, she sits near me at lunch."

"If you got close enough to see Leah wearing a peace locket, weren't you close enough to speak to her?"

"Yes, I did speak with her—a little."

The psychologist shrugged. "If you're sure the book belongs to Leah, why not give it back to her? Why set up this meeting with me?"

Collin realized that question was just as hard to answer now as it was two weeks ago when Herbie asked it. "Well, um —"

"And then, when you give it back to her, you can ask her why she put it into your backpack."

"Dr. Kaufman," Herbie said slowly then looked the woman right in the eye. "How much of the diary have you read so far?"

"I'm at the top of page 11."

"Please keep reading."

She did. As the psychologist moved deeper into the journal, the muscles of her jaw tightened and her eyes narrowed. A slight curl came onto her lip. When she appeared to be about halfway through, she closed it and placed it on her desk in front of her. "They're some pretty shocking things in here, which I assume you've read. You still haven't told me why you didn't give the journal back to Leah."

Collin shuffled his feet on the beige carpeting. "For one thing, I wasn't sure she wanted it back. I mean, why give it to me? I don't even know her... or at least I didn't until a few weeks ago."

"Did it occur to you she might have wanted to hide it, at least temporarily?"

"Who from?"

"This Red Lion, maybe?"

Collin didn't recall seeing Mr. Scanlan in the hallway that Friday afternoon, but then again, he wasn't paying much attention to who was nearby. "Wow, that's possible."

Dr. Kaufman opened a side drawer on her desk and put the journal inside. "This should be returned to Leah, but maybe I'm in a better position to do that than either of you."

Collin and Herbie nodded.

"And maybe I'm the one who should find out who Red Lion is. That might not be easy. Leah may not want to give me his name."

Again in unison, as if they rehearsed it, Collin and Herbie spoke. "We know who Red Lion is."

Dr. Kaufman snapped her eyes on Collin then shifted them to Herbie. "Who?"

This time, only Collin answered. "Mr. Scanlan."

Both teens braced themselves for an unpleasant, even stormy reaction from the psychologist followed by a stern lecture on respecting those in authority but it never came. Dr. Kaufman raised her eyebrows, hinting at nothing more than moderate surprise at Collin's accusation. She rose from her desk, her glasses sliding down her a nose a little, and came around in front of it. She wasn't tall, but standing just a foot or two from where the teens sat, her head seemed to touch the ceiling. "What makes you think Mr. Scanlan is Red Lion?" she asked Collin, folding her arms.

Collin told her about the fight with Blake, being taken to Mr. Scanlan's office and seeing the red lion figurine on his desk. "And that's not all," he added, seeing he was not convincing her. "Mr. Scanlan is Leah's next-door neighbor."

"How did you find that out?"

"I took Leah downtown to the art museum, and when I brought her home, I saw Mr. Scanlan come out of the house right next to hers. Later, when I helped her dad get into a car, Leah shut up real fast when he came over to help."

Dr. Kaufman tapped her foot on the carpet. "I've never heard anything about our assistant principal as bad as what's described in this journal."

"But you've heard something bad about him?" Collin tried to sound calm, reasonable, even though anxiety ate away at his insides.

Dr. Kaufman raised her eyebrows again and gazed at him with an intensity that made his skin burn. *It's as if she wants to answer me but can't. Maybe I should make it easier for her.*

"Dr. Kaufman, I guess without more evidence you need to give Mr. Scanlan the benefit of the doubt," Collin said. "But maybe there's one small thing you could do now."

"What's that?"

"Could you make him stay away from the prom?"

"Mr. Scanlan is going to the prom?"

"Yes, as head chaperone, and I'm afraid what he might do if he sees Leah and me there."

"You're dating her, aren't you?"

"Well, the prom will only be our second date."

"I see." The psychologist returned to her desk and began typing on her keyboard. "The first thing I'm going to do is notify the police of a possible child abuse incident in our school. That's something I'm required to do. As for Mr. Scanlan himself, I can't have him arrested or fired, but I should be able to keep him away from the prom. I'm going to tell the superintendent about this journal and recommend he put Mr. Scanlan on administrative leave until a full investigation is completed." She fell silent for a couple of minutes until she finished typing. "I've also sent a message to Mr. Scanlan telling him about the accusations against him and what I've asked the superintendent to do."

Collin gripped the sides of his chair. "Please don't mention our names."

"No need for that. But I had to let Mr. Scanlan know what we're doing. I can't stab the man in the back. I'm also going to bring Leah into my office and return her journal…we need to see what she has to say. As much as anything, I want to find out why she gave it to you."

"Do you think it will be safe for me to take Leah to the prom?"

"If our superintendent puts the assistant principal on leave, he won't be allowed on school grounds during any school function."

Collin breathed a sigh of relief. "Thank you, Dr. Kaufman."

The two teens got up and headed toward the door.

"Collin?" Dr. Kaufman called out. "I won't tell Leah who gave me the journal."

Collin smiled and breathed another sigh of relief, bigger than the last one. "Thanks."

"I want you to do that."

Chapter 34

For Collin, the rest of the day rushed by in a blur as he struggled with when to tell Leah he was the one who found her journal. A huge selfish worry was that she might break their prom date. He never thought he might get a date, let alone a prom date, with someone so fun to be with as Leah. He settled on Sunday after the prom, because there wouldn't be enough time at school on Monday before Dr. Kaufman talked to her. He reasoned with himself that was the right thing to do since he didn't want to ruin *her* prom experience either.

These choices weighed on him well into the afternoon when he went to see his doctor and his weight loss was confirmed. His goal was achieved, but he was warned he was still slightly obese for a 5'10" teen male. The doc allowed Collin to go off the hard diet for now. Better still, if he could lose a few more pounds by the end of summer by exercising and eating smart, they could ditch the diet and the follow-up appointments for good.

At dinner, an unexpected bonus to prom night came from Collin's dad. Before anyone started eating, he stood up and waved his hands as if silencing a huge crowd. "Ladies and gentleman," he said, smiling, "tonight for the first time, but not the last, you have the pleasure of dining with the new team project manager at UDLS!" Mr. Morris bowed while his family applauded.

"That's great, Dad," said Collin.

"Yes," Mrs. Morris said. "Your father finally found a company that can appreciate his talents."

"I've got some news of my own," Eleanor chimed in. "Roger wants to get back together."

"Is that so?" her father said, the smile vanishing.

"Yes, but I'm not sure I want him back. I'll need to think it over for a while."

"Good for you, Ellie," exclaimed Collin. "Make him sweat!"

Mr. Morris' smile returned, shining out like chrome on a new car. "For the last several weeks, you've all done a lot of sweating of your own, thanks to me. You've had to put up with my grouchiness and complaining, I know it wasn't easy being around me. To make it up to you, I've got a special surprise for each of you. A surprise made possible by the $5,000 signing bonus UDLS gave me."

Both Eleanor and Collin gasped, and their mother all but glowed with joy. It had been a long time since any just-because gifts had been shared.

"First of all, Della my dear, I bought a frame that should go perfectly with the painting you finished last week. It's in the living room, propped up against the sofa."

"Oh!" gasped Mrs. Morris, pushing her chair back. Before she could get up, Mr. Morris put a hand on her shoulder.

"Wait, there's more. Next Sunday morning, you and I are headed to the new Hocking Valley Resort for a day of fun and relaxation. I've already got us booked for a massage, a tennis game and dinner at their five-star restaurant."

"That's wonderful but will we be home in time—"

"It's only an hour and a half away, so we should be home before it gets too late. But if passion gets the better of us and we get a room…" Mr. Morris winked at his wife "…I'm sure the kids could manage one night without us." Both Collin and Eleanor let their mouths fall open in feigned shock.

"And now, Eleanor's turn. I know how you love the Black Keys. Can take them or leave them myself, but anyway I've got four front-row tickets to their concert next month in Cleveland. I thought you could take three of your girlfriends, but I guess one of the friends could be Roger if you—"

"No way," said Eleanor, smirking.

Mr. Morris reached into his shirt pocket, pulled out the tickets and handed them to his daughter.

"Oh thank you, Dad," Eleanor gushed.

"As for Collin…" Mr. Morris got up from the table and walked out of the dining room. When he returned, he held a white brochure with a picture of a car on the front. "I know you're going to the prom on

Saturday and were probably hoping I'd take you and your date. But I'll be relaxing in my quiet house because this is how you'll get there."

He handed the brochure to Collin who saw that the car on its cover was actually a black limousine. Inside were pictures of other limousines, some white and some black, and some big enough to carry a whole football team. "You mean I'm going in a limo?"

"Yes, not the biggest one there but one big enough for you, Leah, Herbie and his date."

"That's fantastic. Thanks a million."

"You've earned it. Not only for putting up with my grumpiness but also losing 25 pounds in 10 weeks. That's quite an accomplishment."

"It certainly is," Collin's mother added. "And the limousine is a good idea. Now we won't have to worry about him getting into an accident coming from or going to the prom."

Collin liked the idea, too, although not for the reason his mother did. *A limo will make Leah see I'm a guy who only wants the best for her.*

"When does your prom start?" asked Mr. Morris.

"They start serving dinner at six," said Collin.

"I'll have the limo here at quarter after five."

* * *

*T*he next day, Collin was more focused on his classes, which was a good thing since he had a quiz in Algebra and an oral report in French. Still, there were times when his brain got lost in a fog, when other students sitting or walking nearby seemed faceless, and when his teachers sounded like the adults in a Charlie Brown cartoon. The question of when to tell Leah about his having read her secrets dogged him as relentlessly as it had the day before. Worse, driving to her home and telling her on Sunday was no longer an option with his dad and mom going out of town that day, using the car. Maybe he could set up an Uber account of his own.

"You'll just have to be ready to pounce sometime during the prom," Herbie told him as they drove to pick up their tuxes.

"Pounce? You make me sound like a predator," Collin complained.

"No, you just need to pick the right time to give Leah the whole story. Riding in a limo to the prom might dazzle her so much, she'll be okay with anything you say."

"I wouldn't bet on it."

"I'm not betting on it either. I'm just hoping that's what happens for your sake."

"I can't see telling her with you guys around either. I'm sure she would want to have her reaction, whatever it is, in private."

On the drive home, with the tuxes hanging behind them, Collin steered their conversation toward dancing—away from the journal.

"Still worried about how you'll do on the dance floor?" Collin asked.

"Not as much as before," Herbie answered. "I've been looking at online dance videos and practicing."

"So what dances have you learned?"

"Oh, let's see… the cupid shuffle, the dougie, one or two others. You should try, too. That way, if you end up falling on your ass, you'll know not to try those dances at prom."

"You think they will play music for ancient dances like that? Suppose they **all** make me fall on my ass?"

"Well, if you can't dance, that'll make it easier to take Leah somewhere and tell her about the journal."

Collin had a feeling no matter what they talked about, the journal would always squeeze in there somehow. An evil power stayed around secrets, they grew bigger and bigger.

After dinner, Collin took Herbie's advice and brought up some instructional dance videos. He passed the older crap, switching to slow dances that would let him get close to Leah, to hold her in his arms. Before long his imagination had him swaying, gliding and sometimes spinning with Leah across the floor, going ever faster. He bumped into his bed once, but didn't slow down.

After a while, Collin focused less on dancing and more on drawing the imaginary Leah ever closer to him. He wrapped his arms tightly around her waist and pressed his head closer to hers. He could almost feel the warmth flowing from her body into his. Could feel her hand pressed against his back and her breath warming his neck. Finally, he puckered up and kissed her, longer and more passionately than the kiss they'd shared in his car after their first date. In the real world, his lips may have been touching nothing more than air, but that hardly mattered. *I can always dream, can't I? Dreaming is being prepared!*

Chapter 35

Herbie came over to the Morris's a few minutes before five on Saturday. Collin thought the dark-gray satin-edged tux looked even better on Herbie now than when he tried it.

"Sir Isaac, you're straight-up killing it in that tux."

"You too, big man. Looking sharp. Dangerously sharp," Herbie said, pointing at Collin's blue bowtie. "Or should I say medium man now?"

"Got your corsage?"

"I got one for Winifred, if that's what you mean." Herbie smiled and held out a wrist corsage made up of three mini pink carnations. "It should look great on her green dress."

"Right. How about your dancing?"

Herbie's smile widened. "I'm actually feeling pretty good about it."

"Really? Can I get a demonstration?"

"Maybe when there's more time… and the girls are with us."

Collin and Herbie were in the early stages of a chess game when Mr. Morris shouted to them that their ride had rolled up.

They grabbed their things and rushed out the front door. What they saw made their jaws drop in unison.

The shiny black limo with whitewall tires and winged hood ornament could have belonged to a billionaire, but here it was ready to take Collin and Herbie to the prom.

"I don't believe it!" said Herbie.

"I hardly believe it myself," said Collin, squinting. "It reflects the sun like a mirror."

"Those tires probably cost more than some cars," added Herbie.

Mr. Morris came up behind them. "Better get going, guys," he said. "I'm renting this thing by the hour, and can only afford it one way. Shoot me a text when you and the girls are ready to go home."

"Sure, Dad, and thanks for doing this."

"Just have fun and don't get into any trouble."

"Us get into trouble?" laughed Herbie. "No way!"

The chauffer, fully in the role with a black cap and matching tie, opened the limo's side door. Herbie climbed in but Collin hesitated. "Do you know how to get to the Scoles' house?" he asked.

"Their address is already in my GPS," the chauffer answered.

"Wow, Dad," Collin said as he followed Herbie into the luxurious vehicle. "You thought of everything, didn't you?"

* * *

The inside of the limo impressed Collin and Herbie even more than the outside. With plush leather seats that could fit up to ten people, a high-quality LCD screen television, a state-of-the-art stereo system and a DVD player, the limo resembled a little luxury condo on wheels. It even had enough room to stand up and walk around.

"Hey, look at this," said Collin, pointing at a mini-refrigerator under the television. "Let's see what's inside." He opened the door and pulled out a bottle of water.

"What? No champagne?" joked Herbie.

Collin shook his head. "My dad isn't that generous – or that stupid."

"Doesn't matter. I'm probably allergic to it anyway."

Collin switched on the TV and for the next several minutes he channel-surfed through baseball games, old movies and real lives of whoever.

When they pulled into the Scoles' driveway, Collin turned the TV off. To make things easier, the girls had arranged to both be at Winifred's house so they could go straight to the prom from there. Better still, coming here instead of Leah's home avoided any chance encounter with Mr. Scanlan. *Who better be nowhere near the school tonight.*

Collin opened the limo's door and hopped out. "Wait till the girls see this," he said over his shoulder to Herbie, rushing to the door.

They didn't have to wait long. Before Collin and Herbie reached the front door, Leah and Winifred burst out, bubbling with smiles, gasps and a stream of oooohs, ahhhs and wows.

"Where did you get a limo?" asked Leah.

"My dad got it as a reward for meeting my weight loss goal."

"You mean you were on some kind of diet?"

"Yeah, didn't I tell you?"

"Maybe I just forgot, because I didn't think you were overweight to begin with."

Collin wasn't sure he believed her, but he was glad she said that anyway.

When Leah scooched into the limo, Collin noticed her blue dress, billowing slightly as she bent down. It fit her perfectly. He suddenly noticed her hair: a different style. A braid over each lovely ear was pulled back into the rest of her hair which flowed in easy waves down her back.

On the way to the prom, the four exchanged boutonnieres and wrist corsages. Collin thought the white rose arrangement he bought for Leah went perfectly with her radiant blue dress. The four teens stretched out their legs and looked at each other. Then they burst out laughing.

"Why don't you pull up some of your dance videos?" Collin asked Herbie.

"Sure." Herbie pulled out his phone and brought up a video clip titled *How to do the Latin Boogaloo*, featuring a fit-and-trim woman in a black leotard.

"What are you guys doing?" asked Winifred.

"I'm just showing Collin one of the videos I watched to improve my dancing."

"Why not cast it on the TV so Leah and I can see it, too?"

"I will if I can figure out how to –"

"Here, let me have it."

Herbie handed Winifred the phone while Collin turned on the TV. A minute later, after alternately tapping Herbie's phone and the TV's remote, the cast was beaming out from the LCD screen.

"How'd she do that?" Collin whispered to Herbie.

"If I knew, I'd have done it myself," Herbie replied.

"Okay," said Winifred, handing Herbie's phone back to him. "I don't just want to watch the instructor. I want to see you dance, too."

"You got it, babe!" spouted Herbie, who then threw himself into the center of the limo, and began gyrating to the strains of a Lucy Grau song.

"Did he just call Winifred 'babe'?" Collin whispered to Leah.

"I think so," she answered. "She doesn't seem to mind."

Maybe Winifred didn't mind because Herbie's surreal dancing

entranced her. When the Lucy Grau song ended, Winifred brought up Walk the Moon's *Shut Up and Dance* followed by Timberlake's *The Other Side*. Sometimes, Herbie's motions followed the beat of the music but more often he improvised in ways that defied gravity and common sense. He jumped and jerked, twirled and swiveled, all the while flinging his arms over his head like a drunk chasing a butterfly. He bumped the limousine's roof a few times, but that didn't slow him down.

"He's a natural," gushed Winifred, her eyes glowing.

"Yeah, but a natural what?" said Collin. As far as he knew, hard dancing wouldn't trigger any of Herbie's allergies, but what about asthma? Besides, Collin thought his friend should save some energy for the prom. "Come on, Sir Isaac. Sit down before you hurt yourself. I think we're almost to the school anyway."

Herbie sat down next to Collin and straightened his boutonniere while puffing out some air to help his breathing settle down. His face had reddened and beads of sweat clung to his forehead. Yet Collin didn't get the feeling his friend was worn out. If anything, he seemed confident, ready for more action.

"I was just getting started," Herbie said.

"What about your asthma?"

"Haven't had an attack in over a month, but I brought an inhaler and med kit just in case." He wiped the sweat off his forehead and grinned. "Just see what I'll do on the dance floor."

"I can't wait." Collin replied. The girls just grinned.

Chapter 36

*T*he limo came to a stop at the bus loading zone and immediately drew a crowd. As Collin and his friends got out, exclamations of surprise and admiration filled the air.

Ronnie, with Janie in tow, ran up to him. "How did you get the dough to pay for this?"

"The dough came from my dad," he answered. "It's sort of a reward."

"I didn't know your dad was Gucci."

"He isn't really, but he got a nice hiring bonus from his new job."

"What does he do? Run a gold mine?"

"Not hardly. He's a mechanical engineer." Collin put an arm around Leah's waist and led her toward the school. Herbie and Winfred were right behind them.

Most of the crowd remained huddled around the limo, peering into its windows or rubbing their hands over its shiny hood. One person, however, held back. "You still look like a loser to me, Morris," shouted Blake.

Collin turned to face his nemesis. "Never said I wasn't a loser, only that I'm less of one than you." Collin eyed Blake for a moment. The guy was rocking a red-and-black tux that didn't fit quite right, but something else felt off. "Hey, Blake! Where's your date? Did she ditch you already?"

Blake flipped him off and shoved his way into the crowd, which turned their attention to the limo, pulling away.

Herbie sidled up next to Collin, smirking. "You think his date actually bailed on him?"

"Nah. He probably came alone, trying to play it cool. Let's head inside."

The prom had been decorated with an Old West-style hotel, jail, bank, saloon, general store and sheriff's office – all made of cardboard – set up at one end of the gym. A stable, with papier-mâché horse heads jutting out, was a little way down from "town" across the gym floor. Next to the stable, gravestones in a cemetery cast gloomy shadows on the wall with the help of floor-mounted spotlights. Dining tables, surrounded by chicken wire cacti and tumbleweeds, were set up near the gym's entrance and along its sides where the bleachers had been folded up. Some tables were set for eight people or more; others for just four or six. There was a table reserved for chaperones, but all the others had open seating.

After strolling through the fake town for a few minutes, the group decided to eat. "Let's sit here," said Herbie, pointing to a smaller table that had a galloping-horse figurine as a centerpiece.

"Great," said Collin. "So, let's order our food."

"Don't you mean our grub?" teased Leah.

"Right, cowgirl."

Each place setting included a small pencil and a menu with little boxes next to the food and beverage choices. Collin marked off green beans, scalloped potatoes, skirt steak and cornbread. Leah chose a tossed salad, sweet potato, skirt steak and sourdough bread. "Look at that," she said, pointing at the menu. "Cowboys called sweet potatoes 'music roots.'"

"Yeah," said Collin, "and for dessert, we can have 'spotted pup,' which is really tapioca pudding and raisins."

Mr. Petrie, their "celebrity" waiter, brought their meals, including Herbie's pre-ordered low-carb, nut-free, soy-free, gluten-free, joy-free plate that looked like something served in a Charles Dickens orphanage.

"You're lucky," Herbie said sadly to Collin. "You get to go off your diet tonight." His face slumped as he stuck a fork into his food. "I'll never get off mine."

"That may not be true," said Winifred. "As you get older, some of your allergies may go away."

"I just hope if my old allergies go away, no new ones take their place."

"Don't worry," said Collin. "You already have every allergy, so there're no new ones for you to get."

While he ate, Collin glanced around at the waiters who scampered back and forth between the tables and several "chuckwagons." Besides Mr. Petrie, there were eight or nine others, all in white aprons and cowboy hats. Mrs. Rowland added a red bandana to her outfit. Mr. Browning wore a pair of black cowboy boots, which made him look bow-legged. The most significant thing Collin noticed about the adults at the prom was the one missing. *No Mr. Scanlan.* He hadn't been at school the day before either. Dr. Kaufman had kept her promise. If Mr. Iron Fist knew what was good for him, he'd be drafting his letter of resignation right now, hiring a lawyer and putting his house up for sale.

Between forkfuls the teens talked about summer plans. Winifred, after an internship, would be checking out Princeton, Herbie would be doing the same at MIT after visiting his mother's family in Jamaica, and Collin would be taking a look at Ohio State and Otterbein.

"What about you, Leah," Collin asked. "Did you find out about your scholarship application yet?"

She sat straight up with a big grin. "I got approved! The letter from the Brinkman Foundation came just a couple of days ago."

Collin's face brightened. "That's great. Congratulations!"

"That is great," added Herbie. "Those foundation scholarships are tough to get."

Leah nodded. "My GPA isn't all that great, but my high score on the State College Entrance Exam got it for me."

"So now you can go to Kenyon like you planned," said Collin, giving her hand a little squeeze.

"Yeah, I'll be visiting the campus at the end of August." She pulled her hand away. "I wonder when the dancing will start?"

As if to answer her question, waiters began to clear away the cardboard buildings, creating a dance floor, while some parent chaperones put up a refreshment table with cookies and a large bowl of orange-colored punch. A bearded DJ wearing a gold shirt and a backwards baseball cap strolled into the gym with two burly assistants and set up shop near the cemetery. Moments later, *Billie Jean* filled the air.

"Time to boogie!" shouted Herbie. Taking Winifred's hand, he swept her onto the dance floor and then began gyrating, spinning and jerking even more aggressively than he had in the limo, sometimes almost colliding with other couples.

"Want to go up there with them?" Collin asked Leah.

"Okay, but only if you don't try any of the things Herb's doing."

"Don't worry," Collin assured her. "I'm not a natural like he is."

Leah turned out to be a pretty good dancer. Collin thought he wasn't half bad himself. They mostly improvised on the spot. But they couldn't begin to keep up with Herbie. No one could. Winifred tried but gave up after she almost fell.

As the DJ's eighth song, Bruno Mars' *Uptown Funk*, faded away, Collin took a deep breath and felt the back of his collar. He could almost squeeze the sweat out of it. Leah looked tired too.

"Is it okay if we sit the next one out and get something to drink?" he asked, adjusting his sleeves.

"Sure."

They walked over to the refreshment table where punch had been ladled into little white paper cups. While he and Leah sipped their drinks, Collin watched Herbie and Winifred throw themselves into the next dance. Herbie's creativity was amazing. He darted his hands upward and then shook them like they'd been electrified. *Wow, Sir Isaac is fantastic. He could win a dance contest.*

By this time, Winifred just swayed back and forth while beaming at her partner. Other couples also began to take notice and moved aside to give Herbie room. Some even applauded and shouted encouragement to him.

"You're slaying it!" cried a girl in a purple-satin dress. "Keep going!"

When the music finally faded away, Winifred grabbed Herbie's hand and led him off the dance floor before he wound himself up for another frenzy of motion.

Collin waved the couple over to where he and Leah stood.

"What made you think you couldn't dance?" asked Collin. "You should go on one of those talent shows."

Herbie picked up two cups of punch and handed one to Winifred. "I'll only go if I can take her with me."

"Hey, I'm nowhere near the dancer you are," protested Winfred.

"So what? You're the one who inspires me."

Winifred giggled. "I don't think you need much inspiration from anyone."

For the next few minutes, the four chatted, watched their classmates dance and gulped punch. After her third cup, Leah ran her tongue over her lips. "You know, this punch has a funny after-taste to it."

Herbie chugged down his fourth, savored it a moment and then shrugged. "Tastes fine to me," he said. "And don't worry. I checked with the lady who made this stuff. Doesn't have anything I'm allergic to. It is basically sugar water with some citrus."

The DJ switched vibes: *Unchained Melody* started and the lights dimmed.

"Ah, a slow number," said Herbie. "Just what we've been waiting for, isn't it?"

Winifred held out her hand and soon the two smartest students at Bridgeview High were locked together, feet shuffling slowly while their heads snuggled together like nesting doves.

Collin put a hand on Leah's shoulder. "Let's join them."

"Great idea," she answered.

What a wonderful feeling it was to have this girl nestled next to him. This girl who wasn't the prettiest one at the prom, nor the most glamorous, nor the most fashionable... but who was, to him at least, the most attractive. Even if he had the choice of being with any other girl that night, he would still have chosen her. They liked the same things, he could talk to her about anything at all, they had matching energy levels. Everything seemed perfect.

The delicacy of her hands, the warmth of her breath on his neck and of course the deep beauty of her eyes somehow combined to make her enchanting. *How does she feel about me?* If the pressure Leah put on his back, *as if she wants me closer*, offered any clue, the affectionate feelings were mutual. Still, Collin knew he couldn't answer that question until he came clean to her, not only about finding the journal but also about learning the secrets it held. *Why did Leah put it in my backpack to begin with?* Sure, he wanted an answer to that question, but Collin wanted something even more important. He wanted to prove to Leah that he cared about her, that he could be trusted, and could -- someday -- be a good boyfriend.

As the song trailed away, Leah eased her hold on Collin's back and whispered into his ear. "Do you want to stay for the next dance or take another break?"

Now is the time. "Let's take a break," he said. "But not by the refreshment table."

Chapter 37

Collin guided Leah toward an empty table the chaperones used earlier to collect tickets. He pulled the table several feet outside the gym along with two chairs. Far off to the right, Luke and Gail were kissing under the light of a trophy case. Otherwise, no one was in sight.

Once seated, Collin took Leah's hands in his. The soft delicacy of her touch, which he relished on the dance floor, sent a quiver through his fingers and up his spine of both pleasure and fear. He studied her face for a few seconds. He saw no suspicion, no mistrust; nothing except a twinge of puzzlement.

"I have to tell you something, Leah. I should've told you sooner, but I didn't know the best time to do that. There really is no best time to say what I need to say, but I can't keep this inside me any longer."

"Are you going to tell me you have my journal?"

The absolute shock of Leah's words hit Collin like a sledgehammer. For a second, he felt like he might fall out of his chair. A little gasp escaped his mouth before he found the composure to respond. "How did you know?"

"Well, for one thing, that whole bit about needing help to find a necklace for your sister seemed kind of phony. Probably, it was a way to break the ice with a girl you liked. I thought Carmen was your first choice and when that didn't work out, you came over to me as a back-up plan."

"You were never a back-up plan, Leah."

"I realized that when I saw your backpack under the table where you eat. It looked just like the one I stuck my journal in."

"So you've known all along I had it!?"

"Right after you told me about getting stuck in a barrel behind a warehouse. I knew you must have figured out who I was from the teachers and classes I wrote about."

Collin felt so relieved he almost collapsed. More than that. He was awestruck by this girl's brain. She didn't seem to be aware of how smart she was. *But... if Leah knew I had her journal...* "Why didn't you ask me to give it back?"

"Partly because I started keeping a new journal on my laptop. This one didn't have as much detail as the first, but it talked about the same things. If I wanted to, I could put this new journal on a flash drive as evidence."

"Okay. What was the other part?"

A thin, almost apologetic smile took shape on Leah's lips. "When it didn't turn up in Lost and Found, I wasn't sure what to think. Maybe the guy who had it was getting turned on by it or trashed it. When I realized *you* had it, I wanted to see what you would do, figured you wanted to help me somehow." She held Collin's hands tighter. "And I was right."

Collin continued to marvel at Leah. There was so much more to her than met the eye, so much about her he wanted to discover. But he knew what he said next might make that impossible. "You weren't the only one whose identity we discovered. We know who Red Lion is, too."

Now it was Leah's turn to gasp. She pulled her hands away from Collin's and clapped them to her mouth. "I didn't think you could do that. I guess I underestimated you and Herb after all."

"We probably wouldn't have found out except I had a fight with Blake and got hauled into Mr. Scanlan's office. That's where I saw the red lion on his desk and smelled his weird cologne. I still wasn't totally sure until I took you home after we went to the art museum and saw he was your neighbor."

"Everything started so innocently—"

"It's not innocent now. You've got to expose him for the monster he is."

"He's no more a monster than I am. A monstrous cheat, anyway."

Collin made a fist to slam on the table, but held back, not wanting to draw Luke and Gail's attention. "Don't say that! No way are you a cheat. Scanlan's the one who's wrong. It's sick for him to force sex on someone, especially a teenage girl, a student, and no way should he have treated you like trash because you went on a date with someone else, no way—"

"A date with someone else?" Leah's face contorted in confusion. "What are you talking about?"

"Isn't that what you did? Make Scanlan mad because you went out with another guy?"

"No! That's not what I meant by cheat. I cheated on a test, the State College Entrance Exam. And our wonderful asshole of an assistant principal caught me."

A rush of understanding came over Collin with the force of a rogue wave. *So that's why she lets Scanlan treat her like a sex slave. It's not out of guilt; it's fear. She's afraid he might keep her from graduating or something. But Scanlan's going after Janie next; for the very same kind of thing. If Leah doesn't help me stop him now there will be a new girl in trouble. I need to know more.*

"How did you get mixed up with Scanlan anyway?"

"Like I started to say, it was all so innocent at the beginning. My parents thought it was cool when he moved next door about five years ago. 'He's got to be a real smart guy to be a principal,' my dad said. 'I bet he could help you with your homework if you needed it.'

"And I did need it, especially in math." Collin nodded and rolled his eyes in sympathy at the same time. Leah smiled in understanding as she continued. "Sure enough, Gerry was right there to help. At first, he came over to our house, later I started to go to his. I also started to help him with chores like raking leaves or vacuuming his floor. He'd give me a few dollars and say, 'Sweetie, I'm so glad we're neighbors. I'd have a hard time getting things done around here without you.' He made me feel really... special. Later, he'd say we were 'friends.' That seemed a little weird, but I didn't think it was wrong. After a while I sort of thought of him as a friend, too."

"What about friends our age? You had some of them, didn't you?"

"Yeah, Sally and Carol. But Sally's family moved to Denver a year ago, and Carol... well, I guess I don't fit in with the new friends she has now. Anyway, Gerry got a little too friendly. While I was watering his garden, he snuck up behind me and kissed me on the neck. When I turned around, he went for my lips. I pushed him away and told him I didn't want to be *that* kind of friend. He apologized and promised not to try anything like that again. But a few weeks later he did try. I was in his garage, putting a rake away, when he suddenly pulled the garage door down. The next thing I knew, he had me against the garage wall and was kissing me on my cheeks and then my lips. For a few seconds, I was too scared to do anything. Then he put his hand on my breast. That's when I screamed and kicked him in the shin. He let go of me and opened the garage door. Again, he said he was sorry. Over and over again, he said how bad he felt and promised never ever to do anything like that again. Said I was just so special he got carried away. I said okay, but after that I didn't go over to his house much. When I did, it was always to do something outside, so I could run away if I had to."

"Did you tell your parents what he did?"

"No, he asked me not to. Almost begged. Said he'd lose his job and go to jail. I said I wouldn't as long he never tried to kiss me again. That seemed to solve the problem but then two things happened."

"I bet your dad's stroke was one of those things."

"Yes, and after that our money troubles started. Even with Dad on disability and Mom doing some substitute teaching, we had trouble paying our bills. That's when Gerry came to our rescue. He started by giving us vegetables from his garden, then later he'd buy us groceries sometimes. I think he might have even paid a couple of electric bills for us. He seemed like the perfect neighbor, but that changed when we took the practice State College Entrance Exam at the end of last year."

"Yeah, I remember one of my teachers saying it would show us where we needed to improve before we took the real exam. How did you do on it?"

"Bad. Real bad, especially in math. I knew the only way I could get into college was by earning a scholarship and the only way I could get a scholarship was to do really great on the state exam. Gerry knew I was worried and once again offered to help me. I said okay as long as he came to my house. We spent hours together on weekends going through workbooks, online guides and other stuff that was supposed to prepare me. Sometimes he'd put his arm around me when he explained something and every so often he'd give me a little kiss on the cheek or forehead. I didn't like this, but didn't say anything. I was afraid if I did, he'd stop helping my family. And with my dad in a wheelchair and my mom working any kind of job she could find, we needed some kind of help about every day."

Wish I'd known Leah sooner. I would have been there for her through all of the troubles. My family could have helped her family, and Herbie could have gotten her ready for the math part of the state exam. Collin knew how Leah's story went from here on, and a part of him didn't want to hear it, but he owed it to her to keep listening. He squeezed her hand, asked if she wanted more punch. She shook her head.

With a hiccup of a breath Leah went into the horrible part of her story. "Gerry's tutoring seemed to help – except in math. For the first grading period this year, I got As and Bs in every subject, except Algebra." She screwed her face into a scowl as if she'd just stepped in dog poop. "I got a D in that. When I told Gerry about the D in Algebra, he said it was time for 'drastic action.' He claimed to have access to a dark website where he could get the answers to the math questions for this year's state exam. He said he'd get the answers for me, if I'd do some 'favors' for him. I was desperate, so even though I knew what he meant, I said okay, but only until I'd taken the exam, which at the time was only about two weeks away. So Gerry got me the answers and we started to…"

Leah's voice trailed off as her lips trembled and tears formed at the edges of her eyes.

"You don't have to say anything more," Collin said into the sudden silence. "I know."

"Of course you do. It's all in the journal. But I thought it would all end once the exam was over. The problem was, I didn't trust myself to remember the answers so I made a little cheat sheet. I pinned it to the inside of my blouse near the neck. By undoing the top button, I could look down and see the answers. On the day of the exam, I got a big surprise. Gerry was the proctor for the exam. He didn't pay any more attention to me than the other students in the room, so I wasn't too worried. While I took the exam, I saw him walking around, but again, he didn't seem focused on me. A couple of days after the exam, he called me into his office and asked me to look at something on his computer screen. When I did, I saw a video of myself taking the exam. Gerry had adjusted a security camera so it pointed directly at me from the corner of the wall and ceiling. The cheat sheet was obvious, so was me getting answers off of it. After that, he…he…"

Leah pressed fingers to her scrunched up eyes, which now welled with tears. When she opened them, the glistening wetness somehow made those eyes even more beautiful.

"He blackmailed you into allowing him to continue abusing you."

She nodded. "He said if I rejected him, he'd show the video to the superintendent and then the Brinkman Foundation. Not only wouldn't I have a chance at a scholarship, I'd probably get expelled from school."

"Your mom and dad—"

Leah cringed. "They think Gerry walks on water, especially my mom. I don't think they'd believe me if I did tell them." Leah let her head droop. "And in my own mind, I began to think I deserved what I was getting. Even if I hated what Gerry was doing to me, I thought it was a good punishment for cheating on a test so important to my future."

A passage from the journal flashed into Collins's mind.

It's my fault. The whole thing is. Red Lion's right to treat me this way.

"So why did you start writing in a journal?"

Leah brought her head back up. "I've had diaries before, so it wasn't something new. But writing in this journal was kind of an escape, a way to express myself without getting anyone in trouble. It worked for a while, but eventually I thought things had gone far enough, that I had paid enough for my crime. I decided to get the school psychologist's help on how to end it. I wasn't going to mention Gerry by name; I was just going to describe him as a 'boyfriend who had ways of getting back at me if I broke up with him.' In the journal, I called him GS once or twice but changed to Red Lion when I saw that little statue in his home before he took it to his office. The name seemed to fit."

A fast dance started to play in the gym. The DJ was getting the dancers to do moves and call back to him with the song. They both glanced at the door to the gym with small smiles on their faces.

"So I made an appointment with Dr. Kaufman for eighth period on a Friday. I put my books in my locker and went to see her with the brown journal in my hand, but before I got to her office, Gerry came around the corner and headed in my direction. I knew if he saw the untitled book, he'd want to know what it was. I had to hide it. The only place to do that was your backpack." Leah took a breath and put her hands back on top of Collin's. "I'm lucky you're the one who got it." She leaned toward him. "Where is it now?"

The irony of his answer was not lost on Collin. "Believe it or not, it's with Dr. Kaufman. She promised to return the journal to you next week. She made it clear I had to tell you I was the one who found it in my backpack and also that I had read your secrets in order figure out who you were."

Leah nodded. "So that's why she sent me an e-mail yesterday, asking me to make another appointment with her."

"Once she gives it back to you, she'll want you to do something for her."

"What?"

"It's the same thing I want; expose Scanlan for the sexual predator he is and get him out of your life forever."

"I don't think I can do that. If I expose him, he'll do the same to me. Show that video of me cheating and get me thrown out of school, so I don't graduate. ."

"Maybe that won't happen. The state exam wasn't part of any course you were taking, it was—"

"It doesn't matter! Even if I graduate, I'll never get the scholarship and go to college... and worst of all... it will humiliate my parents... maybe give my dad another stroke."

"But Scanlan's got to be stopped, Leah. He's a monster, a predator, a pervert and even if you go away to college, he's just going to go after some other girl and do to her what he did to you."

"But maybe he won't –"

"He will! In fact, he's already got his eye on Janie Vilditch. Caught her stealing from a locker. Probably has a video of Janie just like he has of you, and he'll use it to make her his sex slave after you leave for college."

Leah's whole body jerked as if she'd been stung by a bee. "I... I... I don't know. I just don't –"

A sudden commotion erupted from inside the gym.

"Hey, dude. What's wrong with you?" someone shouted.

"He's having a seizure," another voice cried.

Collin bolted up from the chair and dashed inside the gym.

A crowd of students talking over each other and pointing encircled a body near the center of the dance floor. Collin couldn't see who it was, but a voice he recognized suddenly rang out above all the others.

"Somebody help him!" Winifred wailed.

Oh no. It's Herbie.

Chapter 38

Collin pushed his way into the circle of students and chaperones surrounding his stricken friend who lay doubled up on the floor, hands clutching his stomach and shaking.

"I'm sure it's a seizure!" the girl in the purple-satin dress repeated.

"No, it's a heart attack from all that crazy dancing he's been doing," someone else stated.

Collin fought off a wave of panic as Herbie's face reddened and puffed out, his breaths now coming in short, desperate gasps. "It isn't either of those things," he said.

"How do you know?" asked the girl.

Collin ignored the question and strode toward a man who had a phone to his ear. By now, the DJ had stopped the music and all dancing had come to a halt. The circle of students around Herbie widened, some peering at their stricken classmate with concern while others seemed morbidly curious.

The man lowered his phone. "I've got 9-1-1 on the line. Does anyone know what's the matter with this kid?" he shouted to no one in particular.

"It's anaphylaxis," Collin answered loudly to make sure he was heard. "An allergic reaction to something he ate or drank."

"Are you sure?"

"Yes! I've known him for years. He's allergic to peanuts, strawberries, milk, wheat, nearly everything."

The man nodded and spoke into his phone, apparently relaying that information to the 9-1-1 dispatcher. Meanwhile Collin dashed over to Herbie's jacket, which lay over a chair by the table they had picked for their home base. He picked up the tux jacket and began rummaging through its pockets. The wave of panic he fought off earlier returned with a vengeance when all the pockets were empty. *He said he brought his med kit!* Collin finally saw the kit underneath the chair. Not knowing or caring how it got there, he snatched it off the floor and rushed back to where his friend lay.

A middle-aged woman—a doctor or nurse, Collin hoped—knelt next to Herbie, performing CPR.

Oh God! He's stopped breathing!

When the woman finished a set of chest compressions, Collin pulled the EpiPen out of the kit and thrust it under her nose. "Here's what he needs." Without a word, she took the autoinjector, flipped off its cap and thrust its needle through his trousers into his thigh.

The man with the phone took a step toward the woman. "An ambulance is on the way," he said.

"Good," she replied. "I'm a pediatrician, but there's only so much I can do for him here. He needs to get to a hospital as soon as possible. In the meantime, we need to continue with the CPR."

"I can do that," said Mr. Petrie, tossing his cowboy hat aside.

The doctor nodded and rose to her feet. "What about notifying this boy's parents? Someone should do that."

Collin pulled a notecard from the emergency kit and handed it to the man with the phone. "Here are both his parents' cell numbers."

"He'll be all right, won't he?" the question came from Winifred. She knelt down to hold Herbie's hand as Mr. Petrie went to work.

"Maybe. It will depend on what triggered this reaction. Right now, the most important thing is getting him breathing again." The doctor pivoted toward Collin. "You mentioned he was allergic to peanuts, strawberries and other foods. He didn't eat any of those things tonight, did he?"

"No," Collin replied. "He had a special meal brought in that didn't have anything he was allergic to."

"What did he drink?" the doctor asked.

"Bottled water that came with his food… and…" Collin hesitated, then pointed at the refreshment table. "…punch… two or three cups. Maybe more."

"Bring me a cup of that punch," the doctor ordered.

A tall kid in a white tuxedo elbowed his way through the crowd and handed her a cup of punch. She took a sip and raised an eyebrow. "What kind of punch is this?"

"Just a fruit punch," said a red-headed woman standing next to the 9-

1-1 caller. "We made it with raspberry sherbet, orange juice, pineapple juice, and lemon-lime soda. Just basically sugar and citrus, we knew to keep it simple."

"No strawberries?"

"No!" the woman retorted. "I've made that punch dozens of times and never put a drop of strawberry juice in it."

The doctor took another sip. "Well, I think some strawberry juice is in here. Taste it yourself."

Someone handed the woman a cup of punch; she put it to her lips and drank. Her eyes widened. "This doesn't taste like my punch."

The doctor knelt back down next to Herbie. "Well, now we know what happened to this boy. But it looks like... maybe..."

"He's breathing on his own," said Mr. Petrie. "Should I stop the CPR?"

"Yes," said the doctor, "but stay with him and let me know if he stops."

There were sighs of relief from most of the people nearby, but the red-headed woman seemed to crumple, her face contorted with bewilderment. "I didn't put strawberry juice in! I don't know how it got there!"

"Excuse me," Collin interjected. "Do you remember who made the punch?"

The woman frowned. "Just me and a couple of other parents. Oh, and the assistant principal, too. He said he couldn't make it to the prom, but wanted to help us out before it started." Her frown deepened. "I should know his name. Scale, Scon –"

"Scanlan," said Collin, the name spilling from his mouth like vomit.

The woman brightened. "Yes, that's right – Scanlan. But he wouldn't have put any strawberry juice in the punch."

A chill ran up Collin's spine and his insides knotted up. *Wanna bet?* He almost said the words aloud, but swallowed them as fear and confusion flooded his mind. *Just how crazy is this guy, coming to the prom when Dr. Kaufman warned him not to? But wait, he came to the school before the prom started, and none of the parents here knew about her warning. But how would Scanlan know about Herbie's allergy to strawberries? And why go after Herbie when I'm the one trying to take Leah out of his grasp?*

Collin gazed around the gymnasium.

The DJ, his flamboyance gone, sat slumped in a chair behind his turntable, watching. Meanwhile, huddled groups of students and parents surrounded the little vignette of the doctor, Mr. Petrie, Herbie and Winifred, who continued to hold Herbie's hand. *Where is Leah?* In the confusion that followed Herbie's collapse, he'd lost sight of her.

Collin zeroed in on the faces of people in the gymnasium, hoping to find Leah, hoping she just made a quick trip to the powder room.

In the meantime, a pair of EMTs pushing a wheeled cot burst through the doors and hurried over to where Herbie lay. One put the end of a stethoscope on his friend's chest while the other spoke with the pediatrician. *Has he stopped breathing again?* Collin watched, hoping to see some movement, even a slight twitch, that would confirm Herbie was all right.

A text tone pulled his attention to a new message on his cell. It was just four words, but what they said left him in a state beyond afraid, beyond desperate, beyond panicked.

Come to Scanlan's office

For a few heartbeats he stood there numb, oblivious to everyone near him, just barely noticing the EMTs place Herbie on the cot and wheel him out of the gym. Another text tone, another message, this time with only one word.

Hurry

This is it! thought Collin, trying to rally himself.

The final battle where the hero smashes the villain and sends him screaming into oblivion. Except... *I'm no hero. I'm just a scared teenager up against the most-powerful person in this school right now. A guy who's got Leah under his thumb and who could ruin me in an instant. Maybe even kill me... like he nearly killed Herbie.*

Collin shoved his phone into his inside pocket and when he did his hand rubbed against the folded-up piece of paper he'd moved there earlier from his wallet.

Panic released its grip on him and his fear diminished.

He'd almost forgotten about this piece of paper, the best and only weapon he had for ending Red Lion's reign of terror over Leah.

The DJ, reading the room, put on a song with a medium beat: too soon for a fast dance, too weird for a slow dance right now. Some students began to return to the dance floor while others drifted to their tables to relax and talk about the deadass serious thing they just witnessed.

Collin knew he couldn't dance or talk or relax or do anything except what Leah asked.

So he headed toward the gym's single-door side entrance that led to the classrooms, the lockers, the labs, the cafeteria—and Mr. Scanlan's office.

Real life.

Ride or Die.

It was Game On time.

Chapter 39

As Collin made his way to the assistant principal's office, he quickly discovered that when night falls, the inside of a large high school becomes a creepy, mysterious place. The hallways resembled long dark roads to nowhere, classrooms took on the empty gloom of a graveyard and lockers looked like rows of robots ready to march out of the wall. Worst of all, his footsteps created a dull echo that made it sound as if someone was following him. Rounding a corner, Collin nearly ran into a drinking fountain, which stuck out of the wall like a giant fist. On the opposite wall, a grinning girl on a sports poster mocked him; above her, a security camera stared at him like a little metallic cyclops.

Collin's uneasiness over the creepy environs paled in comparison to his dread over what waited at his destination. *What's Scanlan up to? Why did he make Leah come to his office? What is he going to do to her – to me?*

Collin passed the cafeteria, the tables and chairs almost crying in loneliness for the students who brought life and meaning to this facility. Beyond the lunch area, the administrative offices loomed. First came the principal's, followed by the guidance counselors', the athletic director's and the assistant principal's – all locked and silent. The building here was dead.

Except for the last one.

A thin light streamed out beneath that door. Collin walked over, took a deep breath, and squeezed his eyes shut for a few seconds, then opened it. The scene that greeted his eyes seemed eerily familiar: Scanlan seated in a chair that seemed too big for the desk in front of it. Behind the assistant principal and to his right sat Leah, hunched over, face down, one of the braids in her hair hanging loose over the side of her head. Her prom dress, once so radiant, now appeared disheveled and forlorn. Strangest of all, Collin sensed Herbie's presence in this room, though his friend was presumably now on his way to the hospital.

Scanlan stood and gave Collin an oily smile before waving his hand toward a chair in front of his desk. "Have a seat, young man."

Again, Collin was aware of the cotton-candy scent in the air from Scanlan's cologne as he moved next to the chair. He was about to sit when he changed his mind. "I'll stand."

The assistant principal shrugged. "Stand on your head, if you want, but listen carefully to what I'm about to say. But first..." Scanlan sidled over to Collin, tapped the pockets of his jacket until he found his phone and pulled it out.

Collin stiffened as Scanlan dropped the phone into a desk drawer and then moved in back of Leah. "We need to come to an understanding about our friend, Leah, here." At the mention of her name, the man placed his hands on Leah's shoulders, causing her to shrink down even lower.

"Take your hands off her!" Collin could hardly believe the words coming out of his mouth. But he didn't regret them. On the contrary, they were only the first shots he intended to fire at this loathsome power-hungry abuser. Collin was channeling his future self, and his future self was going to be a man who helped people.

"Take my hands off her?" Scanlan chortled. "Why, I can put my hands on her almost anytime I want. I can do that with any kid in this school, including your little friend Herbie."

"Herbie? I knew the strawberry juice was your doing! You could have killed him."

Scanlan twisted his mouth into a smug, triumphant smile. "Just wanted to remind you of what I can do around here."

"How would you know Herbie was allergic to strawberries?"

Scanlan moved away from Leah, opened the top drawer of his desk, and plucked out a brown folder. Opening it, he read slowly, occasionally letting his eyes dart out toward Collin.

"Kessler, Herbert J. 5'5" 104 lbs. Known conditions: hay fever, asthma, gluten intolerance, Type II diabetes. Known allergies: wheat, dairy products, corn syrup, peanuts, strawberries, mold, animal fur, soy, and celery. Prescription medicines required: Chlorphen--"

"Shouldn't that folder be in the nurse's office?" Collin challenged.

"This one is my copy."

"Your copy?"

"Yes. I have a copy of your health record, too. And Leah's and every other student who attends this school." Scanlan put the folder back in his desk and leaned toward Collin, appearing to grow taller.

"I know everything about every student in this school. Every test they take, every grade on their report card, every smart-ass remark they make in the hallways, every piece of food they eat or puke up in the cafeteria. I know about it because my eyes are always open and my ears are always listening."

"What are you, Scanlan? The assistant principal or Big Brother?"

"I'm a lot of things, Mr. Morris. Mr. Iron Fist—"

"Yes, I've heard them before. The strangest one is protector."

"What's strange about it?"

"Makes me wonder who protects us from you."

Scanlan's eyes narrowed into snake-like slits and the spikes of his buzz-cut hair seemed to bristle.

"You're no protector, Scanlan. The opposite. You're a predator." Somehow Collin realized he had passed through fear, he was numb and cruising forward, just doing what was right no matter what happened.

"And what the hell are you? A mediocre student who's lost a little weight but is still a klutz and who spends most of his time living in a make-believe-world of superheroes, super-villains and damsels in distress. Not exactly what the world needs right now."

On the inside, Collin flinched. That punched a small hole in his numb-armor. *He's not exaggerating when he says he knows everything about every student.* On the outside, he held his ground. "I'm not trying to save the world." He moved his eyes to Leah, who seemed to have shrunken to the size of a doll. "Only her."

The assistant principal put forth his hand, a gentle gesture suggesting a desire for peace. "Good. Because in that case, I've got a proposition to offer you."

"What is it?"

"It's simple. You leave Leah to me until the end of the school year. After that, she's all yours—if you still want her."

"You talk about her as if she was a piece of property. She's a person, a human being who you've treated worse than garbage. She's done letting you use her."

"Some people in my position would consider her worse than garbage because of what she did."

"You mean cheat on a test?"

"Not just any test: the State College Entrance Exam. With the help of a cleverly designed cheat sheet, she knew every answer to every math question and ended up stealing a scholarship that should have gone to a more-deserving student."

"If it was actually that big a deal to you, you would have reported her to our superintendent or the Brinkman Foundation. Instead, you blackmailed her into being your sex slave. She's suffered enough from your abuse, so the answer to your proposition is Hell to the No."

"You're a fool," Scanlan snarled. "There's less than a month until this school year is over. After that, she's... well... to put it in words you'll understand... she will have escaped from the big bad nasty assistant principal and will be free to run into your heroic arms."

"The answer's still no. Here's a counter-proposition. You turn yourself into the Bridgeview police and confess to all your crimes, all the abuse you've committed against Leah and I would guess other girls at the high school. Then you turn in all your education licenses to the State Board of Education for permanent revocation. Finally, you offer to pay for counseling services for Leah and your other victims with no limit on the cost."

Scanlan crossed his arms over his chest; his smug smile returned. "And if I decline your counter-proposition?"

"Then I'll turn you into the police myself."

A snicker slid out of Scanlan's mouth and then he put his hands next to each other and held them out in front of him. "Well, if you think the police will arrest me, go ahead and slap some handcuffs over my wrists."

"I've got something better than handcuffs."

"Oh? What might that be?"

"During the months you were abusing her, Leah kept a journal, and in it she—"

"Do you mean this thing?" Scanlan's hand again went into his top desk drawer, and when he pulled it out, he held the familiar brown felt-covered book with the elastic band around its center.

Collin choked back a gasp and swallowed hard. *How did that monster get his hands on that?* He cast a disheartened glance at Leah, who sat frozen in her seat, her head still drooping downward, her face invisible. *How did he get that from Dr. Kaufman?* There wasn't time to find out. *Need to play my ace in the hole.*

"Yes, that journal," Collin answered. "The one that identifies you as Leah's abuser. The one that details the cruel things you did to her. Just like you have your own copy of student medical records, I have my own copy of that journal. Made it at our public library. It can easily be handed over to the police. Here's a page from it, if you don't believe me." Collin reached into his inside pocket and removed the copied page he'd been carrying with him since his last Scarlet Angel dream. He unfolded it, and with a flick of his wrist, slapped it down on Scanlan's desk.

The assistant principal snorted at the rumpled copy and opened the journal in his hand. Slowly, one by one, he leafed through its pages. "If you do have a copy of the journal, then you must know my name isn't mentioned anywhere in it."

"You are Red Lion."

"Me? What makes you think that?"

"From the little red lion figure you have on your—" Collin pointed to where the statue stood on Scanlan's desk... except it wasn't there anymore. His heart began to sink down to his stomach. *It's like he knows what I'm going to say before I say it.* Collin rallied himself. *It's not going to matter.*

"You know what I'm talking about, and enough other people have seen that figure, too, so hiding it now won't do you any good. It will just make you seem more guilty."

"Oh, the little red statuette I once had on my desk?" Scanlan shrugged. "That must mean I'm a sexual predator, right?"

"It's obvious Leah substituted Red Lion for your real name."

Scanlan stuck out his lip in mock pity. "No, kiddo, it's not obvious at all. Let me explain." Scanlan plopped the journal on the right front corner of his desk and seated himself behind it again. "Every student of Southwestern Pennsylvania College receives that little figurine when they graduate. Ms. Gaines at our middle school has one, so does Mr. McBrayer who sits on our school board. There's even a Red Lion Inn at Westport and a luxury motor boat named the Red Lion down at the marina."

"You're BS'ing me, Scanlan." Collin's finger jutted out toward the assistant principal like a switchblade. "You're the Red Lion who's been blackmailing Leah. You're the Red Lion who's been abusing her and forcing yourself on her. And you're the Red Lion who is going to jail for it."

Scanlan threw his head back and grunted out a short, derisive laugh. "I don't think so, boy. No jury is going to convict me because of a journal you say Leah kept; even less on your copy of it. All you're going to do is turn yourself into a bigger loser than you already are, and…" he jerked a thumb at Leah "…ruin her entire life."

Collin wasn't sure Scanlan was telling the truth, but he wasn't sure the man was lying either. With the principal on an extended leave of absence, the man sitting in front of him was the most powerful person in the whole school. He probably had connections with the school board, with city council, maybe even the police. The journal had seemed like the perfect weapon to bring this monster down, but Scanlan didn't act like it bothered him. And yet…

"I'll give you one more minute to consider my offer," said Scanlan. "While you're thinking about it, I may as well get rid of this trash." He reached into his top desk drawer one more time and pulled out a lighter. Flicking it on, he held the copied journal page up to the flame and watched in satisfaction as the paper caught fire and shriveled into ash. Then, taking the blackened remnants between his thumb and forefinger, the assistant principal rose from his chair and leaned over toward a wastepaper basket on the left side of his desk.

And that's when Leah sprang into action.

Up until that moment, she had remained huddled and motionless in her chair, head down, hands clasped in front of her. Collin assumed she was too frightened to say anything, but now it seemed more likely she just bided her time, waiting for the right moment to strike.

Bursting out of her chair, Leah lunged toward the journal on the edge of Scanlan's desk. Grabbing it, she flung it toward Collin. "Take it to the police!" she cried. "It's got his fingerprints all over it. DNA, too!"

In the half second before the brown book dropped into his arms, Collin realized Leah was right. No matter how many Red Lions there were in the world, only one put his grubby hands on *this* journal, making it once again the best weapon for destroying him.

When Scanlan realized what Leah had done, he dropped the burnt paper and charged around the desk toward Collin.

Or at least he tried to.

The last thing Collin saw before dashing out of the office was the monster falling to the floor with Leah, prom dress and all, wrapped around his waist, like an NFL lineman bringing down a quarterback.

As grateful as he was for Leah's quick thinking, Collin knew Scanlan would soon be on his feet again and in hot pursuit. It was a long way to the gym and the dark corridors in front of him looked more foreboding, more treacherous than before.

Chapter 40

Collin barreled out of Scanlan's office, holding the journal between his forearm and ribcage. He pivoted to his right and ran as hard as he could down the way he had come. Unfortunately, he was not very fast. *There's no way I can get back to the gym before Scanlan catches up to me. Maybe I can hide then get past him.*

The cafeteria, with 20 or more tables and dozens of chairs spread out in a large area with no lights on, provided a terrific place to put this new strategy into action. There were no doors to deal with, since the cafeteria opened up off the hallway, so as soon as he came to it, Collin darted in. Zig-zagging his way to the far end of the big room, he ducked under a table and pushed some chairs together to make himself as close to invisible as possible. Then he listened. For a moment he heard nothing, which worried him. *What's going on back in his office? What's he doing with Leah? Maybe I should run for the gym like I was planning to.*

Collin began to scoot out from under the table but stopped when he heard the sound of footsteps coming his way. The steps came in a quick succession of thump-thumps that suggested the person approaching walked quickly but not at a full run. When the footsteps reached the cafeteria, they slowed and then stopped altogether. Collin tried to see through his barricade of chairs, but whoever was out there, *It has to be Scanlan!* was not in his line of sight.

He switched his focus to the path he'd taken to his hiding place. In his haste to get out of sight, he knocked some of the neatly arranged chairs out of place. He could only hope his pursuer didn't notice. A few more seconds passed. Collin clutched the felt book against his side and let his breaths go in and out as slowly as possible so they couldn't be heard anywhere beyond his table. He noticed his now crumpled boutonniere clung to his lapel like a hapless little mountain climber.

The foot thumps resumed and for two terrible seconds Collin thought they were coming toward him. *No! They're growing fainter.* Scanlan was going beyond the cafeteria, following the path Collin would have taken had he tried to return to the gym. The thumps grew fainter until they disappeared altogether.

Collin thought about his next move. He wanted to stay put for a while under this little fortress of table and chairs, but realized he couldn't. In his hurried escape from Scanlan, he'd forgotten about Leah! *What's happened to her?* He had to find out. Plus he was trapped here if Scanlan came back.

Collin tucked the book in the back of his pants, shuffled backward on all fours from under the table, got back on his feet, and worked his way toward the opening to the corridor. With every step, he tried to convince himself Leah was okay. *Scanlan couldn't have had time to hurt her too badly. He came right after me. And once he left his office, she could've escaped.*

Approaching the junction to the hallway, Collin wasn't sure whether he should run to Scanlan's office or walk, but it didn't matter. The second he left the cafeteria he heard the sound of footsteps coming toward him from the direction of the gymnasium.

Why is Scanlan coming back? To look for me? To punish Leah?

There wasn't time to answer those questions.

As quickly and quietly as he could, Collin scurried back to his hiding place. He hadn't quite gotten himself under the table, when the footsteps reached the opening to the cafeteria… and continued on without pausing at all. Collin's fear for Leah came back like a knife through his gut. *Scanlan's going back to get her!* He could only hope Leah made an escape of her own while Scanlan searched for him. The only thing for him to do now was, again, dash to the gym.

Once more, as if caught in a time loop, Collin repeated his exit to the corridor, taking care not to disrupt the alignment of the tables and chairs any more than he already had. He reached the corridor and faced in the direction of the gym. *Should I run or walk?*

A good question suddenly meaningless when Scanlan's voice came out of the darkness. "You're not only a loser, Morris, you're also an idiot. Give me the journal, and you and Leah can go back and boogie at the prom."

The shock of hearing Scanlan's voice no more than 20 feet away gave

Collin something akin to an electrical charge that sent him racing – almost flying – down the corridor toward the safety of others. Rounding the corner by the drinking fountain, he slowed just enough to hear Scanlan's footsteps coming up fast behind him.

Except there was nothing to hear.

Scanlan, if he followed at all, was far behind. *Where is Mr. Iron Fist? Did Leah sneak up and tackle him again or did he go back to his office to molest her one more time? It doesn't matter. In a few seconds, I'll be back in the gym with the journal. I'll tell the chaperones what that monster has been doing, and they'll call the police. Leah will be rescued and Scanlan will be arrested.*

Collin rounded the last corner of the main hallway and immediately realized he would not be getting to the gym anytime soon and maybe not at all. It was clear now why Scanlan had made no effort to find Collin in the cafeteria.

Rather than aggressively pursue Collin, the assistant principal blocked his path to the gymnasium by pulling a metal security gate from one side of the corridor to the other. There were several such gates around the school, but they were usually folded up inside the wall. Far from giving him any security, this one with its crisscrossed bars looming ahead, threatened to ruin any chance he had of getting the journal into another adult's hands.

And now the sound of Scanlan's footsteps reached his ears once more. They came quickly and sharply like cracks of a whip. With no way to go any farther, Collin had only one avenue of escape and only if he reached it before Scanlan. The central staircase wasn't far, about fifty feet behind him, but Scanlan might get to it before he did. *What other choice do I have? None, unless I want that monster to pin me against this gate.*

Collin spun around and dashed toward the staircase. He knew he was moving faster than he ever had before, yet it felt like moving in slow motion, his arms and legs straining, pushing against some invisible force. *It almost feels like Scanlan cast a spell on me like Vor—but no! Get a grip. This is the real world. There's no magic here. It's all up to me.*

Collin reached the staircase and started bounding up toward the second floor. He didn't dare look back to see how far away Scanlan was, but from the sound of the monster's footsteps, he was fast closing the gap between them.

At the top, a few feet from the guardrail, someone—no something—

stood in Collin's way. It wasn't a security gate this time; it was a janitor's cart with mop and bucket attached to one side and various cleaning items hanging around its rim. Still not looking back, Collin grabbed the cart with both hands and flung it down the stairs. He caught a glimpse of plastic bottles, a broom and a dust pan bouncing around as the larger items tumbled down to hopefully hit, or at the very least impede, his pursuer.

Once on the second floor, Collin had to make a quick decision. On the right was a row of classrooms, mostly devoted to science courses; on the left were two doors, both leading to the auditorium's balcony. It proved to be an easy choice. The classrooms would be traps.

Darting through the nearer auditorium door, Collin thought he heard footsteps clumping up the staircase. It occurred to him that Scanlan was just as desperate as he was in his own way. This was a truly dangerous situation.

The balcony, like the rest of the auditorium, was unlit. Better still, the seats were dark green, which blended in well with Collin's black tux. He squeezed himself under the first two or three seats a few aisles away from the door. Then he assumed a sphinx-like position with his legs and forearms flat on the floor and his head raised just enough to give him a clear line of sight to the doors. The floor was gross, with some plates left behind by kids who wanted more privacy than the cafeteria allowed. He pushed thoughts of rat shit out of his mind.

Minutes passed.

The balcony lights suddenly flashed on, re-focusing Collin's attention on another rat more dangerous than the ones with four legs. Scanlan flung open the same door Collin used and stomped onto the balcony. Collin didn't know why it had taken the jackass so long to come into the auditorium, but now he arrived, tie hanging loose and sweat glistening on his forehead. He gazed around a few seconds before resting his eyes on Collin, who realized too late that with the lights on, his hiding place was useless.

Scanlan began walking toward him, his hand outstretched. "Just give me the journal, Collin. That's all I want. You can have Leah right now. Don't have to wait . Just give me the journal, keep your damn mouth shut, and I'll forget about all the trouble you've caused me."

Even if he couldn't see the rage burning in Scanlan's eyes, Collin wouldn't have believed him. *Time to get out of here.* Scooting backward, he caught his jacket on something under one of the seats and when he pulled it away, the journal fell out. By the time he put it back in his jacket, Scanlan was hardly more than three strides away.

Instinctively, Collin reached under the nearest seat, grabbed a lunch-crusted plate, and hurled it toward Scanlan.

"Here! Take the damn thing and stop chasing me."

Collin saw the plate fly several inches over Scanlan's head, and by the time it landed, he had scrambled to his feet. Had he actually thrown the journal, it wouldn't have made the clattering sound the plate did when it hit the floor. Even so, Scanlan whipped around and lumbered toward the noise, and as Collin ran to the nearest door, he caught a glimpse of the assistant principal bending to investigate.

"Damn you, you fat loser," Scanlan yelled when he realized he'd been tricked. One second later, Collin was back in the corridor and heading toward the west staircase... which was blocked by a barricade of desks piled one on top of the other.

Now I know why it took him so long to get to the balcony.

He doubled back toward the central staircase, but stopped in mid-stride when one of the auditorium doors swung open and Scanlan lurched into the corridor. The assistant principal now appeared to be almost as much a monster on the outside as he was on the inside. He'd thrown off his tie and unbuttoned his shirt. The burning rage in his eyes spread across his whole face, contorting it into a look of insane hate.

No choice now. Got to run to a classroom and hope it isn't locked.

Rooms 201 and 203 were latched shut. Collin felt certain Scanlan would catch him and tear the journal out of his jacket. But for the moment, the monster stayed in place, stooped over and panting, apparently out of breath. Room 205 opened. It was a biology classroom with microscopes, slides and dissecting instruments on the tables. In one corner, a complete model of a human skeleton from skull to metatarsals added to the surreal nightmare Collin felt he was in. The room offered no place to hide, but there were windows, which gave Collin an idea.

Scanlan's voice bellowed in the corridor. "Give me the journal, fat ass. Don't make things hard for yourself."

"I don't have it any more," Collin said.

Scanlan charged through the door, eyes blazing and nostrils flaring like an angry bull. "Don't lie to me, you little—"

Before the assistant principal could take one step toward him, Collin threw the journal toward the nearest window. He didn't know what was below the classroom, but wherever it landed, the thing would be out of Scanlan's reach, and before the monster could get down—

Collin gasped as the journal bounced off the window frame and thudded down inside, not outside, next to a row of bottles holding a variety of preserved creatures.

Shit! My arm screws me when it actually matters.

Scanlan remained frozen in place, staring at the spot where the journal fell. Almost mid-way between the two. Maybe he suspected another trick. Whatever the case, Collin took advantage of the monster's delay. Seizing the skull of the model skeleton, he yanked on it with all his might. It took two tugs before the thing broke free of the neck bone. By then Scanlan unfroze himself and began moving toward the journal.

Collin reached the little brown book with Scanlan barely an arm's length away. Grabbing the journal with his left hand, he swung the skull with his right hand and smashed it into the window pane closest to him which had been closed. With jagged glass falling onto his fingers and Scanlan clawing at his back, Collin thrust the skull and journal out into the open air and let them plummet to the ground.

A surge of relief swept over him like cold water over an open wound. The feeling remained even when Scanlan pulled him away from the window and shoved him to the floor.

"Give me the diary before I kill you."

"I threw it out the window. Go outside and get it."

"You're lying again!" Scanlan grabbed the teen by the lapels and dragged him back onto his feet. The stench of cologne-tinged sweat made Collin gag.

"Here, I'll make it easy for you," Collin said. The teen slipped out of the tux's jacket and handed it to the man, who rifled through its pockets and turned it upside down.

"Check my pants pockets, too, if you want." Collin reached into his pockets and pulled out the lining, they hung bright white and empty at his sides.

"You fat little shit!" Scanlan threw the jacket into Collin's face and bolted for the door, banging into a table and spilling a jar of alcohol over his pants. Collin took off after him. Maybe the monster exaggerated when he threatened to kill him, but even if he meant it, Collin knew he couldn't let Mr. Iron Fist get the journal. Besides, he liked this turn of fortune that transformed him from pursued to pursuer.

Outside the classroom, Scanlan swung toward the west staircase, apparently forgetting the barricade he put up there. Realizing his error, he did an about face and scrambled toward the central staircase. By now, Collin was out in the hallway and as the monster ran past, he lowered his back and threw himself with arms outstretched toward Scanlan's legs. He briefly caught hold of the man's pants around the ankles, but let go when a sharp blow from a fist sent him face down into the floor. Pain shot through Collin's nose, making him wonder if Scanlan broke it. Undaunted, he scrambled to his feet and resumed his chase.

Scanlan, meanwhile, skidded on something as he neared the staircase and stumbled to his knees. The same thing happened to Collin when he came up behind the assistant principal. Returning to his feet, he saw a sticky blue liquid puddled up at the top of the staircase and shards of glass nearby. *I must have broken some bottle when I shoved the janitor's cart down the stairs.*

He prepared to resume his pursuit but instead of running away, Scanlan came straight at him!

The assistant principal, smelling like a circus and a hospital, rushed toward Collin with hands like claws and eyes ablaze with fury. He grabbed the teen around the throat and hurled him back into the rail. Collin winced in pain keeping enough composure to throw a punch back, connecting with the monster's chin. Scanlan, retaining some of the strength he had as a wrestler, kept his balance and gripped Collin around the throat again. This time, the monster didn't let go. Collin struggled to breathe. Scanlan's vice-like grip made that impossible. He kicked out with his feet, hoping to hit the man's groin but barely tapped his thigh instead. Desperation quickly morphing into panic swept over him.

He's really going to kill me. As the strength drained out of him, Collin slumped to the floor, his upper body painfully stretched over the top two steps. *Maybe he'll let go of me now.* If anything, the monster's grip became stronger, fingernails digging into Collin's flesh like little knives.

Then, from out of nowhere, an arm swung down toward the monster. A red fist struck the back of his head. This caused the choke-hold around Collin's throat to loosen enough for him to pull in some air. The arm swung down again, faster than before. When the red fist hit the monster's head this time, the hands around Collin's neck fell away completely.

For a moment Collin remained awkwardly sprawled over the stairs, catching his breath and trying to figure out what happened. On one side of him lay Scanlan, apparently unconscious, temporarily de-fanged. Checking himself, he realized he must resemble something non-human, too, with his clothes and skin stained blue and blood dripping from his nose.

His vision cleared. In front of him was his rescuer: Leah. The girl he'd set out to save. In the end she saved him. Her dress was rumpled, her corsage was gone and her once nicely braided hair hung over her face and stuck to her neck. To Collin, no girl ever looked more beautiful.

A red fist? From blood? No, it isn't her fist that's red; it's the thing she used to bash Scanlan on the head! His own red lion statue! Mr. Iron Fist was taken down by the two of them working together.

Leah reached down, took Collin by the hand, and helped him to his feet. He hugged her and then gave her a puzzled look. "I'm happy to see you," he said, "but surprised. Didn't Scanlan lock you in his office?"

"Yes," she said with a very strange look on her face. "Someone got me out."

"Who?"

"Him." Leah pointed several feet behind her. When Collin saw who it was, he nearly fell back to the floor, this time from shock.

"Blake? Blake got you out of Scanlan's office?"

"I sure did," said the crooked-tooth bully, sauntering up to them. "I was taking a break from that boring prom when I heard someone trying to get out of there. I didn't know who was in there, but I couldn't pass up the chance to smash in that asshole's door. I got a fire extinguisher from near the cafeteria and pounded it on the door knob until it fell off and the door opened. On the way here, Leah told me what's been going on." He sneered down at the still-unconscious assistant principal. "Guess this bastard will be getting some detention of his own pretty soon."

"We all better get back to the gym before he wakes up," she said. "The prom's probably over, but some of the chaperones should still be there. We can borrow a phone from one of them and call the police."

"I'll tie his hands up, just in case." Blake, pulling his belt out of his pants, looked thrilled at this prospect.

"We might want to call the custodian, too," said Collin. "I made an awful mess of this school."

Leah kept hold of his hand as they walked down the staircase. "Nope. You've made it cleaner than it's ever been before."

Chapter 41

Herbie pulled the blanket on the hospital bed up to his chest and leaned back on his pillow. "Well, look who's here," he said as Collin and Leah came into his room. "Did a limo bring you over?"

"Not this time," Collin answered. "My dad brought us back to my house after prom and then I talked him into letting us drive over to visit you. I promised the nurses we'd keep it short since they're supposed to let only family visit after ten."

"I'd say someone who saved my life is more than family." Herb paused for a brief, cheesey, sweet moment.

His grin faded. Herb's eyes took in Leah's messed up hair. Then they shifted to Collin's stained clothes and swollen nose. "Damn! What happened after I left? Did Blake get to you?" Herbie entwined his fingers behind his head, ready to listen to another story of Collin getting pushed around.

But the snorting laughter that comment caused let him know this was going to be a totally different story. He listened as Collin recounted the events at Bridgeview High that led to Scanlan's downfall.

When Collin reached the part about getting blue cleaning liquid all over his tux while being choked by the assistant principal, his friend interrupted. "Maybe you should be a patient. You've been punched and choked and knocked down, and your nose might be broken. Go ask the nurse if you can be my roommate." Herbie pointed to the empty bed on the other side of the semi-private room.

"You don't need a roommate," Collin said. "You need to get well and get home."

"That shouldn't be a problem. They're just keeping me overnight as a precaution. If there's no sign of anaphylaxis in the morning, I'll be released. Now finish your story."

"There's not much more to tell. While Scanlan was choking me, Leah came up behind him and knocked him on the head with the red lion statue."

"Yes!" Herbie punched the air. "So the damsel in distress rescued the knight in shining armor. I love it." He shifted his gaze to Leah, standing next to Collin. She still wore her prom dress, but had borrowed a small blanket to put over her shoulders for added warmth. "How did you get ahold of the statue?"

"I saw Scanlan put it in one of his desk drawers before Collin came in," Leah said. "The real problem was getting out of his office because the sick bastard locked me in there after Collin got away."

Herbie's expression darkened, his usual sarcasm sharpening into something colder. "That piece of shit. So how'd you get out?"

"Blake let me out."

"Blake?" Herbie went slack-jawed. "You're joking."

"Nope, he smashed the door knob with a fire extinguisher."

"What was he doing, hanging out in the admin area?"

"I didn't ask. Pretty sure he was smoking weed. Smelled like it anyway."

"Well, that much I can believe."

"After Blake let me out, I wanted to find Collin. I wasn't sure if he'd made it back to the gym or not. Then I saw the security gate pulled across the hall. I knew he must've gone up the stairs to hide, so I went up, too."

"Thank God she did," said Collin. "I might be dead now."

Leah had a look of hate flash across her face. "You'd both be dead if Scanlan had his way."

"Strawberry juice didn't kill me thanks to the nice people here and in the ambulance," said Herb. "Still, it's scary to think of him having access to all our school records. I would have to have 'Killed by the juice of strawberries' on my tombstone."

"Maybe every kid in our school should get a copy of his criminal records," said Collin. "That would only seem fair."

The door opened and Herb's parents came in. There were introductions, hugs, words of thanks and a few tears, and then Leah and Collin left. On the way to her house, they didn't talk much. That was just as well, because Collin's mind bubbled over with questions he wanted to ask – it just didn't seem the right time after all they had just went through. *Will Leah want to be my girlfriend? Will that even be possible, after all the abuse she's survived? How much damage did Scanlan do to her emotionally, psychologically, even physically? Can she let me help her heal from this damage? Would I even know how to do that?*

By the time he pulled into the driveway of Leah's house, Collin had thought of one question he could ask her. One question that had to be answered ahead of all the others. He put his arm around her shoulders and peered into her eyes.

"Would you like to go out with me again sometime?"

There was a slight pause before she answered. "Sure. I wouldn't go out with anyone else."

That caught Collin off guard. Of course, she could go out with any guy who asked her. He was hardly the only boy at Bridgeview High. Maybe the best thing for Leah was to make her aware of that fact. Yet, he didn't want to. He wanted her for himself. *Is that a bad thing?* He wouldn't be anything like Scanlan. He'd even treat her better than most other guys treated their girlfriends. *But what's best for her? I don't know, maybe we can find out… together.*

He walked Leah to the door of her house, put his arms around her waist and kissed her. He held the kiss for a minute. When he finally broke it off, his mind was hazy. One thought remained clear. Whatever his future held for a relationship with Leah, the abusive one she had with the monster was dead, buried and gone forever.

Chapter 42

Collin closed his car trunk and dropped the stack of comic books into the wagon with a thump. He tightened the twine around them and then started pulling the wagon toward Cyril's Comic Book Universe. Leah closed the passenger door and glided next to him.

"How many do you have in there?" she asked.

"Two hundred and fifty-six. Some *Alien Dusk, Western Warrior* and *Meteoria* but mostly *Scarlet Angel*."

Leah put her arm around Collin's waist. "Is that your whole collection?"

"Almost. I kept a few *Scarlet Angel* issues, including the first one that came out about 20 years ago. I'm sure it's worth more than what I'd get at Cyril's. Also three from my grandmother's attic, and a handful of ones I liked a lot. Every other issue is here."

"You know, I'm not sure why you're getting rid of them. Lots of people make collecting comics a hobby."

Collin stopped pulling the wagon and looked at her. "That's just it. Scarlet Angel and these other superheroes were more than a hobby. They were role models for me... even more than that. I was living my life through them; I was hiding by reading them and letting them be all I ever did. I let the bullies win. I don't need to do that anymore. Not only that, I realized that bullies are people too, just not easy to get along with most of the time." They both laughed while picturing Blake.

The two teens continued their walk down the strip mall toward Cyril's. They passed all sorts of little shops before pausing in front of a sidewalk newspaper box with the latest edition showing through its window.

Collin stared at the headline:

School Administrator Gets 20-30 Years for

Multiple Sex Crimes

Without looking at her, he knew Leah saw the headline, too. Neither of them needed to read the story that followed.

For a moment, he re-lived the whole drama of finding the journal in his backpack. The search for the 'girl in trouble,' the search for Red Lion, the date with Leah at the comic book exhibit, the prom and the chase/battle with Scanlan in the darkened halls of the high school... it passed through his mind like flood waters.

Collin had been prepared to give testimony if the **State of Ohio v Gerald Nash Scanlan** had gone to trial. It didn't. Besides Leah, Scanlan's attorney would have had to face the other women who came forward, telling their own chilling stories of the abuse they suffered at the monster's hands when they were in high school.

One survivor now lived out of state, two more were college students in their 20s. All had one thing in common: Scanlan caught them doing something bad: using drugs, cheating on a test, stealing from a classmate. Mistakes that shouldn't have been life-altering. Scanlan usually saw them from the closed-circuit cameras he'd installed supposedly to improve student security or from the tiny cameras and microphones that he placed in strategic locations, including Dr. Kaufman's office. He even had a hidden camera in the girls' locker room, which was how he caught Janie.

Whatever the screw-up, his next move was always the same—threaten to expose the girl's secret unless she gave in to his sick demands. This time, Scanlan didn't get away with it. Charged with rape, assault and a whole list of other crimes, the bastard took a plea deal. It kept him from getting an even longer sentence. In the end? Mr. Iron Fist would be rotting behind bars for the next two decades.

But it wasn't really over. Not for the girls he preyed on. And definitely not for Leah.

She lost her scholarship, but she kept her grades up and made it through the rest of that year and then into a great senior year. At first, she was sure everyone would judge her, whisper behind her back. It had been the bravest thing she had ever done to go back to school after the prom. Once school started, she realized something—other girls admired her and Scanlan had been too much of a sneaky piece of shit for anyone to blame her. She got to graduate with her class, and in the fall, she'd be heading to community college. For right now? She needed to heal.

That's why, as soon as Collin sold his comics, he'd be driving Leah to her therapy appointment. After that, they'd hit his mom's booth at the Bridgeview Art Fair, then meet up with Herb and Winifred for a picnic at the nature preserve.

Leah let out a breath. "How many more creeps like Scanlan are out there? Just waiting to ruin girls' lives?"

Collin shook his head. "No clue. Probably more than we wanna know."

"At least there's one less now." She nudged him. "Because of you."

He smirked. "Nah, because of *you*. I wouldn't even be here if you hadn't had my back."

They kept walking, the wagon full of comics rattling behind them. Two doors away from the comic shop, Collin stopped in front of Roseanne's Ice Cream Land.

"Let's hit this first."

Leah started digging in her purse. "I dunno if I have enough—"

"Chill, I got it. You can even get the extra-large cone with two scoops of your favorite flavor."

She laughed. "Alright, you talked me into it."

As they stepped toward the door, a guy walked out—red jacket, black jeans, double-dip chocolate cone in hand. A blue scarf hung around his neck. He gave them a quick nod before heading toward the parking lot.

Leah frowned. "You know him?"

Collin hesitated, then smiled. "Don't think so."

Shrugging, they headed inside, hand in hand. But for just a second, Collin's mind wandered—back to a dream, one he'd had so many times. A young man, red jacket, black jeans, blue scarf... smiling, waving... then fading away.

Only this time, Collin knew that dream was done.

It was time to make new ones.

ABOUT THE AUTHOR

Clay Cormany is not a young adult, but he enjoys writing YA novels. Besides *The Secrets We Carry*, he is the author of *Fast-Pitch Love* which combines the angst of teenage romance with softball competition and *The Bullybuster*, which also involves a teenage romance story as well as robots and revenge.

Before completing his novels, Clay spent 28 years as a writer and editor for Ohio's State Board of Education. His creative work appeared in the Columbus Dispatch and Spring Street, Columbus State Community College's literary magazine. He also edited numerous books, including a three-volume biography of Christopher Columbus and *A Death Prolonged* by Dr. Jeff Gordon, which received coverage in The New York Times and on PBS.

When he is not writing, Clay enjoys reading, bicycling, and (when he has enough energy) spending time with his grandchildren.

ACKNOWLEDGMENTS

Many fine people offered wise criticism and useful information that made *The Secrets We Carry: Journal of a Girl in Trouble* a better book than it otherwise would have been. The members of my two critique groups — the GEM-C Writers and the Ohio Chapter of the International Women's Writing Guild — helped me every step of the way and with everything from character development to sentence structure. Several members of Angela Rydell's Inlet Beta Readers Club pointed out some word-choice problems and offered sound advice on strengthening the middle chapters of the novel. A comprehensive start-to-finish review by Book Doctor Gretchen Hirsch led me to flesh out some characters and add a few small but clever plot twists.

Great credit goes to two individuals who provided professional guidance on education policy and medical issues, respectively. Melissa Conrath, former superintendent of Worthington City Schools, gave me valuable insight to the disciplinary process an accused school administrator would face. For her part, Ann Connelly, Supervisor of the Ohio Department of Health's School Nursing Program, made sure my descriptions of Herbie's allergies and medications were accurate.

I would be remiss if I didn't acknowledge Trish Lewis, CEO of Van Velzer Press, who decided to publish this YA book despite the author being well beyond his young adult years. Credit also goes to Trish's sharp-eyed young editor Emily Semaya, who helped move the book through its early drafts.

Finally, I would also be remiss if I didn't acknowledge the help I received from two family members. Jonathan Cormany, a comic book enthusiast, helped guide the creation of the Scarlet Angel. And my wife, Rebecca Princehorn, did a final review of my manuscript and identified a number of small but important changes that were necessary. Her love and devotion were, of course, the best thing going for me before, during, and after the writing of this novel.

A WORD FROM THE AUTHOR

Although *The Secrets We Carry: Journal of a Girl in Trouble* is a work of fiction, the problem it addresses is real. Each situation was based on a real incident. During my years as a consultant for Ohio's State Board of Education, I learned about instances of sexual abuse that students suffered at the hands of educators. Although these abusive educators represent only a small group, the damage they do is long-lasting. If you or someone you know has been the victim of sexual abuse (inside or outside a school setting), the resources below may help with the healing process. My thanks to the Rape, Abuse and Incest National Network for putting this resource list together

Sexual Violence Resource List

rainn.org

RAINN is the nation's leading anti-sexual violence organization for adults and children, offering vital resources and support for survivors through programs like the National Sexual Assault Hotline, which provides confidential, anonymous, 24/7 assistance via phone and online chat. RAINN also offers online learning about child sexual abuse and resources for caregivers supporting child victims and themselves.

nsvrc.org

The National Sexual Violence Resource Center supports victims of sexual violence by providing education, resources, and training to prevent and address sexual violence.

www.thehotline.org

The National Domestic Violence Hotline provides 24/7 support for victims of domestic violence, including those experiencing sexual violence within intimate relationships.

victimsofcrime.org

The National Center for Victims of Crime empowers victims of all types of crime by providing them with advocacy, resources, and support.

nationalchildrensalliance.org

The National Children's Alliance supports a network of Children's Advocacy Centers nationwide, which provide coordinated, trauma-informed services.

www.bravemovement.org

Brave Movement helps child victims of sexual abuse connect with local organizations and services for support and healing.

d2l.org

Darkness To Light empowers adults to prevent child sexual abuse and provides resources for survivors, parents, and professionals.

1800runaway.org

The National Runaway Safeline provides confidential support, crisis intervention, and resources to runaway, homeless, and at-risk youth, helping them find safety and reunite with their families, and access critical services

missingkids.org/home

The National Center for Missing & Exploited Children works to prevent child abduction, sexual exploitation, and trafficking while providing critical resources

humantraffickinghotline.org/en

The National Human Trafficking Hotline connects victims and survivors of human trafficking with support services, provides tips to law enforcement, and raises public awareness to prevent and combat trafficking in the U.S.

loveisrespect.org

Love is Respect operates a confidential, 24/7 hotline offering assistance via phone, text, and online chat, as well as providing support and education to young people to promote healthy relationships

Love Books?

SUPPORT **A**UTHORS – buy directly from independent publishers. This puts more royalty dollars into the pockets of your favorite author – and gives them time to write their next book.

Visit us for links to our other books as well as many other vibrant publishing companies to find the book for you; join our Launch List to be the first to know about new books:
director@vanvelzerpress.com

These ARE The Books You've Been Looking For.

www.ingramcontent.com/pod-product-compliance
Lightning Source LLC
Chambersburg PA
CBHW031302120726
47906CB00003B/857